THREE *sweet* NOTHINGS

NIKKI SLOANE

for my husband

KYLE

I fisted my cock, stroking the hard length, and tightened my grip.

My hand ached. I'd been at it a while, and even though my gaze was on my iPad, my mind wandered elsewhere. Fuck, this porn wasn't getting it done tonight. It wasn't real. The girl's moans were as fake as her tits, and the guy kept grunting out his words like a caveman. I tapped the screen, shut it off, and tossed it down on the empty side of my bed in frustration.

Okay, time to get serious. I was tired and didn't want to fall asleep with my dick in my hand. I shifted under the sheets to get comfortable and focus.

I retrieved the memory which never failed to get me off. Ruby Carter's drunken laugh while she was sandwiched between me and her friend Leslie, her tight body pressed back against mine, while I worked a hand up her shirt. Ruby had such perfect breasts, and I remembered the shock when I discovered Leslie had beaten me to them. Our palms met over the top of Ruby's bra, trying to get inside while she squirmed beneath our mutual touch.

Every detail of that night had been committed to perfect memory. I could still smell the sunny laundry detergent that lingered in Ruby's sheets, and hear the breathless moan she gave as Leslie explored, both girls trying something new and eager for more. I didn't know how the stars aligned so goddamn perfectly to bring that night into existence, and I wasn't going to question it.

I pumped my grip, twisting around the head, and then had to flex my fingers to shake the strain from them. Ruby's breathy moans ramped up in my head as I recalled sliding my fingers down the front of her jeans. I'd decided to stay out of Leslie's way up top, and skip right to the best part.

Making Ruby come.

There wasn't anything else like it. I'd fucked women before and after her, but no one compared. She shook violently with the force of her orgasms. Deep groans of pleasure rolled out of her as the waves wracked her body, over and over again. I'd made her come countless times during the ten months we'd dated, but every time she came, it felt . . . new. Like a shocking surprise.

My fingers ached as I squeezed harder, willing my hand not to cramp. Or were they aching because I wished they were buried between Ruby's legs as they'd been then? She was so wet. Making out with Leslie had turned us both on, and then the potential there'd be more had brought us both to the brink.

I'd barely touched Ruby. Just one swipe of my fingertips on her swollen clit, and she jerked. Her shoulders seized and shuddered, followed by a loud gasp, and then she shattered.

"*Fuck*," I whispered in my empty bedroom, echoing Ruby's word as she came on my damp fingers. I was just as close to coming now as I'd been then, but there was no need to hold back tonight. No need to satisfy anyone but myself. One more stroke, and I'd have a mess on my hands.

My phone rang, vibrating noisily on the nightstand and bathing the room in dull light.

Jesus Christ, what asshole doesn't send a text at one in the morning?

I ceased moving my hand when I read the screen. *Payton McCreary.* Although it should probably say Ward now. Her wedding was a week ago, and my independent sister had surprisingly taken her husband's last name. Was she back from her honeymoon already, or was this a drunk dial where she forgot about the time change?

A weird feeling rolled through me. Payton was wild, but not inconsiderate. She wouldn't call at this hour unless it was an emergency. And if that was the case, when did I become the one she called for help?

"Hello?" I said, abandoning my cock.

"Kyle." Relief filled Payton's voice. "What are you doing?"

"Jerking off. You?" I clamped my teeth together. Where the fuck did that come from?

There was no hesitation from her. "Can you finish later? I . . . need your help."

My throbbing hard-on began to flag. My sister was confident, but she didn't sound that way now. Hearing her nervous made me nervous.

"Help with what?" I blinked back confusion as I sat upright.

"I need to talk to you. Can you come over?"

"Now?" I threw off the covers and stood. "Is Dominic around?"

Wait. My mind was slow as the blood began to return to my brain upstairs. She'd told me their honeymoon was short due to Dominic's demanding job.

"No, I'm not at home."

"Okay, where are you?"

She paused. "I'm at the Federal building."

I froze. "You're where?"

"I'm being questioned by the FBI." Her voice was clipped. "My friend is, too."

"Evie?" I asked. Payton had been best friends with Evelyn since college. "Why are you being questioned?"

"Not Evie. His name is Julius, and it's . . . complicated. Can you come, like, right now? I told him not to say anything until you get here."

Things sharpened into focus. Payton wasn't calling me for help as her big brother. I tried to ignore the tinge of disappointment. My sister was a product of our parents. Self-reliant, proud, and headstrong. It made sense she would only need me for legal counsel.

"Yeah," I said, heading for my closet. "I'll be there as soon as I can." I gazed at the selection before me. "How serious is it?"

Payton's voice was thick. "Wear your most intimidating suit."

After passing through security, I was ushered into the FBI office and led down a hallway to a small conference room which probably doubled as an interview space. Gray carpet, a government cheap table, and no windows. My sister sat on one of the worn chairs, staring vacantly at the most wanted list posted on a wall.

Payton looked much younger than her twenty-eight

years, sitting alone with worry etching her face and her shoulders slumped. My sister was attractive. I knew because I'd heard about it from guys during high school, the ones who were dumb enough to tell me how fuckable they thought my sister was.

She'd grown into a gorgeous woman. Even if I'd failed to realize that, her fiancé Dominic was quick to remind. *Husband*, I corrected. How could I forget my little sister was married? My mother hadn't stopped shooting me disappointed looks throughout the evening this past Saturday. I hadn't even brought a date to the wedding.

"God, thanks for coming." Payton leapt to her feet, and in four quick strides, reached me. She threw her arms around my shoulders and squeezed.

"Are you all right?" When she nodded, I added, "Are they holding you? Have you been charged with anything?"

"No, not me. Just questions." She straightened. "I'm glad you're here."

We hadn't been close growing up. I'd had pressure coming at me from all sides, and if I was honest, it pissed me off how differently our parents treated us. I'd resented Payton for how she did whatever she wanted. Mom and Dad acted like I was the better child. The smarter one, but the reality was Payton was more intelligent. She'd figured out how to brush off our parents' disapproval nearly a decade before I did.

Things shifted between us last year when I moved back to Chicago. We'd forged slowly into new territory, getting to actually know each other. She'd let me siphon friends from her, too. The move home from New York had been difficult. Why was it so hard to meet people as a single guy at thirty?

Payton dropped into the chair and gestured to the one opposite her. "You're going to want to sit for this."

I lowered into a seat. "What's going on?"

"Can we talk freely in here?"

"They can't record your conversation with counsel." What the hell had she gotten into?

She pressed her lips together, but then gave a slight shake of her head, surrendering. "The wine club I sometimes work at . . . it's a front. The place is actually a high-class brothel."

What?

I couldn't . . .

My mind was pure confusion. "This isn't Nevada, it's Cook County. Prostitution is illegal."

"Yup." It seemed like she was watching my reaction intently, and her expression was guarded. "My job is to negotiate the purchase price between the clients and the girls."

Emotions clashed inside me. Horror Payton worked at an illegal whorehouse. Relief she wasn't one of the *girls*. "So," I tried to assemble the words and floundered. "You aren't the one sleeping with clients for money?"

"No, no. Not anymore."

The room went still.

What the fuck did she mean?

Payton combed a hand through her hair, pushing it back off her face, and leaned forward on the tabletop. Her expression hardened. "I like money, and I like sex, and I'm really fucking good at it. So, yeah, I was an escort for a while, and I don't regret it." She straightened, and defensiveness flashed in her eyes. "It's how I really met Dominic."

She was right, it was a damn good thing I was sitting down, because her words left me reeling. "Dominic paid to be with you?"

"Yeah." She scowled, like she abruptly thought better of her answer. "No, he didn't, actually. It doesn't matter. That was years ago. After Dominic, I only worked at the club when Joseph needed help managing or if a sales assistant called in sick."

"Wait a minute." I pulled my shoulders back. "Joseph Monsato?"

Again, she nodded. "It was his club up until last year."

Thoughts swam in my brain. I'd been the fifth wheel to Payton and Dominic's dinners with Joseph and Noemi a half-dozen times. Payton had been a prostitute and Dominic was her john, so that made Joseph . . . her pimp? Good God, what was she going to tell me next? "Jesus. And Noemi? Is that how he met her?"

"Fuck, no. She's the reason he gave up the club."

In the onslaught of all the shocking information, my brain focused on the dumb stuff. I *liked* hanging out with Joseph. His dominating personality was one I admired, and there was something . . . *intriguing* about the way he was around his fiancée.

Not just intriguing, but fascinating. He seemed to have command over Noemi, but the smallest word or gesture from her could draw a huge reaction from him. As if he was always dialed in to what she was thinking and feeling. Being around them made me envious.

I wanted what they had.

But now? I felt like I had nothing in common with him. Joseph had sold sex. Fuck, he'd sold sex with *my* little sister, and yeah, even though she'd been willing, the idea made my fist tighten.

"I get that you need time," Payton said, interrupting my

anger, "but we don't have it. Julius needs your help now."

"Who?"

"My friend. He's the club manager."

I broke my gaze from Payton and stared at the table-top marred with scratches. She wanted me to defend a pimp? I struggled. "Okay, putting all the personal shit to the side for a minute, how exactly is the FBI involved?"

"Earlier tonight I negotiated a deal between a woman and some asshole, and after I left the room, it went to shit. The guy tried to kill her, and he would have done it if Julius hadn't stopped him." Payton took a deep, preparing breath. "So, apparently, this woman, who I thought was my friend, is actually an undercover agent, and the ass-hole is a congressman. Or, he was. Don't think they let you stay in office when you try to strangle the fucking life out of someone."

"It was a sting operation to bring down the club?"

"No, I don't think so. Regan—" A scowl crossed her face. "The *agent* has been working at the club for over a year."

If that had been the goal, the feds wouldn't need that much time to shut down the club. It meant the sting had been set up to trap someone else. The congressman? May-be other high profile players in Chicago?

"Did you witness the assault?"

"Not in person, but Julius has video of the whole thing."

Her eyes hinted at something and I understood in-stantly. "Julius has it. Not the FBI."

"He's smart." She rose from her chair, forcing me to do the same. "He knows how valuable the video is." Pay-ton stepped closer. "Look, I know this is a lot to ask, but will you help him? Julius saved Regan's life and called the ambulance, knowing it was going to destroy his club. He's a good guy.”

My gaze fell to her hand, which gently gripped my arm.

“Please, Kyle.”

I'd failed Payton as a brother most of my life. I wasn't going to do it anymore.

My voice was strong. “Of course. Where is he?”

ONE MONTH LATER

Spoons. I was actually getting ready to write a motion about spoons.

Keith and Elizabeth Gillespie had been in the process of divorcing for more than two years. Their union had begun forty-three years ago, and I was certain they'd despised each other at least that long. So why had they gotten married in the first place? Keith said the sex, *even now*, was fantastic.

They fought over everything as I struggled to separate their assets. Last month it had been the window treatments. Now it was a set of collectable spoons from a trip they'd taken to Rome. In 1997.

Two years ago, I'd been at a top-tier firm in Manhattan, arguing cases that mattered. Now, I'd been handed the Gillespie's joke of a divorce, a case from the bottom of the barrel. Punishment for not coming to James, Franklin, and McCreary after I'd graduated law school as my parents expected me to. It'd been five years and they still weren't over it.

I spun in my office chair, turning to glance out the floor-to-ceiling window. I stared at the black tinted windows of another high-rise. If I leaned forward in my chair, there would be a break in the buildings and I could see a sliver of Lake Michigan.

"Kyle."

My father stood in my doorway, one hand on the door frame. Robert McCreary's hair was graying and had gone completely white at the temples. It made him look trustworthy, when the truth was he was a shark.

"What's your schedule for New Year's Eve?"

My parents wanted to spend the holiday together as a family? That'd be a first.

"I don't have anything yet. Why?"

"Your mother double booked us for a fundraising event and a midnight cruise with the partners." He didn't pause long enough for me to protest, since I knew what he was about to say. "We need you to go to the fundraiser for us."

"Uh, pass."

He stepped into the office, pulling my door shut. "The school's unveiling their new McCreary theater, so a McCreary has to attend for the press release."

I bit back the swear word I wanted to let loose. It wasn't like they could ask Payton. She didn't even hyphenate her new last name with her maiden one, as if she couldn't wait to get rid of it.

And my parents wouldn't forgo anything with their precious partners. The plain expression on my father's face said he wouldn't take no for an answer.

I scrubbed away the wrinkle that was developing on my forehead. "All right, all right." The old me would have just gone with it, but not anymore. If I was giving up my holiday to perform a symbolic ribbon cutting, I deserved something in return. "But I get my pick from the client list next time I have an opening."

Displeasure was an ugly expression on my father's face. I didn't blindly accept his demand, and it was as if I had insulted him. He didn't have a choice, though. His grimace faded into resignation. "Agreed."

As he exited my office, my focus returned to my computer screen. I'd done what I could to ensure this was the last goddamn motion I ever wrote about spoons.

Soldier Field was thick with Bears fans, anxious for football. After taking an escalator, two elevators, and following a winding hallway, I arrived at the box suite. I'd taken Julius's case pro bono, which allowed me to keep it under the radar from my parents, and as a thank you, Julius had invited me to watch the game with him. The Chicago Bears versus their arch rival the Green Bay Packers.

Tickets would have cost a fortune, but not for Julius. He'd played football in college with Tariq Crawford, a cornerback for the Bears. At least a third of the fans I'd passed coming up here had Crawford's number on their jerseys.

I hung my coat in the space just inside the door and stared through the deep room out the glass to the stadium beyond. Players warmed up on the field, which was starting to yellow from winter.

The suite was half-full with people, more women than men, and a few children sat at a side table, engrossed in their tablets while adults mingled by the marble-top bar. Fancy-looking appetizers waited under heat lamps, while a black and white portrait of George Halas looked on.

Julius was already seated in the tiered leather seats facing the sloping window. He looked at ease as he stared at the field, and I wondered how many times he'd seen this view before.

"Hey," I said.

"You made it." Julius came to his feet and gave me a strong handshake. He was a bear of a man, who could look intimidating if you didn't know him. His dark skin had a sheen on the dome of his shaved head, but when he flashed a warm smile, it became contagious.

I'd helped him through negotiations with the FBI. His club continued to operate under the FBI's supervision, and as long as he fully cooperated, he received immunity, along with all of his staff. Including my sister.

Once his case was over, he'd stopped being a client and had become my friend. Payton had been right; it was impossible not to like Julius.

When he sat, I took the empty seat beside him. "You and Tariq must be tight."

His face took on a strange cast. "Yeah, these are actually Court's tickets."

"Who's he?"

"Courtney Crawford." Julius's pause wasn't dramatic, but caught my attention. "She's, uh, Tariq's wife. She said she wasn't going to use the tickets, so he gave them to me."

A game against the Packers? "This is a big game to miss."

"Yeah."

What he didn't say, and how he looked off in the distance, spoke volumes. Was trouble brewing in the Crawford marriage? There was more to the story there, but I didn't ask.

We kept the conversation light and focused on the game. When the first quarter was coming to a close, Tariq flattened a running back and sprung the ball loose, sending all the players scrambling for recovery. The suite erupted in shouts, but Julius's was the loudest.

"Do you miss playing?" I asked when the roar in the crowd finally receded.

"Nah. Maybe, but then Tariq talks about two-a-days, and fuck that. Or Court will text how he comes home looking beat to shit."

Julius made a face and took a long sip of his beer, as if trying to shut himself up. What was this reaction? He didn't want me to know Tariq's wife had texted him?

I should have left it alone, but I was curious. "How come she's not here?"

"She . . ." He sighed. "Ain't a secret, I guess. It's not working between them anymore." He glanced around the room, checked that no one else was listening, and leaned closer, his voice going low. "Tariq's my boy and all, but she can do better."

The picture snapped into focus.

"Holy shit, Julius," I whispered, stifling my grin. "I'm guessing Tariq doesn't know, or he wouldn't have given you the tickets."

"What are you talking about?"

"You want to fuck his wife."

Julius could say whatever he wanted, but his dark eyes went enormously white, and it confirmed my suspicions.

"No, man, it ain't like that!" Once again, his gaze swept around to make sure we were safe. "She's just a friend."

"Yeah, a friend you want to stick your dick in."

I probably shouldn't have teased him. He was humongous, and I'd seen what he could do when he put power behind his fist. Former Congressman Bennett's jaw was likely still wired shut. But I believed Julius was a gentle giant.

"Fuck you, Kyle." His voice was warm. "Yeah, I wished she'd noticed me instead of him at OSU, but it's a done deal." He took the last sip of his beer. "She's off limits."

Was he relieved to have his secret out? It felt good he'd shared it with me, and I wasn't going to tease him further. Instead, I stood. "You want another beer?"

"Yeah, sure."

Discussion between us was relaxed up through halftime, even as the Bears fell behind on the score. Courtney Crawford had been a cheerleader at OSU, and Tariq had staked his claim on her before Julius got a chance. He'd been carrying the torch for her a long, long time.

"So, man, I gotta ask," Julius said. "No lady for ya?" He made a face like he was displeased with his assumption. "Or guy?"

I chuckled. "No, no *woman* on the horizon right now."

"I wondered," he said. "Taylor came at you hard at Payton's wedding, but you didn't go for her."

Taylor, one of Payton's coworker friends had been beautiful, as all of Julius's girls were. At the time, I hadn't known what she did, but I'd pretended I was immune to her non-stop flirting. "She's nice, but she was . . . a lot."

I didn't have anything nice to say, so I wasn't going to. It'd been clear after the first thirty seconds Taylor and I had nothing in common, and the attempt at conversation became painful.

The leather seat squeaked as I shifted in it. "Since I got back from New York, it's been a challenge meeting women I click with."

"Why'd you come back?"

I still hadn't found a convincing lie to tell about it. I stared at the man beside me, whose dark eyes were curious and free from judgment. I could tell him. I'd figured out his secret, and he'd seemed relieved. Maybe sharing with him could do the same for me.

"There was a woman I got involved with. I thought it was just sex, but she thought it was . . ."

"More," he said, nodding.

I put emphasis on it. "A lot more."

Sharon had thought it was the jewelry in a little black box kind of more, which I couldn't have been further from. I understood loyalty and commitment, but what we had wasn't in the same ballpark as love.

"We messed around for a few months. When the fun began to fade, she upped her game, and said she'd do *anything* I was into. I'd been curious about . . . well, shit. The kind of things that go on at your club. So, when she offered to let me explore that, like a fucking idiot, I took her up on it."

"That don't sound like it went well."

Even though I knew he wouldn't bat an eye, it wasn't information I liked volunteering. "I bought a kit off of Amazon, like handcuffs and toys. Don't judge me."

He flashed a smile. "She wasn't into it after all?"

"No, she seemed to be. I mean, she said she was, during." I paused, remembering my confusion afterward. "I thought we had fun, and that's all it was. In the morning, she pulled a one-eighty. It had been a tactic on her part, and she was really fucking pissed when I explained we weren't on the same page."

The memory of Sharon's words echoed in my mind. *"I endured your stupid fetish for nothing?"* she'd yelled at me.

Fetish?

All I'd done was spank her a few times and used some dirty phrases. That night wouldn't have even earned the #hardcore tag had it been a porn video.

"When Sharon didn't get the commitment she wanted, she lost it. She said what I'd done to her made it too difficult to continue working together."

"Oh, shit." Julius sobered. "You worked together?"

"Yeah. She was a senior partner at the law firm I worked at. Basically, she was my boss." I picked at the label on my beer. "I knew it was stupid to get involved, but I did it anyway." It was painful to admit. "I fucked up, big time."

For a long moment, he was quiet, as if contemplating.

"It happens," he offered, his voice sincere.

"Sharon blacklisted me as revenge. Finding another job at a decent firm was impossible." I left out the part where I'd been forced to retaliate, and rather than have her reputation sullied, Sharon paid me to leave New York quietly.

I had slinked back to my parents' firm and tried to be grateful for the job, but it was a struggle.

What wasn't a struggle, was hanging out with Julius. Conversation rarely lapsed, and when it did, the silence wasn't uncomfortable. We grimaced together as the Bears fell further behind in the score, and took turns groaning about the officiating.

"Gotta ask," I said, late in the fourth quarter, "what are you going to do about Courtney if and when she's a free woman?"

"Nothing," he said, resigned.

"Because of Tariq?"

"Nah. Tariq's not good enough for her," his expression was serious, "but I ain't either."

Tuesday felt like a Monday, and I had to get a second cup of coffee to get me going. I was walking back from the coffee maker when I glanced at the conference room at the center of the office suite.

It was all glass. A strategic design, in case the firm ever became outnumbered during a discovery or deposition and needed to call for reinforcements. My father sat across the large table, his arms crossed on the tabletop, and leaned forward to listen to the woman sitting on the side opposite him. I couldn't see much of her other than her blonde hair that was cropped short.

Usually he met clients one-on-one in his office which was designed to impress and intimidate. I took a detour through the front lobby.

"Why's my dad meeting in the conference room?" I asked the administrative assistant who manned the desk.

"He has a client in his office, so he had me put Ms. Crawford in the conference room," she said. "She actually asked for you, but your father said you were full and he'd handle it."

"Courtney Crawford?"

The assistant nodded.

"The fuck he will," I muttered under my breath.

I moved as fast as my full cup of coffee would allow and pulled open the door, catching my father's attention. He scowled, but I jerked my hand to the hallway, giving him the signal, *"We need to talk out here."*

"I'm sorry," he said, rising to his feet. "Please excuse me for a moment, Ms. Crawford."

She turned her head, giving me a view of her profile, and if I wasn't so fucking pissed at him, I might have grinned. Oh, she was cute. The image of Julius pining after this petite little white girl was so sweet my teeth almost hurt.

Dad waited until the door closed before speaking. "What is it?"

"That's my client you're meeting with."

He had the nerve to look confused. "It's another divorce case. I thought you wanted your pick so you could avoid them."

Bullshit. This was a high-profile divorce. Tariq Crawford was worth millions, and if there wasn't a prenup? My father was trying to poach from his own son, and I narrowed my eyes. It was funny how work always came first with my parents over family. I felt compelled to remind him it was the same for me. "She asked for me by name, *Robert.*"

"I was just trying to do you a favor." He balked at me

using his first name, but I wanted to reinforce our professional line.

"Okay, thanks, but I've got this."

He shook his head and put his hand on the door, signaling he was going back in. "It's fine. I've already started with Ms. Crawford. Tell you what, you can take a look at the client list for—"

"I won't do the New Year's fundraiser."

He stopped dead in his tracks, the door open a few inches. He pushed it back closed and turned to me, anger flashing in his eyes. "I don't like being threatened."

"Yeah? You're in the wrong job, then. I don't like clients being stolen from me."

The ensuing argument probably played out in his head just as it did mine, while we stared at each other wordlessly. He wouldn't win, and the moment he knew it was clear on his face. He pressed his lips together and drew in a deep, resigned breath.

I followed him into the conference room and waited as my father introduced me. Courtney had big blue eyes and long lashes, giving her a doe-like look. Her blonde hair was swept aside. Minimal makeup, or artfully applied to look that way.

"Well," my father said, collecting up his tablet, pen, and paper. "I apologize you'll need to go over this again with Kyle, but you're in good hands."

I set down my cup of coffee and sank into the seat. "It's nice to meet you, Ms. Crawford. I'm told you asked for me?"

She nodded, fidgeting with her hands. Her ring finger was bare, which was a good sign for me. It was hard when the client hadn't come to terms with what was going to happen.

"Julius," she said. "He told me you helped him with some legal issue a few months ago."

The blank expression said she had no idea what. She didn't know what Julius did for a living? His comment about not being good enough for her made a lot more sense.

"Yes, I did," I said. "But I can't discuss that. What can I help you with?"

Her eyes grew wet with tears, but she blinked them back. "I need a divorce attorney. A good one."

I smiled and hoped it was sincere without being cocky. "Perfect. I'm both."

RUBY

How the fuck did my glasses always get so dirty? I rarely wore them. I'd forgotten to order contacts and torn the last pair I owned this morning while trying to put the left one in. Fuck my life. The black rimmed glasses were cute, but cheap.

I was still polishing them during the elevator ride up, then into the opposing firm's lobby, and all the way to their conference room. The smudge would not come off, and it made me look like a crazy person. I'd wipe the lenses, peer through them up at the light, and then go right back to wiping.

I sat in a chair and didn't even know where we were. Henry was the lead on this case, and he grabbed me out of the pool of junior lawyers, mostly because I was a woman, and therefore, assumed I would be excellent at taking notes. Sexist pig. He gave me no information other than the guy was a football player and *hot shit*.

We rode in the elevator together, and it turned out Hot Shit's name was Tariq Crawford. He looked unhappy and uncomfortable in his gray suit, but I figured it was from the legal proceedings about to occur rather than his attire. I didn't pay much attention to sports, but I knew professional players had to dress nicely when they traveled. He probably had a closet full of expensive suits.

Or maybe a hotel room. I wasn't sure what kind of

divorce this was.

He was attractive. Tall and lean, with dark skin and beautifully black, expressive eyes. He wore his hair in clean dreads which were gathered in back, and gave him a professional and serious look.

The conference room wasn't empty. A tiny blonde woman sat across from me. The only thing in front of her was her phone, and her pained gaze flew to Tariq. So, obviously, the wife. She was cute, and I would bet when she smiled, she was dazzling. But she wasn't smiling today. Her eyes were full of sadness.

Sitting next to her was a gorgeous piece of man. His charcoal slim-fit suit hung perfectly on his shoulders, and the purple-plaid tie was knotted exactly so at his neck. A short beard, if you could call it that, wrapped around sexy lips. His brown hair was mussed nicely, calling me to run my fingers through it and make the curling ends lay just a little flatter. The maple color of his hair and scruff set off the blue in his eyes.

Which were staring at me with something like horror trapped inside.

Oh.

My.

Shit.

"*Kyle?*" I eked out.

He seemed to swallow hard. "Hey, Ruby."

No way. No fucking way. I tore my gaze from him and glared at Henry. He could have warned me the only man to ever break my heart was representing Crawford's wife. Only Henry didn't know a thing about me because he was a sexist pig, and even if he weren't, my history with Kyle wasn't something I liked to share.

Henry raised an eyebrow. "You know each other?"

There was a long pause where neither of us said anything. I wasn't about to do it. Leave-y McLeaverson could.

Finally, Kyle spoke. "We, uh, went to law school together."

That was what he'd boil it down to. I'd waited five years for contact, waited for his apology. So when I finally got to hear his deep, sexy voice and the first words weren't, *"I'm so fucking sorry that I'm a piece of shit asshole,"* I almost reached across the table and slapped him. Instead, I glanced at the door. How much trouble would I be in if I bailed on Henry? I wasn't sure I could stay here.

Not with the way Kyle made a tidal wave of memories crash against me.

Or the way he looked now, wearing the hell out of his gorgeous suit.

Henry attempted to clear his throat, but it was obvious to everyone this was his call for my attention. I put my reluctant gaze on him and watched one of his bushy eyebrows lift. His expression said it all. *"You fuck this guy?"*

I ignored his questioning look, and glared back to Kyle, choking on my temper. I forced myself to be professional. "What happened to New York?"

His lips parted as if about to say something, but he produced no sound. I didn't know why I was surprised. He'd left me without saying a thing. Ten amazing months with him, and I didn't even get a goodbye. Not a goddamn word.

No, I wasn't bitter at all.

"It's . . . not relevant right now." Kyle straightened his pad of paper and turned his attention to Henry. "Should we get started?"

Fucking unbelievable.

I took notes, fueled by rage, and pretended I wasn't thinking about the asshole across from me in the gray suit, or how I wanted to strangle him with his perfect tie. The marriage was breaking down due to irreconcilable differences. The couple was frosty, but cordial. Or maybe it was the open hostility between Kyle and me overshadowing it all.

I stayed silent during the meeting. It didn't appear to be a contentious divorce, and everyone was civil until the final moments.

"Alimony," Kyle said, flipping to a new page in his pad.

Henry looked offended. "What my client has offered is more than fair."

"To who? Your client? He just signed a contract for twenty-seven million over the next six years."

The wife drew in a deep breath, signaling her discomfort. She appeared uneasy about the money, but I pushed it from my mind. My focus was on our client, not Kyle's.

It was the first time Mr. Crawford spoke in the meeting. "Nene."

Her gaze went to her soon-to-be-ex-husband. "Don't, Tariq. I hate that nickname."

"Since when?"

She made a face. "Since always."

"I'm going to be sending over a revised figure," Kyle said to Henry. "It's reasonable." There was a threat laced in his words. *Don't push back, or I'll hit you hard.* I knew Kyle well enough to believe he'd do it. Should I warn my colleague not to challenge him? I hadn't worked much with Henry, but I was fairly certain he'd be decimated if he went head-to-head with my ex-boyfriend.

When the meeting was over, I packed up my things

as quickly as possible. It'd be poor professionalism to flip Kyle the bird, so I'd need to make a run for the elevator bank before that happened. The risk grew greater every second I remained in his presence.

"Ruby." The irritatingly sexy voice caused me to hesitate. "Do you have a minute?"

I shook my head and jammed my tablet into my bag. No, I didn't have a minute. He'd had five long years to talk to me; my phone number hadn't changed. I was done giving him my time. I slung my briefcase strap over my shoulder as I stood. *C'mon, Henry. Move your ass!* My middle finger itched to raise up and announce how I thought Kyle was number one—a number one asshole.

His voice was surprisingly forceful. "Ruby, a word."

"Yeah? How about *fuck you*." It burst out from me and detonated in the room, blanketing us in horrifying silence right after the Crawfords joint gasp.

"Well," Kyle said, grimacing, "that was actually two words."

I expected him to volley a barb at me or turn to Henry and demand I apologize, but he said nothing. As I hurried toward the door, I had the fleeting thought Kyle might chase after me, but I cursed myself for being stupid. He wasn't any good at goodbyes. He'd made it oh-so-clear how silence was his favorite way to go.

"Jesus Christ, Ruby," Henry groaned as soon as the elevator doors shut, sealing me in with him and Tariq. I sank down into my shame faster than the elevator car could carry us to the ground level. "What the hell?"

"I'm sorry, I wasn't prepared to see him. My temper got the better of me, and I promise it won't happen again."

It was quiet for a moment, and I watched the numbers

change as we descended. The elevator car was stifling.

"What'd he do to you?" Tariq asked quietly.

Was he being polite, or genuinely curious? I was so scattered, I felt compelled to answer, only . . . How did I do that?

"We were together for almost a year, and then he . . . vanished." It was a massive oversimplification, but it would do. I'd been in love with Kyle, and although he was never able to say the words back to me, I'd believed he loved me, too. Boy, was I naïve.

He was a year older than I was and about to start his final year of law school when I'd bumped into him at Randhurst University's bookstore. We'd both reached for the same textbook, and the moment was still so vivid. I still remembered how excited I'd been when he struck up a conversation. How thrilled I'd been when he asked for my phone number. Well, he'd more or less demanded it, but I didn't need much persuasion. He was smart, and funny, and holy fuck, gorgeous.

Our relationship had been wild and amazing. We clicked on every level, or so I thought. Conversation, politics, and the two of us in the bedroom? Oh yes, we definitely were in sync there.

When his job offer from the firm in New York came in, it thrust us into a strange territory. I couldn't leave law school with only one year left and follow him, and more importantly, he hadn't asked me to. We danced around talking about it for a month as his graduation loomed.

Neither of us were interested in doing the long distance thing. I firmly believed long distance relationships only worked out if they started off with distance from the get-go. There was no way we'd survive an eight-hundred-mile wedge being driven between us. I loved Chicago, and Kyle had made it clear he wanted to get the fuck out as soon as he had his diploma.

Planning to say goodbye to him the day after his graduation had torn my heart into two. How was I going to kiss him, watch him climb into his car loaded up with everything he owned, and leave me? What if I broke down and asked him to stay? Could I survive him saying no?

It never got that far.

The sadness at the memory was instantly replaced with fiery rage. Fuck him for making me think about that horrible afternoon. He hadn't answered my repeated knocking on his apartment door, and the curtainless window showed the place was vacant. The guy across the hall said Kyle had finished moving out and left a while ago.

My heart shredded further when I'd called his cellphone and it'd gone straight to voicemail. I sat on his doorstop and cried my stupid eyes out until there was nothing left but anger. Some at myself for being a fool, loving an asshole, and getting played, but most of it was aimed at him.

What a fucking coward.

I could breathe again when the elevator stopped and let us out. Henry dismissed me with a glare, wordlessly telling me I was on my own for getting back to the office.

It was sleeting outside and my feet froze in my heels instantly, so every step across the slick pavement was extra treacherous. It was close to lunch, and I didn't have any appointments today. My pathetic frozen dinner in the freezer at work could wait. I'd treat myself to dessert first.

Despite my attempts not to think about Kyle, I somehow typed his name into the browser on my phone while I waited in line to drown my sorrows at Mac Bakery. Why wasn't I more interested in the macaron flavors they were offering? Instead of looking at the hand lettered chalkboard menu, I peered at the tiny screen of my iPhone, demanding it tell me what he'd been up to since he'd fled Chicago.

Since he'd pulverized my heart and left me a bawling mess on his doorstep.

Google didn't have answers. There were a few mentions of him regarding casework, starting last year, for his parents' firm. What had happened to bring him back to the city, and gotten him to work for his parents? He'd acted like he'd work anywhere but with them.

"What can I get for you?" The woman behind the counter stared at me expectantly.

There were rows of perfectly formed French macarons stacked behind the glass. Each flavor sounded divine. Peanut butter. Chocolate mint. Birthday cake. It went on, and on, and I wanted them all in my mouth. How the fuck was I supposed to decide?

I got a box of six, swearing to myself I wouldn't eat more than two before returning to the office. While I waited for them to be packaged, I glanced once more at my phone.

Huh.

I wouldn't have pegged Kyle for a philanthropist, but then again, I obviously didn't know him. On New Year's Eve, he'd be the guest of honor at some fundraising party at the Opulent Hotel. Black tie, five hundred dollars a plate.

God, he'd look great in a tux.

Wait. No.

In fact, hell-to-the-fucking *nope*. Fuck him in his tuxedo-wearing ass. I hoped he'd choke on a gourmet hors d'oeuvre. That was the last I was going to think about Kyle

McCreary. I paid for my macarons, snatched up the bag, and flung the door open, scurrying out into the cold.

KYLE

I spent Christmas Eve at Payton and Dominic's place, sitting off to the side while the rest of her coupled friends celebrated together. Noemi, Joseph's fiancé, was considerably younger than everyone else. Even if she'd wanted to distance herself from the group, Joseph wouldn't allow it. His arm was always around her shoulders, or a hand rested on her hip, holding her against him.

Holding her close.

Not that the girl wanted to be anywhere else. She seemed to hang on Payton's every word, like my sister could do no wrong. Did she know what Payton used to do for a living? She had to. Her future husband created the club. He'd run it for years before selling it to Julius.

The glass of spiced eggnog in my hand was getting warm, and I ignored it. I stared out the enormous floor-to-ceiling window of my sister and her husband's apartment which usually had a magnificent view of North Beach, only it was snowing and overcast tonight. The only thing I could see in the window was the reflection of twinkling white lights from the Christmas tree.

Sitting in a chair across from me was a large guy, who appeared more out of place than I was, except he was attached to the redheaded FBI agent. I wasn't sure which name to use. She'd been Special Agent Andrea Adams during the deposition, but everyone here called her Regan, her enormous boyfriend included. So I'd stick with that.

The cuffs of his sweater were pushed back, revealing a sleeve of ink on one arm. I wasn't a tattoo person myself, but the pattern was interesting.

"Is the design yours?" I asked him, trying to make conversation. Payton had said the guy was an artist.

His voice was deep, matching his large form. "Yeah."

Before I could compliment it, Joseph's head turned toward us. "That reminds me, Silas. If I wanted to add to my tattoo, would you have time?"

Noemi's face skewed with alarm. "What are you doing to your tattoo?"

"Relax," he said, hushed. "I'm not going to change the overall design. I just want to revise the wording." Joseph's dark eyes lit with amusement. "I wouldn't dream of jeopardizing your favorite part of me."

She tucked a lock of blonde hair behind her ear, revealing a serious expression. "It is the only reason I'm with you."

"Oh, is it, now?" Joseph's voice was playful, but contained an edge beneath. His hand slipped from the small of her back, coursing down until it rested on her ass, and then he squeezed so hard, she bit her bottom lip. As if silencing a yelp of surprise. "Because I can think of some other parts of me you like. Should I keep those to myself?"

She leaned in close, whispering. I couldn't hear it, but her lips moved to form what appeared to be, "No, sir."

Victory ran through his expression.

Watching the exchange made ugly jealousy churn deep inside me. Their partnership filled me with envy. I was aggravated I was having difficulty finding a woman I wanted to spend time with both inside and outside of the bedroom. Would I ever find one who was interested in the same things I was?

You've already met a woman like that.

The annoying thought slid into my brain like a seemingly innocuous line of text buried in a contract. Only those little words had major ramifications.

Yeah, I had met a woman like that, but Ruby hated my fucking guts. And I was just as angry and caught off guard as she seemed to be.

The petty streak in me was pissed she looked even better than when we'd been together at Randhurst. She'd have been easier to ignore if my cock hadn't leaped to attention at the sight of her. It'd been ten days since the Crawfords' meeting, but I remembered every detail of the event with painful clarity.

A strange prickle worked its way along my spine as I'd glanced at the brunette alongside the male attorney representing Mr. Crawford. My gaze started at her nude heels and moved swiftly upward as she shed her tan coat and unwrapped the plaid scarf from her neck. Beneath, she wore a navy fitted suitdress which clung perfectly to her, flaunting her hourglass figure.

Her hair was the color of dark chocolate and curled into soft waves, falling past her shoulders. I made it all the way to her face before I recognized her. The glasses threw me off. Black rimmed, hipster glasses were tucked beneath her bangs, giving her a sexy yet studious look.

I didn't want to see Ruby again. *Ever.*

My scars from her had healed, or so I thought. Her gorgeous eyes, hidden behind the thick lenses, peered at me, and it tore open the wound so it was as fresh as the moment I'd driven away from Chicago.

"Kyle?" she'd said.

Her face flooded with shock, followed instantly with contempt. Our time apart hadn't softened her feelings toward me either, it seemed.

Fine with me, I lied to myself. I could pretend the woman across the table meant absolutely nothing, even though she'd crushed me. Jesus, she was still crushing me now with those pouty lips and fire blazing in her eyes.

I'd held it together until the end of the meeting. Tension and unease grew with every moment Ruby came closer to walking out the door. What if I never saw her again? Was this how I wanted my last memory of her to be? She put her things away in a hurry.

"Ruby, do you have a minute?"

She shook her head, refusing to look at me, and it made me angry. How could she say no to one lousy conversation, after all this time? With what we'd had, didn't she owe me at least that?

Her denial made my skin burn hot, and I couldn't contain my frustration, so it came out more forceful than I wanted. "Ruby, a word."

"Yeah? How about *fuck you.*"

Awesome. Add that to the list of sweet nothings she'd lobbed at me.

I watched her storm out, and after her boss's unnecessary apology, I was left alone in the room with Courtney, who perked one eyebrow upward.

"That was a nice change of pace," I said, gritting my teeth. "Usually it's the husband who's cussing at me."

Courtney gave a sad smile.

I'd spent the rest of the day in my office, trying not to let Ruby's angry voice ring in my head. I also forced myself not to seek out her email address from her firm's website. I'd heard a joke once that an app existed where anytime you tried to call your ex, the phone would play Nickelback.

I didn't download it, but whenever I got the urge to hunt for her contact info, I hummed "How You Remind Me" as punishment, and it seemed to work. But I could not stop thinking about her. Ruby Carter dominated not just my waking thoughts. I'd nearly flung the alarm clock across the room yesterday when it interrupted my dream moments before sinking my dick into a wet and waiting Ruby.

"What's with the face?" Payton asked, drawing me back to the Christmas party. Her scolding gaze was fixated on me. "Still pissed about the white elephant game?"

I glanced at the box where I'd set the cooking apron decorated with a lobster body and the two matching claw oven mitts. "What do you mean?" I said. "I love it. I'm so relieved no one stole it from me."

Payton grinned and plopped down on the couch, scrolling through her phone. She brought up the picture she'd taken when I'd modeled my prize, and zoomed in on my face, complete with idiotic expression. "See how awesome you look in it?"

"If you show it to anyone else, you're dead to me."

"Ooh." She faked a sheepish look. "Yeah, I Instagramed that shit twenty minutes ago."

"Okay, well, it was nice knowing you."

Payton pocketed her phone and gave me her full attention. "Let's talk New Year's resolutions."

"I don't need any. I'm already perfect."

"Ha!" She practically snorted. "That's not what those products on your bathroom counter say."

This again? I blinked slowly. "That's the kettle calling the pot black. There's at least as much shit on yours as there is mine."

"I'm a woman. That's normal for me. Is that why you don't have a girlfriend? Are you worried she'd be crushed under an avalanche of metrosexual products if she stays at your place?"

Dominic lingered nearby, listening in. "Payton, it's Christmas Eve. Cut him some slack." As my brother-in-law took a swig of his beer, I was somewhat grateful he was on my side. That was, until he added, "Maybe looking good doesn't come as easy to your brother as it does for me."

"Asshole," I said. "We know who's better looking. I have the dollar to prove it."

It was a running joke between us. A few nights after my sister and Dominic had returned from living abroad in Japan, I'd taken them out to dinner, and Payton made the bet the waitress would find her fiancée more attractive than me.

I'd lost that one, but won the dollar back when we asked the hostess. It had passed hands countless times, but currently was tucked in *my* wallet. It'd been the bartender the last time we'd gone out for drinks. He'd winked at me right after, and although I didn't swing that way, I'd still take it as a win.

"Okay, Mr. Fucking Perfect," Payton said. "My New Year's resolution is to find you a special lady friend. And by lady friend, I mean someone you can stick your dick in."

"Jesus." I swallowed hard and choked on the spit. "You're my sister."

"Yeah, and you're my mopey big brother who clearly needs to get laid. I can offer Dominic up as a wingman, but he's too distracting. The wedding ring only slows the hoes down." She glanced across the room. "Joseph. He needs a new project."

I wasn't sure how to feel about Joseph. As time went by, I was coming to terms with the club and Joseph's role in all of it, but he'd set my sister down a path I wasn't happy with.

"I don't care to be referred to as a *project*, and you don't seem to understand how resolutions work," I said. "You can't set one for someone else."

My sister shrugged. "I do what I want, Kyle."

Yeah, wasn't that the fucking truth?

Black and gold balloons were suspended in netting over the dance floor of the Opulent Hotel's ballroom, waiting for the clock to hit midnight and start the new year. Round tables covered with black tablecloths and gold napkins surrounded the hardwood tiles on three sides. The simple, temporary stage was on the fourth, and held the deejay booth.

I'd done what was required of me at the fundraiser twenty minutes ago. The superintendent gave a long speech, and I'd been called on stage to accept a plaque and handshake as the school's gesture of gratitude. It'd been awkward, holding the man's hand and my smile for a long moment while pictures were taken.

Did I need to stay all the way until midnight? I took a sip of my drink, which was far more Coke than bourbon, and glanced around the room. Frank Sinatra sang from the speakers and couples had partnered up on the dance floor, swaying to the music. Cocktail dresses sparkled in the soft chandelier light.

I needed to get out of here before the balloons rained down on all the happy partygoers. I was starting off another year in Chicago alone.

Fuck it.

Payton's resolution for me was stupid, but true. I could call Julius and ask for a wingman, but I was pretty sure he was holding out hope for Courtney. I'd had dinner with him right after Christmas, a casual thing to watch a college bowl game. How long would my new friend wait after the divorce was finalized, and would he make a move at all? Or would Julius wait forever to see if Courtney was interested in him as more than a friend?

I could call Joseph as well. After Payton had pitched her "project" to him, he'd set his gaze on me and seemed pleased. But I didn't need help or a wingman. There was no reason to go trolling bars, or list myself on dating websites. I was done kidding myself. I already knew what I wanted, and I hated it.

There wasn't a ring on Ruby's finger.

Sure, we were both still angry, but there'd been feelings between us before. Strong, deep ones. What would have happened if I'd stayed in Chicago? Would there be a ring on her finger now?

I stared down at my drink. Maybe it was stronger than I thought.

Whatever. I'd convinced her to give me a shot once. Could I do it again? And . . . did I really want to? There were days when simply hearing her name scraped at the hole left where she'd ripped my heart out.

At that exact moment, the universe tilted on its axis.

A woman in a pale pink dress stood at the bar, her intense gaze locked onto me. My knees softened and I tightened my grip on my glass, fighting against the weak response. Her dark hair was pinned up, and her lips were stained a vibrant red, the same shade as her name.

Ruby.

Chapter
SIX

RUBY

Breath halted in my lungs. Kyle's tuxedo was simple. Maybe it wasn't even a tux, but a jet black suit he owned and a matching silk tie. He looked out of place, standing alone with his fingers curled on a glass tumbler, while everyone else mingled around him.

The moment he saw me, hairs lifted on my arms. Every nerve ending in me fired up to the ready. As anticipated, he looked amazing, and it pissed me off. What was I doing here? Was I really this stupid? I must have suffered PTSD last time I'd seen him, because I'd forgotten his magnetic effect.

The flood of emotions overtook me. Desire. Longing. And on top of it all, heart aching pain.

He stood still as a statue, watching me. His expression was confusion, and then it shifted into a blank one. To someone else it might look empty, but I'd seen him preparing for mock closing statements. There was definitely a lot going on behind his eyes right now. Was he deciding on the best way to bail?

No, I convinced myself. He'd wanted to talk to me last time. It was doubtful my "fuck you" comment had made much of an impact to change his mind. I shifted my weight on my nervous legs. Should I stay here by the bar? Could I walk up to him without giving away I was falling apart inside?

Shit. *Shit!* I had a plan, but it ran screaming with terror from my brain as soon as Kyle took a step toward me. This was when I was most dangerous. When my thoughts turned off, my temper made itself home.

I spun on my heel and faced the bar. "Get it together!" I whisper yelled to myself.

The female bartender, who was mixing a drink, paused and looked at me.

I plastered on an apologetic smile. "Sorry, not you. You're fine." I pointed to the bottle of chardonnay on the counter. "Can I get a glass of that?"

I couldn't hear his approach over the music, but I sensed it. A shiver ran down my spine when he spoke. "Ruby."

"Kyle," I responded, my voice flat and even, which was a small miracle. I refused to turn and look at him. Instead I watched as the bartender poured my drink, and I fumbled in my purse for a tip.

"What are you doing here?"

"Getting a drink."

He had no response, and it left me without options. I took the glass from the woman, dropped my tip in the jar, and forced myself to look at the man who'd callously squashed my heart.

"You look beautiful." He spoke almost like he was mad about it.

His compliment was the last thing I expected him to say, so it was suspect. When my plan abandoned me, I switched into emergency backup mode, which was all defense. "Fuck you."

He wasn't fazed and let the barb roll off him. "I believe you mentioned that already."

"Yes, but I feel strongly, so it bears repeating."

"All right. Noted."

I struggled with what to say next as he took the final sip of his drink and plunked it down beside me on the bar. His hand lingered on the glass. He was close.

Too close.

"You wanted a word last time we saw each other." My voice was tight. "So let's hear it."

"Did you come here for that?" He glanced around the room as if taking in the expensive decorations and setting for the first time. "You could have called me, or my office—"

I shook my head. "Don't go thinking I spent any money. I crashed this." Sneaking into the event had been easy. I'd shown up after dinner was over and pretended I was with a group of women returning from the restroom. Security was incredibly lax as we closed in on midnight. "And I borrowed this dress from a friend."

"Okay, then." Kyle's gaze wandered appreciatively down my figure. "Please tell her thank you for me."

I rolled my eyes so hard I was sure to sprain them, but inside, his compliment created a flutter of warmth. Damn him. The truth was I felt like a million bucks in this dress. The skirt was layers of chiffon with a peekaboo slit halfway up my thigh, and the bodice had a plunging neckline. The dress gave excellent cleave, and Kyle sure hadn't missed it.

Good. I wanted to show off what he'd walked away from. "You come by yourself?" I asked it as a jab, but really, for some insane reason I wanted to know.

"As did you, it seems. Did you leave the boyfriend home alone on New Year's Eve?"

I clenched a hand into a fist. "No, there's no boy— No." Crap, I was better than this. "And you? Why come alone?"

His expression was devoid of emotion. "There wasn't

anyone I was interested in taking."

When the conversation lapsed, his gaze dropped down to my breasts. I let him ogle me for another moment and then set my fist on my hip. "You wanted to talk. Well?"

He needed to get on with it. For years, I'd thought I didn't need closure, but it was likely because I never thought I'd get it. I couldn't stop thinking about what he would have said if I'd let him take me aside and talk to him. It plagued me every moment since, only quieting when I'd made the idiotic decision to seek him out at the fundraiser. At least here I had the element of surprise, and neutral ground.

Would an apology, if he offered one, do anything to lessen the damage he'd caused?

Kyle's focus left me and he seemed to survey the ballroom critically. "Not here. It's going to get loud in twenty minutes."

I didn't want to spend twenty minutes with him. I didn't trust myself when his face looked good enough to wrap my thighs around. "Twenty minutes? Come on, counselor, we both know you can finish in five."

His shoulders snapped back, but otherwise he didn't seem fazed. "How can you be sure? Usually you've forgotten your name after the first two."

My mouth hung open. He pulled out his wallet, dug out a few bigger bills, and made a production of dropping them into the tip jar so the bartender would see.

"Can I grab a bottle of champagne and two glasses?" he asked her.

It sounded like he was only asking as a courtesy, and confirmed it when he didn't wait for an answer. He stepped to the side of the bar, where two servers were pouring champagne into rows of flutes, took two glasses from the end, and plucked an unopened bottle from the large ice bin.

Kyle didn't wait for me to follow, and I hurried to keep up as he headed for the exit.

"Where are we going?" I tried to walk steady and not spill my nearly full wine.

We cleared the doorway and he continued at a fast clip toward the elevator bank. He slapped the button for 'up,' and turned to look at me. "Upstairs."

"Seriously? No. I'm not going up to your room."

"Okay, not a problem. I don't have a room."

The elevator doors peeled back, revealing an empty car. I took too long to decide what to do, and Kyle made the decision for me. He crossed the champagne flute stems in his hand and gripped the neck of the bottle all in one, so his free hand could touch me in the small of my back and urge me forward into the elevator.

I sucked in a sharp breath at the contact.

It was silly. He wasn't a stranger; he knew me *intimately*. This delicate touch wasn't sexual, and yet the muscles tightened in my belly. My heart skipped faster. It felt like he hadn't touched me in a lifetime, and yet my body remembered like it had happened only five minutes ago.

I spun around to face the doors and watched my last chance to escape fade away as they slid shut.

The air was thick being alone with him, but I refused to look at him. Instead I watched the numbers climb as we rose toward the top floor. Where was he taking me? If there was a bar at the top, that didn't make much sense. It'd be just as loud as the ballroom at midnight, and they wouldn't let us in with Kyle carrying the champagne.

My throat tightened as I spoke. "When did you come back?"

"About a year ago."

Even though I already knew the answer, it wounded me all the same. He'd been in the city, working for his parents' firm for more than a year. We had mutual Facebook friends. If he'd wanted to find me, he easily could have. But why would he want to find me, after he'd so cleanly severed my heart?

I washed the hard lump in my throat down with a healthy dose of my wine. Coming to the fundraiser had been a stupid idea. Maybe the dumbest thing I'd ever done, and I'd once gone to a Baha Men concert.

The elevator halted, and Kyle gestured to the opening doors. I hurried out of the confined space, but then pulled to a stop. "Again," I said. "Where are we going?"

Kyle moved swiftly to the hallway and swung left. The sign announced rooms were to the right, and the pool was to the left. The . . . pool? On the top floor?

"Shit," he groaned as we approached the door. "It closed at eleven."

Sure enough, the pool hours listed on the glass door declared the pool area closed. He cupped a hand to the glass and peered inside. It was too dark for me to make anything out, but he straightened abruptly and rapped his knuckles loudly on the door.

"What are you doing?" I said.

"There's a guy in there cleaning up."

I stood back as a man in a hotel uniform pushed open the door and flicked an irritated gaze at Kyle.

Only the irritation evaporated when Kyle pulled out his wallet and shoved a handful of cash toward the man.

"Mind if we have a private party in there?"

The janitor didn't mind at all. He snatched up the bills and jammed them in a pocket. "Clean up after you're done. The door will lock behind you when you leave."

My mouth gaped wide as Kyle held the door open for the man, who pushed a cleaning cart out and toward the elevators. It rolled with a squeaky wheel.

"Happy New Year's, folks," he added, disappearing around the corner.

"You, too," Kyle said, his voice soft, and his deep gaze set on me. The way he looked at me was unsettling. I felt hot and twitchy. He used to look at me that way, and I had loved it.

Once upon a time, I'd loved everything about him.

You hate him now. He crushed you. Don't let him continue to do it.

I marched into the pool area where it was steamy, and instantly began to sweat. I surveyed the room and felt my eyes go large. "Oh my God."

Because the place was stunning. The ceilings were tall and reflective, making the room feel much larger than it really was. The infinity pool wasn't very big, but it didn't matter. No one came here to swim laps. Surely people came to soak and enjoy the view. The far side of the room was mostly glass, separated with columns that were illuminated by uplighting. The pool's edge was almost to the windows, giving the impression it was right against the glass.

The Opulent Hotel was a modest height, barely considered a skyscraper, but it boasted a fabulous view of the other buildings nearby, the skyline beyond, and the edge of Lake Michigan.

"My sister Payton got married here," Kyle said. "I

remembered the pool was something else."

It was lit with two underwater lights, and the water cast shadowy ripples all around. "It's amazing."

I flinched when the cork popped on the bottle of champagne in Kyle's hand. I'd been too distracted with the view to notice he'd set about opening it.

His tone was sheepish. "Sorry."

I turned to glare at him while he poured the glasses of sparkling wine and set them on a table positioned between two lounge chairs. "So," I snapped, "you do know how to apologize."

Kyle shrugged out of his suit coat, probably sweating worse than I was in the hot room, and laid it gently over the chair back. "Do *I* have something to apologize for?"

"Are you shitting me?"

His gaze narrowed, and I wanted to scream. Did he honestly think what he'd done was no big deal? I couldn't handle it if that was the case. Being this close to the pool was a bad idea. A vision of holding his head under the water until he stopped moving flitted through my evil mind.

"You want to finish your wine first," he asked, "before we get into it?" He leaned over and braced his hands on the back of the lounge chair, waiting.

I stared at him for a long moment and decided his suggestion was a solid idea. I slammed the wine, hoping the time it took to drink it would bring me to a calmer state, or slow my reaction time down and give him a better chance to escape. Because I was still considering the most efficient way to get him underwater.

Then I was thinking about how he'd look wet. Goddamn it.

"You remember the last conversation we had?"

His tone was casual, but something was off. There was tension buried inside his voice, and I moved slowly to set my empty wine glass down.

"You said you thought you'd be finished loading your car in another hour." That was the last thing he'd said before a hurried goodbye on the phone. I'd had no idea it was all the goodbye I was going to get.

He paused. "That's it?"

"If you want to get technical, you sent me a text message the next day demanding I delete your number. I didn't respond."

His expression was strange as he picked up both the champagne glasses and held one out to me. When I took it, I was careful not to brush my fingers over his, even though I had the weird desire to do so.

"Okay, it didn't take me an hour to load up." His tone was dry. "As you established earlier, I can finish faster."

I ignored the humorless joke. "Yeah, I figured it out when I went to your place and you were *already gone.*"

The glass was chilled in my hand, but it did nothing to subdue the fire that flared wildly until it was all I could feel. Maybe I didn't need closure from him in the form of an apology. Perhaps all I needed was to tell him about the colossal pain he'd inflicted.

"God, Kyle. Do you have any idea what that was like? How much it hurt? I sat outside on the front step of your place, bawling my stupid eyes out." I didn't want to relive the memory, but it was unavoidable with him standing there, staring at me. I'd been too upset that day to drive, and my car had been far down the street, anyway. The shock and grief was physically debilitating, making it impossible to get to.

"On top of everything, it was so embarrassing! All your neighbors saw me, and I couldn't stop crying like a fool. Fuck, it hurt just to breathe." It'd felt like part of me was dying. Maybe it was. Kyle had damaged a section of my heart that still hadn't recovered.

His expression was bizarre, as if torn between confusion and concern. So much time had passed, yet I shook violently just as I'd done then.

"Why?" I demanded, my voice breaking with emotion. "Why'd you do that to me? Didn't I mean anything to you?"

There was no sound in the room. Light bounced off the water's surface, casting ripples of blue beams on him while he stood motionless, holding his glass of unsipped champagne.

Then, he blinked slowly. "You meant a lot to me, Ruby. *A lot.*"

Why didn't he just stab me with a knife? It would have been less painful than his words. "Then, fucking *why*?"

He was calm, my total opposite, as I was coming unglued. Kyle took a tiny step forward, but it felt enormous, like he was right up against me. "The plan was to meet at your place," he said quietly. "When I told you I'd be done loading my car in an hour, I think you misunderstood."

Confusion coiled in my mind. "What are you talking about? We were going to meet at your apartment."

His shoulders rose as he drew in a deep breath, and his expression turned sad. "Do you actually remember discussing it, though? Because, honestly, I don't. I assumed you knew I was heading your way."

I stared at him, trying to process. In a professional setting, we excelled at communication, but personally? It was never our strongest suit. Had we said specifically where we were meeting? I'd been so twisted up about saying goodbye . . .

Wait a minute.

Wait one fucking minute.

Had I spent the last five years hating him for a misunderstanding that might be my fault, at least partly? My tone verged on horror. "What are you telling me?"

"I drove over to your place," he said. "I waited hours for you to show up so we could say goodbye."

Shock cemented me into stone, and Kyle destroyed me all over again, but he didn't seem to notice. He leaned over and clinked our glasses together.

"Cheers."

KYLE

It was a dick move, but I wanted to watch Ruby stomach some of her own medicine. I took a drink of my champagne while she simply stood there, dumbfounded.

Her recovery was quick, and her anger came right back. "I called you," she accused. "I called you a bunch of times."

"Yeah, you did."

That seemed to piss her off more. "You didn't answer."

"When I first got to your place and you weren't there, I thought it was because I was early. After a while, I got worried, and that's when I discovered my battery was somehow dead."

It wasn't like I could ask to borrow someone else's phone and call her. I didn't have her number memorized.

"I couldn't remember where I packed the charger, and my car . . . Everything I owned was in there. I had to tear it all apart to find it, right in the street outside your building." My stomach churned with unease, like it had then. "Shit, I was worried about you the whole time, thinking any minute your car was going to turn the corner and we'd laugh about how stupid I looked with my shit all over the sidewalk. Only you never came home."

Her eyes had gone impossibly wide, and she reached out, latching a hand on my forearm. The turmoil in her voice cut into me. "Because I was waiting for you at your place. I had no idea—"

"I knew you wouldn't blow off saying goodbye to me," I said, getting louder and more worked up than I meant, because this was the heart of my issue. "Hell, you'd told me you loved me, Ruby. So something awful must have happened to stop you from coming home."

"Oh, God, Kyle—" Her face twisted with hurt.

"So, I finally found the charger buried in a box, and then got someone to let me into your lobby so I could plug into a wall outlet. As soon as I had enough power, I saw the twelve missed calls from you." My hands had been shaking as my mind ran all sorts of awful scenarios. "And there was the one voicemail."

She straightened abruptly, pulling away like I was on fire. Her expression shifted and she whispered it with dread. "I was so angry. I . . . I don't even remember most of what I said."

"Yeah?" I spat out. "Well, I do."

Her recorded tirade was like being run over a mandolin grater. Every sentence she spewed was another pass on the metal edges, taking chunks out of me.

"Whatever it was," she gasped, "I didn't mean it."

Irrelevant, logic screamed at me. It was too little, far too late, and technically not even an apology. I put up a hand, waving her comment away. "Forget about it. It was a long time ago."

I would act like I'd moved on, and pretend it was all water under the bridge, but that was what it would be. An act. Her words were still sharp in my mind. I'd cared about her so damn much. If I'd been able to fit my feelings for her into a tidy little box, the word *love* would have been scrawled across the side in black marker.

"What did I say?" Her expression was a mixture of fear and desperation. "Please, you have to tell me."

"You opened with a strong barrage of insults. All the different ways I was a pussy. I'd thought it was some sort of a joke at first, but then you said where you were, and I figured out what had happened."

"That," she whispered, "I sort of remember. There was more?"

Oh, yes, there was. "You said you were glad I was leaving so you could move on and find a better guy who deserved you. I was just a good fuck you were having fun with." Her face went ash white, but I pushed on. "Then, you told me you never really loved me, and you'd only said it because I was pathetic and so, so desperate to hear it."

Ruby banded an arm around her stomach like I'd slugged her in the gut. Yeah, that was similar to my reaction the first time I'd heard it. She gasped, drawing in her breath as if it were painful, and her gaze dropped to my feet.

I tossed back the rest of my glass of champagne, giving me something else to do rather than stare at the woman who looked like she was going to be sick. If I was capable of falling in love, it should have been with Ruby. But it hadn't happened.

At least, not for her.

The silence stretched between us, so tense I couldn't tolerate another moment. "Coming up here was a mistake."

She shook her head and lifted her gaze to meet mine, her eyes wet with tears. "I'm so sorry. I was hurting and I didn't mean it, not a word." She spoke it with conviction. "You have to know that."

Part of me wanted to believe her, but I steeled myself. "You made it pretty clear I didn't know you at all."

"What do you mean? I loved you."

Her expression made an emotion flare in me that I refused to acknowledge. "What evidence do you have to prove it?"

Her lush lips parted and her face twisted into a look which announced what I'd demanded wasn't possible. "How do I prove that I loved you?"

Each time she said it, the words dug deeper into the spot where I'd stored away all my emotions about her. Ruby needed to be careful. I didn't have as big of a temper as she did, but there was a lot of pain and anger hiding behind my front, and if it cracked, I might say something hurtful. There was no upside. It'd only make us both feel worse.

"Forget it." I set my empty glass down on the table, no longer interested in the remaining alcohol in the bottle. Champagne had been a terrible choice to dull the senses.

"I don't want to forget. I mean, for fuck's sake, we almost had a threesome."

For once, the steamy hot memory didn't do anything to warm me, and my voice filled with ice. "Don't you dare act like I pushed you into that. We both know who instigated it, and besides, all it does is support the argument how I was just a fuck buddy to you."

"No." She planted herself before me, defiance etching her face. "No. I loved you. All that shit I said was lies, just a defense mechanism. It fucking destroyed me when you left."

I closed my eyes and centered myself. She was an attorney, which meant she was smart and skilled enough to know how to persuade. She could shade the words just so, spinning and twisting until things were seen her way.

But I was an attorney, too, which meant I was immune. Clever words or, God forbid, tears, weren't going to shock me into seeing anything other than the facts.

"You didn't seem too destroyed later that night," I said.

Panic visibly poured through her. "What are you talking about?"

"After your voicemail, I lost it. I packed up my shit and drove off because I was so angry. I wasn't thinking. Hell, I got a speeding ticket in Indiana and almost got arrested when I ran my mouth at the cop." I'd been lucky to avoid jail. "By the time I hit Pennsylvania, I'd cooled off enough, and I called you to explain what happened. To apologize for leaving."

Ruby went cold. "You did?"

"I shouldn't be surprised you don't remember. You sounded wasted."

She'd looked scared when I'd mentioned the voicemail, but now she looked terrified. "What happened? What'd I say?"

I felt bad she'd spent the last five years not knowing what happened, but that wasn't my fault. "It doesn't matter."

"It fucking matters, Kyle."

Anger heated in my veins. "I don't want to talk about it. It's done. Let's just move on."

Could she see how serious I was? It'd be a waste of time to argue with me, because I would win.

Her expression fell. It appeared she understood, but she didn't look happy about it one bit. Her gaze went severe, but she bit back her words, and my heartrate ticked up a notch. There was calculation going on behind that gorgeous face of hers. *Whatever she throws at you, you can handle it.*

"All right," she said, her tone cool and calm. "What happens now?"

I tried not to mentally stumble over her shift in tactics. "I feel like we owe each other a real goodbye."

Not the goodbye we'd planned to exchange five years ago, though. I was a lot of things, but not a masochist, and kissing her would only bring pain. I loved my memories of her lips and all the different kisses they'd delivered. Sexy, passionate, sometimes sweet. What if I kissed her now and it didn't live up to what had grown legendary in my mind? It wasn't worth the risk.

"Dance with me first."

I froze. "What?"

"It's New Year's Eve. I got all dressed up, and . . ." She appeared to stopped fighting what she wanted to say. "I thought this conversation was going to take place on the ballroom dance floor."

A calculated move. She looked unbelievable in her dress, which she'd probably worn to distract me, and it was working. She'd caught me staring at her chest more than once, and her satisfaction was evident. Fuck her for flaunting what I couldn't have. She wanted me to look, so I did.

I glanced out the window, staring at the skyline. It had begun to snow, and fat snowflakes wafted downward. The only light in the room came from the shimmering pool, so the view was even better without our bright reflections competing against it. We were only two muted shapes in the glass.

"There's no music."

"A smart guy like you? I'm sure you know how to work Pandora."

I didn't want to dance with her. The idea of letting her

get close was dangerous. But her eyes flared with a challenge, and I wasn't one to back down. If she thought this ploy was going to work, I'd show her how wrong she was.

So I went to my suitcoat I'd left hanging on the chair back, dug out my phone, and picked the first station I found that would work. I propped the phone against my empty glass and stood.

Ruby watched me wordlessly as I unbuttoned my cuffs and began to roll back the sleeves of my dress shirt. It was warm in the pool room, but it climbed to a thousand degrees when I looked at her. The song playing from my phone sounded like Michael Bublé, a slow, jazzy number.

Alarm was loud and incessant in my brain.

The dim lighting. The sultry music. The view. Everything about the environment was seductive and romantic. I stepped up to her, opened my arms, and invited her into my embrace. The only consolation was she seemed to hold her breath as she set her warm hand in mine, as if she was as wary of this as I felt.

I'd fucking swear my body remembered the feel of her. My arm slipped behind her back and rested comfortably there, as if happy to be home. Her hand not clasped in mine lay gently on my shoulder. But tension made me stiff, and I focused on the movement rather than the girl in my arms.

I took my first step forward, and she followed my lead. My mother had taught me a basic dance pattern once, and I fumbled through the sequence, rusty, but good enough. Ruby's face was tipped up toward mine, but I refused to look at her. Instead, I stared out over her head, eyeing the buildings beyond the glass.

Bublé serenaded us as the snow outside continued to

fall. We'd turned two rotations before I felt myself start to slip. My posture softened and I drew my arm in, pulling her closer. No, dammit. I couldn't slip further. The ache for her, which had dissipated over the years, was back and stronger than ever.

She slid her hand up my shoulder, moving it up until it cupped the back of my neck and demanded my attention. Her soft, delicate fingers were more powerful than anything else, and I had no choice but to obey.

My heart stopped. Even shining with unshed tears, her eyes were breathtaking. I was right back in that bookstore, staring at her as we argued over the last used copy of an intellectual property textbook. She'd been so pretty with her bangs falling over her eyebrows and annoyance skewing her face. There was no way I was letting her leave the store with that book and without getting her number.

The steam in the room seemed to thicken, slowing everything down, especially my thoughts. Ruby pressed further into me, and I allowed it. I could feel every inch of her against me as we swayed to the music, and I was greedy for more contact. Our hands let go at the same moment, so I could move mine to join my other in the small of her back, wrapping my arms around her. She encased my jaw in both hands, and I didn't want to think about why she was trembling.

She didn't blink as I leaned closer. She didn't even take a breath.

Color burst off in the distance, lighting the night sky, and we turned together to look at it. A series of fireworks exploded in reds and brilliant golds, and rained down over Lake Michigan. It had to be the New Year's Eve fireworks display over Navy Pier. Which meant—

"Happy New Year, Kyle." It was barely a whisper.

I turned my head to look at her, and her mouth sealed over mine.

Chapter
EIGHT

Ruby's soft lips pressed against my mouth, and everything went offline. Her kiss shut me down faster than a sustained ruling on an objection. Desire took command. I tightened my hold on her so she was fitted against me, and then I kissed her back.

Her kiss was sweet and slow, but mine was an assault. When her lips parted, I slipped my tongue inside her warm mouth, taking possession. Claiming and branding her, like she was mine. I deepened the kiss, pushing into her, forcing her head to tilt back just enough so she'd welcome me further.

I wasn't in control. I'd told myself I wasn't going to touch her, and definitely wasn't going to kiss her. Everything was unraveling, and I hated it. I poured my frustration into my movement, dominating and taking from her. Ruby's soft moan fed into my desire, and it pumped through my bloodstream.

Five years I'd wondered what our kiss goodbye would have tasted like. I imagined it would have been a lot like this. Our kiss dripped with longing and need, and burned with heartache.

No.

I braced my hands on her shoulders and pushed her back, severing the connection of our mouths, and we stood staring at each other with disbelief, gasping for air. The heat of the room was to blame for the mistake of that kiss. Or maybe the music. And certainly her dress.

"All this time," she said, "I believed you left without saying goodbye."

"I did leave without saying goodbye." My hands were still holding her shoulders. Why was that? Why hadn't she squirmed away, and why the hell couldn't I let her go? "So, goodbye, Ruby."

Her expression hardened into pure determination, and she took a step toward me. Like a strange dance where she was leading, I backed up to keep my arms straight and not allow her to come closer.

"I loved you. You know I did. Even when you *never* said it back!"

The wall inside me eroded and I finally dropped my hold. Anger and hurt seeped through the cracks, making my voice build. "If that's true, how could you think for one fucking second I'd walk away from you like that? Jesus! Did you consider any other scenario where I wasn't an enormous asshole?"

Her mouth hung open.

The silence should have calmed me, but instead I grew angrier. "I waited for you at your apartment because I *knew* you wouldn't blow me off. I mean, the thought never even crossed my mind." My tone was as dark as the sky outside. "But it seems like me abandoning you was the only thought you had."

"That's not fair. We were supposed to meet at your place, but it was empty and you were gone. What was I supposed to think? If the roles were reversed, you would have thought the same!"

"No, I wouldn't have. And I definitely wouldn't have jumped on the first piece of ass I could find twelve hours later."

"What?"

Fucking hell. "I could barely get a word in when I called at two a.m. You were too busy telling me about the guy you'd brought home from the bar."

Her expression twisted from outright shock to confusion. "I didn't. I would never—"

I had to point out the obvious. "You don't even remember talking to me, so . . ."

"No." She shook her head vehemently. "I went out with my sister, yeah. But I was so drunk and miserable, she took me back to her dorm room." Her tone was sharp as a knife. "I slept on her floor, very much alone, and woke up to the text message from you."

I wanted to believe her, but my lingering anger was hard to overcome.

"If I said I was with anyone else, it was a lie. Just an extension of the shit I said earlier." She gazed at me with fresh hurt. "I was drunk and defensive. I can't believe you thought I'd really do that."

"You realize you're telling me you lied repeatedly, and in the same breath I'm supposed to believe you when you say you loved me?"

A noise of frustration tore from her throat. "I've gone five fucking years hating you for the wrong reasons."

"Because there are right reasons to hate me?"

"Oh my God, right now there are." She jabbed her finger in the center of my chest. "I said awful things. I'm sure I did. They were lies and I'm sorry." Her voice carried weight. "I'm *sorry*. I was too torn up over you to even remember what I said, which is the fucking proof you want." Her finger needled further into me. "It should have been obvious I was hurting. And drunk."

Was her finger going to burrow into my skin? I moved backward to get away, but she charged forward, staying on me.

Her face twisted with a mixture of sorrow and rage. "You leaving like that wrecked me. I know I'm not easy, and I'm sorry I lied, but do you realize how much pain you could have spared us with a five-minute conversation when I was sober? Why didn't you call me again?"

Who was being unfair now? "Are you serious? I called you. I tried, Ruby. What more do you want?"

She peered at me with disbelief. "You . . . gave up on me."

Maybe that had a hint of truth, but her words then, whether they were lies or not, had hit too close to home. The sting from them was sharp and cut deep. My parents loved me and Payton in their own way, but it was detached and cold. Love to them was loyalty and financial support. It was constant criticism to help me improve and be the best I could be. I'd been left to figure emotions out on my own.

"It took me months to get over you. How could you think I'd go out and just fuck someone else?"

"Well, you thought I was the type of asshole who'd leave you, so I guess we're even."

She groaned loudly, her annoyance boiling over, and slapped her palms against my chest. I wasn't surprised when she shoved me backward. She hardly put any force behind it, and it barely made me move. However, I was surprised when there wasn't flooring under my foot, and I fell.

For a suspended moment, I hung in the air and clawed futilely for something to stop my descent. I only realized what was happening as the lukewarm water rushed all around me, filling my nose, mouth, and ears.

The pool wasn't deep, and I got my feet under me, bursting from the surface of the water and wiping at my eyes. I reeled and found her staring at me like she couldn't believe what had happened.

My mind went haywire, but focused first on the essentials.

My phone was still playing music on the tabletop, and my wallet was in my suitcoat pocket, so both were safe. My watch was water-resistant up to ten feet, but my pants were dry-clean only.

White-hot anger shot up my spine.

I trudged through the water to the side of the pool, set a slippery hand on the tile, and tried to climb out. When I faltered, Ruby pulled up the skirt of her dress, bent, and offered a hand.

"Shit, here," she said.

I grabbed her wrist and tugged, sending her face-first into the water, but not before she let out a satisfying scream of surprise, which was followed by an equally satisfying splash.

Ruby emerged from the water sputtering and her shoulders tight to her ears, her expression pure shock. The water line was at my shoulders, and her dress billowed around her beneath the surface. Her mouth gaped open.

"I can't believe you fell for that," I said.

She snarled it. "I was trying to help you, you asshole!"

"Says the asshole who pushed me in first."

"I wasn't trying to push you in, it just happened." She ran a finger under each eye, wiping away the faint streaks of mascara.

"Do you have any idea how much my shoes cost?" I asked. "Or my belt?"

But my annoyance stalled as I watched her arms moving furiously under the water. Ruby wasn't as tall as I was, which meant she couldn't stand. I had no idea how good of a swimmer she was, and the dress tangled in her legs.

"Goddamnit," I groaned, sloshing over to her. She went rigid as I wrapped my arms around her waist and hauled her up against my soaked chest.

Her tone mirrored my annoyance, and she squirmed in my embrace. "What are you doing?"

I ignored the question and plodded toward the stairs at the far end of the pool.

I was halfway there when she spoke again. "This is all your fault."

The water was shallower now and I dropped her like an anchor, moving to a safe distance. "No, this is your fault. You fucking kissed me."

She stared at the ceiling for a moment, beyond exasperation. "It's tradition to kiss someone on New Year's." Her gaze focused on mine like a laser. "Should I mention you kissed me back? With a whole bunch of tongue?"

Now it was my turn to make a noise of frustration. I needed to get out of the pool. A drenched Ruby wasn't any less enticing, and perhaps she was more. Water droplets clung to her skin and trailed down between her breasts. Lucky water drops. I wanted to follow them with my mouth.

The adrenaline from the unexpected fall was finding other places to go, mainly my cock. My dress shirt was plastered to my body and the tie weighed a ton, a sopping noose around my neck.

"Don't look at me like that," I said, working loose the knot.

"Like what?" She said it begrudgingly. "Like I hate that

your kiss was the hottest thing I've had all year?"

My cock twitched in agreement, but I gave a short laugh. "The year which just started two minutes ago?"

She slapped her hand against the surface of the water, splashing me. Her jaw was set, but Christ, she looked hot like that. Water dripped from the loose ends of her pinned up hair, and the pink dress was nearly see-through when wet. Her nipples stood pointed to attention.

She seemed to be seething. "You're the worst."

"But not at kissing you, apparently."

"Fuck you, Kyle."

Something inside me snapped. The first few times I'd put up with it, but I was done with her repeated insult. I moved as swiftly as the drag in the water would allow, and shoved my hand into the hair at the back of her head, grabbing a handful of pins with the strands. I tugged her head back firmly and stared down into her wide eyes.

I'd never been aggressive with her before. I'd still been finding my way with women back then and how much they wanted when it came to roughness. But now a dark need took hold, urging me to show her how inappropriately she was behaving, and to do it in a way as if she were mine.

"Oh," she whispered and the softest of moans followed.

Not in pain. This was distinctly pleasure.

A lightning bolt sizzled through me. I blanked for a moment, my vision going hazy. She *liked* this? Fuck me, did she want more? I laid my palm against her chest, my fingers resting softly around her neck. Not trying to choke her, but to signify control. I'd made it so she couldn't look anywhere but at me. It was only fair, because I could focus only on her.

Beneath my fingers, I felt her swallow hard. And when

her eyes hooded with desire at my action, I was done for. I leaned down and crushed my lips to hers.

RUBY

Kyle's mouth, fused with mine, was fire. All of my rage and pain melded together with our heat into an inferno that left me breathless. At least we were standing in water, so when we combusted, nothing else would go up in flames.

I skimmed my fingertips along his broad chest, which was covered in the soaked white dress shirt. It had become transparent to both my delight and horror. He looked even better than I remembered. All tight and toned, and daring me to touch.

But I hated him.

He'd put me through the wringer tonight. The high of realizing he hadn't left, only for him to send me crashing down to the low that he'd left me another way . . . In the fucking dark.

The kiss he gave me now wasn't like the one right after midnight. That one had been impressive, but this was so powerful and raw, I cried out against his mouth. I didn't want him to stop like last time. I needed him and this brutal kiss, even though I despised the desire in me.

I hooked an arm around his shoulders and shoved a hand under the water, gathering up as much of my skirt as I could while not breaking our connection. When I was free and the dress was out of my way, I wrapped my legs around his waist.

He groaned in approval and stalked back into the

deeper water so I was mostly weightless in his arms. The frantic sounds of our lips moving against each other echoed off the surface of the water, and could just be heard over the music.

I wanted to rip his heart out like he'd done to mine, and I was okay with tearing off his clothes to do it. Floating in his arms while we burned together left me dizzy. It was as if he was consuming my heat, feeding off it, and returned it back to me a million times hotter.

Kyle kept his hand locked in my hair, but the other drifted down the length of my spine and curled under the wadded skirt around my hips. His tongue plunged into my mouth when he squeezed my ass and pushed himself against me.

"Oh, good God," I whispered, my voice weak and needy. As soon as it was out, I sucked in a breath. I hated how I was responding to him, and that I was letting him have such power over me.

If it were any other man, it'd be fine. I loved a guy who would take charge during foreplay and sex. But I knew if it was someone else, the likelihood of him having a fraction of the impact like Kyle did was next to nothing. No one compared. He'd left me hurt and broken, and unable to find any kind of replacement.

So I hated him.

I hated the way I loved his mouth against my throat, sucking and biting until I was a quivering mess. Breath came and went in shallow bursts as his fingertips grazed down my neck, abandoning his grip in my hair, so he could slip beneath the shoulder strap of my dress.

Goosebumps lifted on my skin, fighting to get closer to him.

He inched the damp fabric to the side, sliding it off the curve of my shoulder as he lifted me higher. So gravity made the strap, heavy with water, tumble down my arm. It peeled away from my skin, exposing my bare breast that was just above the waterline.

Kyle went . . . nuclear.

I gasped as his hand closed over me, and he pinched my nipple between the side of his hand and his thumb. His pinch was hard and sharp, sending a bolt of pleasure all along my body to the tips of my toes. There wasn't time to think. His mouth covered mine and stole my breath.

He moved us so fast through the water, it made a wake and it sloshed around the pool. When we reached the side, his hips pinned me against the wall with one thrust, and I reached back with a hand to clutch the ledge. I couldn't watch what he was doing to me as his hurried, forceful lips moved down my neck, working a steady line to what was exposed. I didn't need any more reminders of how good he was with his hands or mouth.

His tongue found its intended target, and he swiped it over my erect nipple, making my gaze turned upward. Big mistake. The ceiling was dark mirrored glass, and I could see us perfectly from above. Our clothes were stuck to our bodies, my arm was braced on the ledge, causing me to arch my back into him, and his mouth roved over my bare breast.

If pulling down one strap of my dress was Kyle's undoing, seeing the undeniably sexy image of us was mine. I couldn't get the other strap down fast enough, and as soon as he realized, he was helping me any way he could.

When had I ever been so out of breath? I was panting and trying not to moan as he had both hands on my now topless body, the dress floating around my waist. The water wasn't warm, but it wasn't cold either, and I was grateful not to overheat. I clung to him, fisting my hands in his hair so I could hold his mouth against me. The burn of his whiskers rubbing on my sensitized skin was almost too much.

"Oh," I gasped.

Kyle bit down, giving me a sharp edge of teeth, and my body responded instinctively, grinding against him. A noise of satisfaction came from his chest, and he bit down a second time. This one was much harder, and earned a bigger reaction from me.

I curled my hands around his tie and yanked him up, intending to kiss him, but his expression was distracting. His eyes were hooded, and every inch of his face was drenched in lust, like he was high.

As our lips smashed together, I clawed at the knot of his tie, but then his hands were there, undoing it. So my fingers raced down the buttons of his shirt and flung it open. I wanted to put my damp hands on his heated, bare skin. I needed it pressed against mine right this second, more than I'd ever needed anything else.

He didn't take off the shirt. He tossed his wadded-up tie onto the pool deck with force, and it made a sopping noise as it collided with the ground. That was as far as Kyle made it before closing in on me.

"Shit," I breathed as we made contact. I shuddered with relief as his smooth skin flattened me against the hard, cold tile at my back. He didn't hesitate, like he hadn't even heard me. His face was between my breasts, teasing me with kisses and licks, and sucking until the ache for him between my legs was painful.

No. You hate him!

The thought vanished as his hand closed on my knee beneath the water and began to slide up my thigh. I arched further into his hot mouth, encouraging him in all ways. I whispered it so softly, there was no way to know if he could hear. "Yes."

He was hard. The bulge of his erection pressed to my center, grinding against me in a pleasurable and tortuous way. I knew exactly what it felt like with nothing between us. How much I enjoyed it when he slid inside me and let me ride into oblivion. I remembered every goddamn inch of him.

My father quit smoking fifteen years ago, but told me once if he could start smoking again without any health risks, he'd do it in a heartbeat. That's how strong the addiction was, lingering even after all that time. I didn't fully appreciate those unwanted cravings until Kyle. Years taught me how to deal with the urges, but the cravings for him never went away.

His palm crept along my thigh, gliding through the water and over my skin, reaching the edge of my panties in a single breath. Where the hell was the air? He drew back, leaving our lower bodies connected, and stared down at me.

The expression he held was fascinating.

His blue eyes matched the water rippling around us, and my heart twisted. I wanted to pull him closer, but also push him as far away as possible. The twinges of regret hadn't started yet, but I sensed them looming in the distance, waiting to strike. How much damage had I done to myself by letting this happen?

"Reach back," he said, his tone firm. "Grab onto

the wall."

Kyle's presence was commanding, and so crazy hot, I did exactly as he asked, and for the briefest of moments, surprise flashed in his eyes. Like he hadn't expected me to do it without question or hesitation. But of course I did. I'd always been in over my head when it came to him.

He studied me as his fingertips slipped down beneath the waistband of my panties, and although his lust-filled expression didn't change, I could sense he felt like we were approaching a threshold. The point of no return. And he wanted to make sure I was okay with crossing over it with him.

I bit down on my bottom lip, held my breath, and gave the faintest of nods.

The slow, gentle lover he'd been before was gone. As he once again gripped my hair in his right hand, keeping my gaze locked onto him, his left hand continued downward in my panties and two fingers pushed roughly inside my aching body.

I liked this new version of him so, so much better.

The intrusion forced me to suck in a breath through clenched teeth. It was an enjoyable stretch, but a lot to take in at first, and my eyes sharpened on him. He watched every tiny breath I took and the hints of pleasure I was sure to be showing in my eyes. He studied me like he was going to be tested later and wanted a perfect score.

I whimpered when the fingers began to move, giving him a sound of contentment. Already my body was tingling and buzzing. Could he feel how turned on I was, since we were floating in the water? His heavy eyes made me think so. His chest rose and fell with steady but hurried breaths.

When he leaned forward and set his forehead against

mine, I was aware I had lost some sort of battle. What was wrong with me? He'd just admitted he'd let me suffer needlessly for years, and I was, what? Letting him do whatever he wanted? Rewarding him?

"I hate you," I whispered, not meaning it. It was a final futile attempt to convince myself of the lie.

"Do you?" he whispered back. He brushed his lips faintly over mine, teasing a kiss. "Or is it another lie?"

I groaned as his fingers thrust, and I saw flashes of white behind my eyes. God, he was so good with those fingers. I remembered every inch of him, and I suspected he knew all of me as well. Kyle knew exactly where and how to touch me to make me come out of my mind.

My tone wasn't the least bit convincing. "No, I'm pretty sure I hate you."

He looked smug. "Then, prove it."

KYLE

Ruby was pissing me off, but she was going to have to take a number and get in line behind myself. What the fuck? Currently I was standing fully clothed, more or less, in a pool, finger fucking my ex while she lied and told me she hated me.

She was topless. At least I could use the insanity plea because her body was freaking insane. Perfect, big breasts with tight, dark nipples contrasting against her pale skin. I'd barely choked back the groan when she'd let me pull her dress down. She was so fucking beautiful, it hurt. It made me weak, and all thought drained from my mind.

Existing in this state was strange. I didn't analyze, I just acted. Did what I felt and wanted. I was rougher than I'd ever been with her, and fuck me, it wasn't scaring her off. Ruby's pupils had gone large and her skin flushed. Her legs had spread wider.

If that wasn't enough evidence to suggest she liked it, there'd been that almost inaudible *yes* that came from her. My dick had grown so hard, it turned to steel. It only added to my frustration. Of course she was into it. We'd clicked so perfectly in bed before. As my tastes had matured, it seemed hers had as well.

"Prove it?" she repeated.

I pushed my fingers as deep inside her as I could get them. It was a tight fit and her body clamped down, like she was trying to squeeze pleasure from me. Jesus, it was so fucking hot.

"Yes." I pumped my fingers faster, and her hips below the water moved to match my tempo. "If you hate me, you'll push my hand away, get out of this pool, and leave." Her expression fell at the idea, and I was relieved. That wasn't what I wanted, not in a million years. I strived for a mocking tone. "But you're not going to do that, are you, Ruby?"

I ground the heel of my palm against her clit, sliding my fingers in and out of her pussy, and watched her struggle to keep her eyes from rolling back into her head. Okay, good. She was still a fan of that maneuver.

"Because," I continued, "you don't want me to stop."

When she didn't answer me, I made a face of displeasure, and slowed my hand until it wasn't moving. Instantly she let go of the ledge behind her and plunged her hands in the water, wrapping them around my wrist.

Fire burned in her eyes. "Don't you dare stop, asshole."

Holy shit. An evil grin spread across my face. "You'd only hate me if I did."

"Yes," she breathed, her eyes slamming shut.

She squirmed on my fingers and I clenched my fist tighter in her hair, trying to hold back from losing it. I wanted to bury myself between her thighs and see if she was as unbelievable as she had been in my memories. Kissing her was better than I remembered; would sex be, too?

Would watching her come be even more spectacular? I needed to find out, so I focused. I drove my fingers inside and curled them to the spot she liked best, and Ruby jerked in my hold.

"Shit." Her raspy curse was sexy as hell, and I kept

at the spot, tapping it with my fingertips. She was up on her tiptoes, leaning back against the side of the pool, her breasts bobbing right at the surface of the water. She bucked and thrashed, sending waves away from us, and sometimes splashing me. But she didn't notice. She was too far gone in the sensations.

Her bottom lip trembled and her hands urged me to go faster still. When she got right up to the edge of orgasm, I held my breath. Should I let her come, or should I draw it out longer? Once she had satisfaction, would she climb out of this pool and leave me?

Outwardly, I held it together, but inside I was shaking with need. Need for this woman, the only one who'd gotten close to being my future.

Her nails suddenly dug into my wrist. "Fuck me, Kyle."

Yes. I swallowed thickly, my head swimming in lust. "I'm glad you decided to revise your statement." Her '*fuck you, Kyle,*' which had started this whole thing, echoed in my head. One simple word swap and everything flipped on its side.

There were tugs at my ruined two-hundred-dollar belt as she tried to get my pants open. I withdrew my fingers from her and curled them around her panties, yanking down. As I tossed her soaked lingerie onto the deck beside my tie, warning lights flashed in my head. This was a very bad idea, but it was too late to stop—

Fuck!

My wallet.

It was all the way on the other side of the room, tucked inside my suit jacket. I had at least one emergency condom in there, but it was a thousand miles across the pool deck. She'd been successful in getting the belt open and my pants unzipped, but I stopped her there. I scooped her up under her ass, ignoring her cry of surprise, and trudged toward the stairs, a man on a mission.

One of her arms hooked around my neck, clinging to me as we moved. "Where are we going?"

"My wallet's up on the chair."

Her whine of frustration was exactly how I felt. She jammed her hand between our bodies, down inside my boxers, and when her fist closed around my cock, I couldn't keep going. Her long, tight stroke drew a shudder and a moan from me. "Jesus."

"We could . . ." Her gaze went to the chair, and then flew back to me, her eyes evaluating. "How many women have you been with since me?"

"What?" My brain wouldn't work right when she was touching me. Heat pumped in my veins, with lust as the accelerant.

"I'm still on the pill, and we didn't used to use condoms." Her lips pressed into a line at the same instant her bare tits pressed against my chest. It shot warmth straight to my groin. Beneath the water, her fist stroked once more. "How many, Kyle?"

The honest number came out before I could stop it. "Three."

Her hand paused and she went rigid. I'd confessed to her once how I'd been kind of a whore when pursuing my undergrad degree. She repeated the word like she surely hadn't heard it right, because how could that be? "*Three*?"

We'd made it into the shallow end, so I let go of her legs, dropped her on her feet, and cupped both hands on her face. I walked her backward toward the stairs. "Yeah, three. And I always used protection. You?"

"Of course, I was always safe." She blinked, as if not quite recovered from her surprise.

When the backs of her calves hit the stairs, she fell to sit and I chased after her. "Your number, Ruby."

I'd revealed too much and tried not to grind my teeth as I set a hand on a step beside her hip, keeping my lips near hers. There was a perfectly good explanation for my number, such as a long-term committed relationship, and I hoped she'd assume that. It wasn't my real reason, though. I'd lost myself in my job in New York, trying to forget her. It'd been impossible, and I'd had hardly any interest in dating in a new city where I didn't know a soul.

When I'd finally gotten back up on the horse, sexually speaking, it'd been lackluster. No chemistry, no strong desire. I'd felt nothing other than a few minutes of empty pleasure. So I was more than a little curious to hear if it had been the same for her. My ego wanted to believe I had destroyed sex for her like she'd done for me.

She tried to stall by kissing me, and I let her because, fuck me, kissing her got me hard. I knelt on the bottom step between her parted legs and was throbbing in her hands as she resumed jerking me off. I was supporting myself on one arm, and palmed her breasts with the other, sliding over her wet skin.

Her tone was quiet and cautious. "More than three." She arched up, stretching into me. "Always safe, though. I'm good. If you tell me you're good, then we're good."

The statement suspended for a moment. So, we were both clean and okay about fucking with nothing between us, but were we *good*? I didn't want to be hung up on her number, so I forced the thought from my head. All that mattered was she was here, beneath me right now, her legs spread wide around my hips.

"I'm good," I said.

"Then, please hurry." Her voice was full of need and her hands clawing at the waistband of my boxers.

I grinned. Her begging tone sounded so goddamn good. She worked the elastic down over my hips, freeing me from my underwear, and she slumped down on the stair, scooting to the edge so it'd be easier for me to take her. Competing ideas battled in me. I didn't want to wait, and yet I wanted to hold her here. To draw this moment out.

Even under the water, her skin was like silk. I trailed my fingers down her naked chest, over the dress bunched at her waist, and further until I hit the junction of her legs. She was hot like fire, and slicker than the water. I teased the pads of my fingers over her swollen clit.

Ruby shifted restlessly on the stairs, and whined as if what I was doing felt good but wasn't enough. And it wasn't. We both craved more. She wound her hand around me and dug her fingernails into my ass, pressing me forward.

"Please," she whined again. "Fucking give me that cock." Her mouth got me every time. She looked so cute and innocent, and I loved the contrast of her conservative librarian appearance and her dirty-talking sailor language.

I ghosted a kiss on the side of her neck. "Always whispering such sweet nothings."

Then I lifted up on my arm, steadied myself, and rubbed the tip of my dick against her entrance as if asking permission to slip inside. Really, I was teasing her again. I couldn't see all that well what was happening beneath the surface. Although the water was clear, Ruby wouldn't hold still, and the ripples bent and distorted the image.

My gaze traveled upward, over her tits that dripped

with water, and then it settled on her face. Her mascara was faintly smudged under her eyes, but the rest of her makeup seemed in place. It exaggerated her pretty blue eyes, which were cloudy with desire.

I needed to watch. Had to figure out what she was thinking as we came together.

She slowly drew a deep breath when I pressed the first crucial inch inside. Her eyes widened as I moved further, burying myself deeper. Holy. Motherfucking. Shit. Had she always felt this good? So wet, and hot, and tight? Her expression mirrored what I felt. Surprise and enjoyment.

Her moan was soft and erotic. It was a sound like she'd finally gotten what she'd been waiting a lifetime for. The muscles in my abs quivered as I pushed slowly all the way to the base and she was fitted perfectly around me.

"Jesus, Ruby," I whispered.

Yeah, she was way better than I remembered, and we hadn't even started fucking yet. I held still, my knees digging into the ridged step, and tried to soak her all in. She was undulating beneath me, her eyes half closed, but her gaze pinned on me. So utterly gorgeous, my sorry excuse for a heart ached.

Why the fuck did things have to go down the way they did? I disliked Chicago, but I would have stayed for her.

Christ, all she had to do was fucking ask.

Pain mixed with frustration at the situation, and clouded like a dark storm in my head. I withdrew slowly and sank into her once more, pissed off at how good it felt. All these years I'd missed this. I was still angry at her, but I was angry with myself for walking away.

"Oh, God," she gasped. "More."

I gave her a gentle thrust, creating a small wave in the

water. Her eyes fluttered closed and her head tipped back, exposing the long line of her neck, so I took advantage. I skimmed my teeth over her skin and felt her pulse roaring there. Her heart seemed to be beating as furiously as mine.

My next thrust was serious. Her pussy clamped tight around me and a groan rolled through my chest. I latched my non-supporting hand on her hip and drove into her. Everything in me was searing with pleasure and chanting for more, and I moved my hips in time.

The water sloshed around us like a turbulent sea, and she cried out. It came from her sounding desperate and thirsty. Her hands flew up and she laced her fingers together behind the back of my neck, holding on for the ride. It was insane.

"Fuck," she moaned. "Oh, *fuck*."

I beat my hips against her in a punishing rhythm, and she responded in kind, rocking into me. Her trembling thighs gripped me tightly, encouraging me to plunge back inside on every stroke out I made. Our kissing was broken occasionally as one of us had to gasp for breath.

As much as I loved looking at her, my knees were grinding against the step and the position was murder on my back. I pulled out and climbed to my feet, gripping her waist and hauling her to stand before me. She squeaked a noise of surprise, but I spun her in my arms, pressing my chest to her back, and snaked my hands around her body. The water was up to our thighs, keeping our undone clothes floating there.

I let my hands wander and play for a moment, just a moment, before I planned to bend her over—

"I loved you," she said breathlessly. "You know I did."

It was a needle dragging on a record, and my hands

stilled. I didn't want to think about love right now. "Enough."

Her head turned, giving me a view of her profile, and a water droplet rolled down her throat. "Kyle, I loved—"

"*Enough.*"

Pushed too far, a dark force took over. I put my hand in the center of her back and shoved her forward. Her hands flew out and caught the handrail at the steps, clinging on. And then I did something I'd never done before, I acted completely without thought.

Only instinct.

The sound of my palm cracking against her ass cheek, followed by her sharp gasp, were as loud as a cannon in my ears. For the longest second of my life, nothing happened. It took another full second for terror to seize me.

What the fuck did I just do?

Chapter
ELEVEN

Ruby's hands were white-knuckled on the railing, but her pale skin where I'd struck her was already blossoming pink. She turned her head to face me and blinked in shock, her kiss-swollen mouth hanging open.

Oh, Jesus. Any time I'd spanked a woman, it had been playful and soft. This one had been aggressive and backed by a dark desire to punish.

Her response was uneven. "Again."

What?

The force of her word knocked me back. Her shocked look melted into something else. She wasn't hurt, or scared, or pissed. She seemed curious. I choked the nervous words out. "You want me to spank you again?"

Even bent over like that, I could see her chest heaving. She swallowed so hard, it was audible. "Yes."

I held my breath. Sharon had turned on me the morning after. I didn't want a repeat of that, ever, and definitely not with Ruby. "You sure?"

She nodded. "Do it."

She took her gaze off me and looked forward, signaling she was ready. Tension rolled through me as I stepped up to her. Should I strike her as hard as the last one? I pussied out at the final second and slowed my palm, smacking her bare ass with little more than a slap.

"Harder."

Was she talking directly to my dick? I reared back, and this time, I delivered it like I meant it. As the warmth of her skin and the sting of the impact radiated up my arm, I expected guilt to follow, but I felt oddly good. Something was wrong with me. I wasn't supposed to want to spank her. I wasn't supposed to enjoy hitting someone else, and I could argue that what I was doing right now was assault.

"Please." Her pleasure filled moan cut those thoughts into shreds. "More."

Fuck me. I slapped her flesh, watched her jolt, and reveled in her noises of surprised enjoyment. Everything about my action and her reaction was unexpected.

Her back bowed, as if presenting her pink-stained flesh to me. "I like the way it feels."

Oh, God, so did I. I shrugged out of my dress shirt and cast it aside, where it floated away. Then I steadied a hand on her hip, delivered one final stinging blow, and plunged my dick into her, needing to reaffirm our connection.

"Oh, shit, yes." Her hands gripped the railing so hard it squealed.

The slide of my cock in and out of her body was intense. My brain fried from the heat, was rendered useless, and I fucked her like a savage. I wove a hand into her hair and yanked her head back, but she grunted in satisfaction. The rougher I got, the more she seemed to like it. I gathered up the dress, fisted it at her waist, and twisted it in my hand, cording it tighter around her body so I could use it for leverage.

"You're so deep inside me, I love it."

I choked out breath, forcing myself to stay in the moment and not lose it. Ruby hadn't come yet, and not only was that important to me, the fuck if I was going to miss her show. I ground my pelvis, rubbing against her, and sucked down air between my clenched teeth.

Because it felt so very good, and it was with *her*.

Since I had her head pulled back, her gaze was on the ceiling, and her startled cry drew my gaze up. We were two dark figures fucking in the water, and seeing my domination of her like this damn near sent me over the edge. Relief trickled down my spine as she seemed to be building toward her end.

Her whole body began to quake, and her moans increased in frequency and volume, bouncing off the walls in the large, open room. All I could hear were her cries of ecstasy as she came, rushing toward her big finish. Inside, her body pulsed and throbbed, choking my dick. I slowed to enjoy the sensation but didn't stop, because I knew I could prolong her orgasm and I wanted it to last forever for her.

She shook uncontrollably and her muscles in her arms strained on the handrail. One scream from her lips echoed in the room and tore straight into my core, injecting me with lust. Then another scream, which trailed off at the end when she must have finished cresting.

Her tremors slowed and she relaxed with an enormous sigh.

"It's the sexiest thing ever," I said between tight breaths. "No one comes like you do."

"That's because no one," she panted, "makes me come like you do."

Her statement caused her muscles to tense, her whole body tightening like she'd said something she didn't want to reveal. But why? Didn't she know how amazing that was to hear? Why did we communicate best when we were fucking? Maybe we were too distracted in each other to worry about anything else.

I released her hair and trapped her waist in my hands, then increased my tempo. My gaze slipped down the line of her spine, past the dress, over her rose-colored skin where I'd spanked her, and to the place where my cock disappeared inside her body. The reflection of the water played around us.

If my mind had its way, we'd remain here all night. I'd fuck her until our hands where shriveled and pruning, and then maybe I'd fuck her some more on one of the lounge chairs. But my body, it had very different ideas. It begged for release, and I couldn't hold it back much longer. Everything ached for it.

Even though she'd come, she still seemed to be enjoying herself. Ruby's soft, satisfied moans as I thrust relentlessly into her caused a swell in me to begin. My chest tightened and I dug my fingers into her, denting the soft skin around them. I pumped as deep inside as I could get, wanting to lose myself. I was greedy and needed one more blissful memory with her.

Breath came and went so rapidly from my lungs, I became lightheaded, but then things began to tingle. The pressure built, pleasure grew, and I climbed until every cell was screaming to tip over the edge.

She must have recognized how close I was. One of her hands came off the railing and clamped down on top of mine. "Yes," she said, her voice hurried and excited. "Oh, fuck yes, Kyle."

The orgasm tore through me, a hot torrent of pleasure, and I slowed to a jerky stop, buried deep. I panted for air, strangling off a moan. Goddamn, it was amazing. The pleasure continued to roll through my body and left me shaky as it went.

It might have been the best orgasm of my life.

My heart went from pounding, to speeding along, and then finally slowed to a normal tempo, and I held on to her hips as I caught my breath. Now that my body was satisfied, my brain fired back online.

Ruby collapsed forward on the steps, and she was shivering. First order of business was getting her out of the pool and warm again. I could handle that, and I did up my pants. She didn't fight me as I tugged the dress slowly down, and slipped it off her.

She rested naked on the steps, not looking at me, which was a very bad sign. I set her dress up on the deck so it was a puddle of wet fabric, and took her by the arm, turning her to face me.

Her gaze focused on my chest, not meeting my eyes until I slipped my hands under her and lifted her into my arms. That certainly got her attention.

"What are you doing? Put me down."

"I will," I said, clambering up the stairs. Water ran off us and dripped with every step I took. I bypassed the lounge chair closest, and went to the one at the end that had a thick, striped cushion. I deposited her there, sat down beside her, and grabbed a handful of plush towels from the stack on the table beside it.

She shivered once more as I unfurled and laid it over her, and I watched as she tucked her bottom lip between her teeth. A nervous, unsure Ruby wasn't my favorite version, but I'd take it. At least she hadn't fled. I might have taken off her dress to prevent that.

I hadn't fled either. There was no desire to do so. I stared at my shirt floating in the water and her high heels resting at the bottom of the pool. So the second order of business would be getting stuff as dry as possible. She curled up under the makeshift blanket of towels and watched me wordlessly as I got back into the pool and fished everything out.

"Roll it up in a towel," she said quietly, gesturing to the dress in my hands, "then wring it out that way." When it was done, I hung it on the back of a chair. Not sure how dry it would get, but it was better than nothing. I did the same with the rest of our clothes, feeling her heavy gaze on me.

My shoes squished with water. That should make walking outside later in the snow fun. I sat down on the lounge chair beside her and tugged off my shoes. The longer we went without speaking, the more the tension grew. It was already as thick and overpowering as the humidity in the room.

At least she wasn't shivering anymore. I pulled off my socks and wrung them out, and when it was done, I suddenly wished I had something else to do. Ruby seemed to be waiting for me to finish moving and start talking, but for once in my life, I hadn't the faintest idea what to say.

"Thanks," she said over the edge of the towel draped on her body. "I mean, for hanging my stuff out to dry."

"Sure."

My brain knew what I was supposed do. I should peel back the long towel hiding her body from me, and slide in beside her on the narrow chair where there'd be barely any room for both of us. We'd burrow under the towels and drink warm champagne, and try to fix this space between us.

I wanted that.

I wanted her in my arms, yet I couldn't seem to move. I lied to myself and said it was indecision, and wasn't fear she'd reject me.

This was stupid. We'd just had sex. Mind-blowing sex. *Get off your ass and get over there.*

Ruby's gaze lingered on mine, and slowly she withdrew. The longer I sat motionless, the further away she felt.

"It stopped snowing," she said, gazing at the windows.

"Yeah."

The silence was painfully taut, weighed down with all the things we weren't saying.

"It's getting late," she added.

I pressed my lips into a line and nodded. Warning lights were flashing in my head, alerting me that this was going south and I needed to correct course immediately. But I didn't know how.

"I think, uh . . ." she said, shifting to sit up, "I should get dressed."

I blew out a breath and my eyebrows tugged together. "Okay."

Goddamnit. What was wrong with me? I didn't want that to happen.

Ruby wrapped the towel tightly around her and padded on her bare feet over to the dress that was still dripping onto the textured floor. She moved slowly, as if giving me every opportunity to stop her. Instead, I sat hunched over with my elbows on my knees, staring at the ground while I listened to the sounds of fabric swishing and rustling.

As she dressed, I tried to pull my thoughts together and force my confusing feelings into words. I'd hung onto my anger for so long, it was hard to just let go.

Her towels were tossed into a laundry bin. She slipped her feet into her heels. Time was running out on me, and it drove me to my feet. "Ruby."

The damp pink dress clung to her like it was painted on. Even though she wasn't tall, she looked statuesque on her heels, framed by the large windows behind her. Like she was a work of art.

She waited expectantly, and maybe with a kernel of optimism, for me to say something, but I faltered. I didn't usually have a problem with words. I could wing a closing argument if needed, as long as I had the bullet points I wanted to hit. Making the transitions between them was easy. But when it came to her, nothing was simple.

Her shoulders fell, and hope visibly drained out of her.

"Thank you for telling me," she said, her tone containing a terrible sense of finality to it. "There wasn't anyone else for me. It's five years too late, but . . . I'm sorry I lied." Her expression was devoid of any emotion. "Goodbye, Kyle."

Her words paralyzed me. I stood stock still as she walked steadily to the door and went through it, never turning back to look at me once.

Chapter

TWELVE

RUBY

Grant's apartment door swung open as I made my way down the hall, carrying Morgan's dress in a garment bag in one hand, and a box in the other.

"Happy New Year," he said. "Let's hear it, then. Feel better after giving McAsshole a piece of your mind?"

Normally I enjoyed Grant's South African accent, but now I grimaced. We had become friends my final year of law school, and although he'd never met Kyle, he'd heard all about him.

No. *Better* was definitely not the word I'd use after my evening with my ex. Trampled, maybe. Or gutted.

As soon as I stepped inside the apartment, I could tell things were different. I set the box down on the kitchen table. Didn't there used to be a picture on the wall over this? Everywhere I looked, it seemed like something was missing. "What's going on?"

Grant stroked a hand on the back of his neck. "Yeah, Morgan and I had a disagreement."

I hung the garment bag in the closet. "About?"

"What's all right to text to other people and what's not."

My movements slowed as I stared at my friend. All the traces of his girlfriend had been removed. There was hurt in his eyes, and I immediately went on the defensive. "What the fuck did she do?"

"Sometimes she'd text me pics where she'd be," he

made a face, "sans clothes."

Surely his girlfriend sexting him wasn't a problem. I gave him a skeptical look. "Naked pics, okay. What's the issue?"

"I wasn't the only guy she was sending them to."

I sighed, and pretended I was speaking directly to his girlfriend. "Oh, Morgan."

Sadly, this didn't surprise me. Morgan was a pretty girl, but her beauty was her favorite thing about herself. Not only was she vain, she needed constant validation. Like, hourly updates on how good she looked.

She was a backup meteorologist for the weather on channel seven, and had met Grant when he'd stepped in as a line producer for the morning news. I'd gotten along with her well enough, but hanging out with Morgan was exhausting, and I thought Grant could do better.

He was a great guy. A few years younger than me, smart, and good looking. He'd also dated my sister for a nanosecond, so I'd never viewed him as a prospect. He was like a brother. He'd come to the States to get his college education, and wound up staying on a work visa. Last year, I'd helped him through the U.S. citizenship process.

Even though I didn't like her, Grant had cared about Morgan, and I freaking hated to see him hurting. I'd have to stifle the urge to throat punch her if I ever saw her again in person.

"She swears she wasn't cheating on me," he said. "She told me hearing from other guys about how nice she looked made her feel better about herself."

I paused. "Other guys? More than one?"

"Some of which we work with. Even if I was all right with her sending those kinds of pictures to other people, which I'm not . . . my coworkers? She didn't consider how foolish it made me look. So, yeah, I'm done." He crossed his arms over his chest and leaned back against his kitchen table. "Just finished my New Year's cleaning. If that's a thing."

"Well, shit," I deadpanned. "I feel just awful now about ruining the dress she lent me."

Grant straightened. "You did what?"

I unzipped the garment bag and pulled the sides open, revealing the dress. The pink silk had dried with water stains all over it. The chlorine probably hadn't helped, either. "A dry cleaner might be able to fix it. Or I can just buy it from her, I guess." *Please don't let it be crazy expensive.*

Grant gazed at the dress and gave half a chuckle. "What happened?" Then his gaze drifted over to the box. He lifted the lid. "Oh no." He peered at the dozens of cookies inside, stacked in alternating colors. He shut the lid and locked his gaze on me. "Your night obviously didn't go well. Did you sleep much?"

A few years ago, after too much wine and an evening on Pinterest, I discovered a tutorial on making French macarons. My first attempt had been a disaster. Puffy cookie shells with cracked tops. But I wouldn't be beaten and kept at it, figuring out the perfect temperature for my oven, and how to fold the delicate batter so I'd get shiny, perfect shells with chewy centers. I was obsessed with making them in different colors and flavor combinations. Creating the sandwich cookies had become my therapy.

Grant knew this. One look at the box announced my fragile mental state.

"Yeah, I slept," I said, trying not to be defensive. "I got an early start."

He meandered to his fridge. "Care for something to drink while you tell me about it?"

I took a glass of water and sat down across from him in the living room of his studio apartment. I wasn't sure where to start. When I'd asked to borrow a dress from Morgan, I'd had to reveal what I needed it for. Grant had seen me at my worst. We'd met just two months after Kyle had left, when I'd been working my way toward rock bottom of a not-great time in my life.

So while Grant understood my desire to get closure, he'd also been worried about the emotional toll there'd be for me to get it. I'd sworn to him I was strong enough now to face Kyle. The one good thing to come out of my breakup with him was I'd grown tough and hardened my heart.

"The suspense is killing me," Grant said, leaning back and casting a thick arm on the back of the couch. "I take it you spoke with McAsshole."

"I did." I took a sip of my water. "He, uh, filled in some gaps in the story."

"Gaps? What kind of gaps?"

It burst from me suddenly, rapid-fire. How I'd left the awful voicemail that had driven Kyle away, and then the second lie I'd told which was the nail in the coffin for our relationship. In hindsight, my New Year's Eve plan had been stupid. If I hadn't kissed him, he would have kept his lips to himself, and we wouldn't have ended up in the water where he gave me the fuck of my life.

Followed immediately by the most awkward ten minutes of my life.

It had been like he'd shut down after he'd gotten out of the pool and dried off. Kyle just stood there, not saying a word. I couldn't tell if he wanted me to stay or not, but it became perfectly clear when he let me walk away. He hadn't uttered a word to stop me. Once again, he gave up.

When the conversation lapsed into silence, Grant's gaze drifted over to the closet. "So, the dress? What happened?"

"We, uh, fell in the pool." It wasn't a lie, but I wasn't about to tell him about what happened afterward. It was embarrassing how fast I'd jumped on Kyle's dick.

My face must have given too much away, because Grant frowned. "Are you okay?"

"Yeah. It was just a lot, seeing him again." Once again, not a lie. My emotions were horribly twisted, and the hardest part was I still wanted him. I wanted to know why he was back. Why he'd only slept with three women since me.

And what the hell he thought about the moment when I turned to him in the pool and whispered, "*Again.*" I shivered now from the memory. It wasn't just the burning sting from his spanking I'd enjoyed; it'd been so much more. All those lies I'd told had made something dark inside me crave punishment from him. Like I deserved it. There'd been relief at his command over my body.

Grant raked a hand through his long, mahogany-colored hair, pushing the strands back. "Any chance McAsshole wants to play a little rugby?"

I smiled. Grant was on the Chicago Lions rugby team. I didn't understand the desire to play the rough sport and get himself beaten up on weekends during the season, but I fully understood the effect his teammates in uniform had on me. I mean, *goddamn.*

"No," I said with a light laugh. "I don't think watching you knock Kyle flat on his ass would make me feel much better."

"And who cares about that?" Grant smiled. "It would make *me* feel better."

"Aw, you're sweet. Speaking of sweets, the macs are raspberry lemon, caramel apple, and blueberry."

"You keep at this, and my team's going to demand I marry you."

I shrugged. "I keep telling you to drop some subtle hints that I'm single."

"I do, but it always comes out as 'stay the hell away from my friend.' It's strange. Must be a cultural thing, or my accent."

He'd always been protective of me, so it came as no surprise when he'd decreed I wasn't allowed to date any of his 'meathead' teammates.

I glanced around the apartment, once again noticing the pictures he'd removed. "And you?" I asked. "How are you doing? Are you okay?"

"Yes." His expression was sincere. "We'd been over for a while. I think all we really liked was the idea of each other. Which, fuck me, sounds bloody awful." In his accent, it came out like, "*sounds bladdy awful.*"

Lord knew he wasn't going to get any judgement from me. This morning had given me perspective, but last night? If Kyle had asked me to go home with him, I'd have done it.

All he would have had to do was fucking ask.

KYLE

Unlike most Italian restaurants, the smell of garlic did not cling to the air. The place was understated. Subtle hints of Tuscany in the décor, as opposed to the obnoxious, over the top decorating you often saw in the chain restaurants. The food was excellent without being pretentious.

Joseph sat on the other side of the wooden table, carefully swirling the red wine in his glass, and studied the legs of the wine intently as they streaked down the sides. His dark-eyed gaze was focused, like nothing else existed in that moment.

It was unavoidable, thinking about sex around him, not just because of the club he'd built. A seductive power radiated from him. Our waitress had gotten flustered while taking his order, and I doubted it had anything to do with the fact Joseph was the owner.

How often did he look at Noemi that same way? Did she melt beneath his intense stare?

He set the glass down after taking a sip and considering its flavor. "I'm not sold on this wine. It's sweet for a red, and expensive. I don't want to get stuck with several cases I can't sell."

He gestured to the glass, wordlessly asking me if I wanted to sample it.

"No, thanks." I shook my head. "I'm on the clock." Not that anyone would care if I took a sip of wine during my lunch hour, but Joseph had called me here to discuss business, and I had a self-imposed rule to never drink while working.

"Of course. Thanks for fitting me in."

Which hadn't been too difficult. His restaurant was in the Loop, so I was able to cab it over from the office, and he could kill two birds with one stone. Our meeting over lunch allowed him to check in with his staff while discussing . . . whatever it was he wanted to talk to me about.

"Noemi's father," he said, "with the help of his legal team, took the liberty of drafting a prenup for her."

"Ah." Joseph's future father-in-law was worth well over a billion dollars, and he'd been grooming his oldest daughter to take over for him at his media company. "I'd be happy to take a look and offer advice before you sign."

A slight smile turned up at the edge of his lips. "That's not necessary. I already signed."

"Oh." If he had, there wasn't anything I could do to help.

"I don't have an issue with the prenup. I know it's irrelevant because there's not a chance in hell Noemi and I will get divorced, but regardless, it's smart business to protect her assets."

His expression was . . . odd. Like he was amused.

"I've explained this to her," he continued, "but my fiancée refuses to sign. It's not the principle of a prenup that bothers her. She's smart and she's seen both of her father's marriages fall apart. Her objection is the way Tony presented it to us. He announced he wouldn't come to the wedding unless we signed a prenuptial agreement."

I didn't know them all that well, but I had a very good idea how that went over with the engaged couple.

"I'm not marrying her for money," he added, his

amusement spreading into a full smile. "I own three businesses and have investments well into seven figures. I may not be as wealthy as the Rossos, but I'm doing all right."

"Sounds like it."

"Noemi says he doesn't respect me, and refuses to let her father hold power over us. So, she won't sign the prenup he had drafted for her. I need to present her with one instead."

Realization clicked into place. "You want me to write a prenuptial agreement for you and Noemi, that's basically a *fuck you* to the most powerful man in Chicago?"

"Yes. Are you in?"

I chuckled. The idea of doing it was wildly appealing. "Sure, why not?"

"Great. I'll email over the draft we have, along with the language I'd like to see changed." He settled back in his chair and a curious, interested expression washed over his face. "Payton asked me to help you get laid."

"Christ." I scrubbed a hand over my jaw, and my beard bristled against my palm. "I don't need any help, thanks."

"Oh?"

This meeting was all sorts of multitasking for Joseph. He could check off wine tasting, prenup, and Payton's ridiculous resolution for me all in an hour. I was so annoyed, it distracted me from thinking before speaking. "Yeah. I just got laid a few days ago. New Year's Eve."

His dark eyes sharpened, and I doubted much got by him. "How was it?"

How was it? Just the best sex of my goddamn life. "It was fine."

He cut off his laugh. "What a glowing endorsement. Are you going to see Ms. Fine again?"

I'd hoped every day Ruby would reach out, although I knew she wouldn't. Didn't stop me from checking my email instantly anytime I got a notification, though. "I'd like to, but that's going to be a challenge."

His eyebrow arched upward. "Why?"

"She's an ex."

He asked it like he was interviewing me. "And how often do you fuck your exes?"

"I don't." My hands were resting on my thighs, and I tensed them into fists. "It's complicated."

"It always is." Joseph withdrew his ringing phone from his pocket, glanced at the screen, and promptly shut it off. Then he set it screen side down on the table with a soft thump, giving me his undivided attention. "Why is she an ex?"

"Do you really want to talk about this?" His calm demeanor was irritating. I'd deflect. "Why are you my sister's ex?"

He actually grinned. "I'm not. You'd have to date someone for them to become an ex. And me? I didn't date." Before I could ask how he became attached to his fiancée, he added, "Noemi came out of fucking nowhere. I didn't stand a chance."

His statement was sort of sweet, but I couldn't focus on that. "Payton said you two—"

"Fucked? Yeah. You may not be aware, but two consenting adults can have sex outside of a relationship."

"Watch it. One of those consenting adults was my little sister."

He lifted a hand, signaling surrender. "It was a while ago, and Payton and I are different people now."

Yeah. People in love, who I had little in common with.

"Your reaction about your ex makes me wonder what happened," he said. "Humor me, I'm curious."

I rubbed away the crease in my forehead. Who liked admitting their mistakes? I'd made plenty with Ruby, starting with taking off for New York without saying goodbye. When I'd called her after, had I even told her what had happened? Or had I been too blinded with anger when she'd slurred out the lie she was with another guy?

I tried to sum up my relationship with Ruby as quickly as possible, giving Joseph the highlights and lowlights. He listened patiently, not interrupting or giving me any hint of what his thoughts were. When it was done and I'd told him about my verbal impotence when she left me by the pool, I awaited his feedback and watched him take another sip of the wine he'd deemed too sweet.

He rested his elbows on the table and steepled his fingertips together. "Sounds like the sex was better than fine."

"*That's* your takeaway?"

He ignored my tone. "Was it?"

"Yeah, of course it was!" I had to bring down the pitch of my voice until it was even again. "Jesus, I don't know which was hotter. Getting to have control, or the way she was into it. But, Joseph, she—"

"You're wrong." He leaned forward and his tone dripped confidence. "You do need my help. You want to see this woman again?"

I pressed my lips into a thin line. "Yes. And no."

"You're still mad about what she said."

I frowned. "It's not the words anymore that are the problem."

He nodded in understanding. "You don't know if you can trust her."

"We both got burned. Wasn't a whole lot of fun, and I'd like to avoid it happening again."

Joseph's gaze went beyond me, as if he was considering, and then his attention snapped back like he'd pulled an idea from the air. "You could arrange a way to build trust." His expression was cryptic. "It's unconventional, and she may not go for it, but from what you've said, sex doesn't seem to be an issue."

Was he serious? "No, it's not an *issue*."

"Good. Then use it. Make it clear you can't have anything more than a sexual arrangement until you've both forgiven each other and the trust is there."

I stared at him like he was insane, but perhaps I was, since I considered his suggestion. "Okay, how the hell do I work that into conversation?"

"You don't. Something like that needs to be spelled out with exact language." Joseph's mouth lifted into a half-smile. "I think that'd be easy for a man who writes contracts for a living."

RUBY

Morgan's dress was twelve hundred dollars. She'd worn it as a presenter at some broadcaster awards ceremony last year. Since she wasn't going to use the dress again, she was surprisingly cool about it. I delivered the silk gown to a dry cleaner and tried to explain what happened. The Korean woman didn't appear to understand a word of it, but she nodded enthusiastically and announced, "Thursday, you pick up."

Kyle had cleaned me out of almond flour and egg whites. I'd set down the box containing my last batch of macarons in the office break room this morning, and my associates swarmed. It got me to crack a smile. At least my misery brought happiness to others.

Since my macaron making supplies were depleted, I told myself that was enough. I was done thinking about Kyle McCreary. I was successful for the majority of the day, until an email arrived in my inbox from 'k.mccreary' followed by his firm's domain name.

> Ms. Carter,
>
> There is business my client needs to discuss, but due to its sensitive nature, I would prefer not to document it. Please call my assistant at the number listed below and arrange a meeting at your earliest convenience.

Thank you for your time,

Kyle McCreary

I fought back the rising anger. The email was professional, but so very him. I drafted and deleted three nasty responses before composing the right one.

> Mr. McCreary,
>
> I am no longer involved in the Crawford divorce as it is a conflict of interest. In the future, you should contact Henry Reed directly. I will forward your request to him.
>
> Sincerely,
>
> Ruby Carter

I fired off the email, and was stunned when his response was immediate.

> This is unrelated to the Crawford case.

A strange tickle developed in the back of my throat, which I tried to swallow away.

> What is it regarding?

This time either his response was slower, or the clock ground to a halt. I held my breath when the new message popped in.

> Please see my previous email about the sensitive nature, and call my office to schedule the meeting.

I actually hissed at my computer screen.

Never had I been so incredibly annoyed and curious at the same time. What the hell was this about? Life would be just great if I didn't see him again, even in a professional capacity. There were plenty of attorneys in Chicago. I'd gone more than a year without running into him, and it stood to reason I could go the rest of my career without it happening.

I dragged my feet about making the appointment, knowing if I wanted answers, I'd have to do it. Did he have a client he wanted to push off on me? Was this some sort of offering as a way of apology? Like throwing work my direction would make everything better?

Because if so, fuck that. I snatched up my desk phone and punched in the numbers with force.

"James, Franklin, and McCreary. This is Suzanne. Can I help you?"

I took a deep breath. "Yes, Suzanne. This is Ruby Carter, calling from the Law Offices of Sterns and Clifford. I need to set up an appointment with Kyle McCreary."

"Sure, please give me a moment to pull up his schedule." There was a short pause. "It looks like the only thing he has available is tomorrow at four. Does that work for you? He's booked solid next week."

I clenched my teeth. I didn't want to meet with him, and definitely not on a Friday, an hour before close of business. If his office was anything like mine, the senior staff cleared out early, and the junior associates were scrambling to finish work before the weekend.

"Is he available during his lunch? I'm fine with meeting outside the office." In fact, neutral ground was preferable.

"Sorry, no. His schedule is tight."

I sighed. "All right, please put me down for tomorrow at four."

"Do you need directions to our office?"

"No, thank you," I gritted out. "I've been before."

I wanted to add last time I'd been there, I'd told the younger McCreary to fuck himself in their conference room, but I refrained.

The couch in the lobby of James, Franklin, and Mc-Creary looked expensive, and I perched delicately on the edge. The receptionist had offered to take my coat while I waited, probably to avoid my snow-damp wool from getting anywhere near the fancy leather furniture. My shoes were safe. I'd changed out of my lace-up sneakers into leopard print pumps during the elevator ride up.

I wore a thin, three-quarter length sleeve black cardigan over a white blouse, both tucked into a camel colored pencil skirt. I'd rolled up the sleeves to my elbows and left several of the top buttons undone on the blouse. I'd also tamed my hair up into a top knot, so the weather couldn't get at it.

I wasn't going to dress like I was an attorney who charged five hundred an hour, because I didn't, and my wardrobe reflected that. Instead, I looked the part of a business professional, but there was also a hint of sexy. At least, I hoped. It was cold in the lobby, but I was already sweating and hadn't even seen Kyle yet.

Approaching footsteps made me clutch my slim brief-case tighter. When he stepped into view and his gaze land-ed on me, my heart clogged my throat. He wore a pale gray suit, once again, slim cut to show off his lean form. The fabric was a matte silver. Beneath was a plain white dress shirt and a sapphire blue tie.

He looked handsome and devastating.

I pushed myself to my feet just as he thrust his hand out. "Ms. Carter. Thanks for meeting me."

A handshake? Was he for fucking real? I gave his dick a handshake with my vagina just a week ago.

I stared at his offered hand for a full second before finally taking it. He wrapped his fingers around my palm with a sure grip, and then closed his other hand on top. It was unadulterated domination and, judging by the enjoyment in his eyes, he knew it.

The shiver that slipped down my spine was unstoppable, and it was embarrassing when the corner of his mouth twitched up into a smirk. Yeah. He definitely caught my reaction.

"It's cold in your lobby," I announced, my voice as tight as his grip still holding my hand.

"Sorry about that." He released me and gestured to the hall. "Please. My office is this way."

I straightened my posture and held my chin high as we marched down the corridor, determined to appear unaffected when the proximity of him had my heart racing. The urge to look around the office was strong. I'd left in a hurry last time and had been too flustered to realize since this was his family's firm, there was a good chance Kyle's parents were in this office.

I'd never met any of Kyle's family. His sister had been studying abroad the year we dated, and the relationship between him and his folks was strained. He didn't talk much about them.

Most of the offices we passed were closed and no light spilled from beneath the doors. As I suspected, the weekend exodus had begun. Down the line of offices, one door was open. He cast a hand out, but I hesitated before crossing the threshold. *This is a professional meeting. Be a professional, Ruby.*

I stepped inside.

Kyle's office was nice enough. For starters, it was an office. I was still sharing a room with three other junior associates. He had a window. The pane of glass stretched from floor to ceiling, and the fading January sunlight cast a warm glow in the room. If our meeting lasted more than thirty minutes, it'd be dark when I left.

His computer monitor and keyboard occupied most of the large desk, but otherwise it was bare. A diploma from Randhurst law school hung on the wall. There was a half bookshelf below it, which held mostly books, and one framed family photo. I forced my gaze onto something else. Anything else. I needed to treat Kyle like he was just another attorney.

As he closed the door, I set my briefcase down on the seat of one of the chairs facing the desk, and sat in the other. There'd been a strange click as he'd shut it, as if he'd locked the door behind us. My surprised gaze found his, but his expression was plain.

He moved to his desk and sat. "How've you been?"

"How've I been?" I gave him a dubious look. "I'm fine. What did you want to discuss?"

For a long moment that stretched between us, he was silent. Then, he leaned back in his chair, pulled open a drawer, and produced a stapled packet of paper. As he reached across the desk to hand it to me, tension seemed to coil in him. The document was serious.

"What is this?" I grasped the packet and waited for him to let go. A cursory scan said it was a contract. The top sheet was full of dense paragraphs.

Finally, he released it. "It's a partnership agreement."

"Partnership agreement?"

"I'm proposing a mutually beneficial arrangement."

Was he purposefully being vague? "Between which clients?"

He blinked slowly. "It'd be for us, Ruby."

FIFTEEN

Kyle's expression was stoic, but I watched the rapid lift of his shoulders. He was nervous, which of course, made me very nervous.

"How's that, now?" I asked, dumbfounded. My gaze fell to the agreement in my hands, and as I began to read, all my blood rushed to my toes.

Holy. Fuck.

"What am I reading?" I gasped.

His gaze didn't deviate from mine, even as I looked down at the papers and back up to him. His intense stare pinned me to my seat while his tone was soft. "Take as much time as you need."

I tried to keep reading, but the phrase *'partnership of a sexual nature'* short-circuited my brain and now I couldn't interpret a goddamn thing. "Okay, seriously." I dropped the document on his desktop and jabbed a finger at it. "What the fuck is this? A joke?"

"No. I can't stop thinking about New Year's Eve. I want that again. I want more."

Air constricted in my lungs, making everything in my body feel tight, yet weightless at the same time. What exactly did he mean? "More . . . sex?"

"More sex, more of you. More of us together, seeing how much further we want to go sexually. There are things I want to explore, and I think you do, too. This agreement lays the foundation for us to do that together."

I stared at the document. "For fuck's sake, you put it

in writing?"

He lifted an eyebrow. "I communicate better this way, and I believe the same can be said of you."

He did have a point about our shitty communication, but still. This was so fucking insane, I had no idea what to say. I wanted to see inside his crazy head and figure out what he was thinking. Yet he gave nothing away.

"Everything is open for discussion," he said. "Except the last paragraph."

He wasn't going to elaborate. I picked up the agreement in a shaky hand and tried once more to read. The first paragraph outlined during the duration of the agreement, we were to remain exclusive to each other. The second was about both partners being willing to play whenever the other wanted to, within reason.

Meaning if I signed this bat-shit crazy proposal, I could call him up anytime, he'd come running, and would have to put out, unless he had a valid excuse. And the same would apply to me. I kept reading, because how could I not? It was the most ludicrous and exciting legal document I'd laid eyes on.

The third paragraph stated we would provide our partner with a willing list. This would detail all the sexual avenues we individually wanted to explore, and gauge our level of mutual interest.

Cold crept over my skin as I skimmed the final paragraph. The proposed partnership was about fucking only. Any discussion of a relationship outside of the sex would nullify the agreement. This meant there'd be no hurt feelings, no messy emotions, and certainly no use of the L word.

Okay. I hated him, right?

So why was I feeling one iota of disappointment? I

wasn't about to enter into this ridiculous agreement, and besides, I'd been foolish enough to fall for him once. I wasn't going to do it again.

Kyle's gaze on me was crushing. I pretended not to notice as I turned to the next page. Well, yep. There was no dancing around it with legalese here. The willing list was a menu full of sexual debauchery. My face heated as I scanned the page. Some of my darkest fantasies were on here. Only . . . "Where are your answers? This is blank."

Heat flared in his eyes, and my body threatened to turn into liquid. "You want to see my willing list?" He placed his palms on his desk and pushed up to stand. He spoke the words with so much weight, I felt each one pressed against me. "You want to know every dirty little thing I want to do to you?"

I squeezed my knees together. The agreement was no longer in my hands. At some point, it had fallen to the desktop, and now my fingers curled around the armrests of the chair and dug in. He stalked around the desk, coming closer. I wasn't moving. My gaze never left his. Yet I felt like I was prey fleeing from a predator.

And I'd never make it. I couldn't outrun him.

The chair creaked as he leaned over and set his hands on the back. It trapped me beneath him, his tie dangling close to my face, and as I forced myself to suck in a breath, I caught the delicious, woodsy scent of his cologne.

"All you have to do," he said, "is sign."

"I'm not signing that." My voice was a ghost.

His was seductive and confident. "Oh, yes, you fucking are." He dropped his lips to mine, and I was too stunned to move. My body reacted to his soft kiss, and silently protested when he drew back. "You haven't put ink on it yet, but you will. You told me you would when you asked me to spank you *again*."

The muscles in my core contracted at the memory, trying to squeeze back the rush he gave me. "I was drunk."

"Bullshit."

"I'm not signing it."

"Bullshit." He hovered over me, his mouth a breath away and teasing a kiss, all while a smirk rolled on his lips.

"I'm not interested in casual sex."

"Bull *fucking* shit, Ruby. Besides, there won't be anything casual about it." His expression turned serious. "At this time, I'm not willing to offer more. You don't want that anyway. You *hate* me." His lips sealed over mine, and there was a hint of tongue. His tone was mocking. "Remember?"

"Why?"

He looked thrown. "Why . . . do you hate me?"

"No. Why aren't you willing to offer more?" I didn't want a relationship with Kyle either, but I needed to know his motivations.

"Honestly?"

Was honesty possible? I nodded.

He straightened and leaned back against his desk. "We both made mistakes, and neither one of us has forgiven the other." He folded his arms over his chest and shot me a hard look. "You trust me enough to fuck you, but not enough to date you."

My mouth fell open, but no noise came out. He was terribly right, but I didn't love having him point it out. It made me sound '*bladdy awful,*' as Grant would say. "That's . . ."

Kyle's expression was pragmatic. "The truth. I don't fault you for feeling that way. As I said, we both made mistakes."

It wasn't exactly an apology, but hearing him admit fault knocked me sideways. How could he be so rational and logical with the damn partnership agreement sitting right there beside him?

"You told me," he said, "no one else makes you come like I do. I like that. Let's keep doing it."

Oh, good God. I took my hands off the armrests and smoothed my sweaty palms over my skirt. "Kyle." I rose onto my heels and issued a grateful sigh in my head when I didn't teeter. I tried to readjust, and steeled my tone. "Mr. McCreary."

I was standing eye to eye with him, far too close. The long lashes around his beautiful blue eyes were lulling me in like an insect to a Venus fly trap. Every cell in my body wanted him, but my mind? It was less sure.

His tone was confident. "You need a pen?"

"No, thank you. I'm not interested in your partnership offer."

I expected him to seem disappointed, but excitement lit like fire in his eyes. "No?"

"No."

"Prove it."

I bent to grab my briefcase, but his voice caused me to halt. "Excuse me?"

"You heard me."

His hands caught my hips at the same moment his mouth landed on mine. His indecent tongue possessed and slid deep, stroking against mine, sending pleasure jolting down between my legs. His mouth was hot and soft, gentle yet dominating. The fingers on my hips clamped fiercely, holding me in place so he could wage his attack.

God, this man knew how to kiss.

His lips pressed to mine, moving urgently and demanding. Without my approval, a tiny moan slipped out. Kyle reacted like it was a starting pistol. He gripped my waist and turned me so suddenly, I was spun around before I understood what was happening.

My hands flew out and I braced myself on the desktop as he bent me over with a shove. "What are you—"

He was faster than lightning. The sides of my skirt were jerked up over my hips, exposing my black thong. I'd worn it to prevent panty lines, and as the cool air washed over me, I felt essentially naked from the waist down.

I tried to right myself and push the skirt down, but he coughed loudly at the same moment his open palm smacked hard against my ass.

SIXTEEN

Kyle's spanking sent me flying forward onto my elbows. Flames licked at me from this shocking act, and it took me a moment to realize his 'cough' was perfectly timed to cover the slap of flesh meeting flesh.

Holy shit. He was willing to do it, right here in his office.

I glanced over my shoulder to look at him. He was staring at my ass, probably watching the blood rush to the skin and color it. I'd be damned if he didn't look powerful. And sexy as hell.

But this was madness. Someone was going to catch us.

Once more I attempted to straighten, and this time his cough was louder. It disguised a strike that stole my breath. My mouth rounded into an "*oh*" and I clenched my hands into fists.

As much as I wanted to deny it, I liked this. I liked it a *whole fucking lot*. This was wrong and I wanted him to keep doing it.

"You know what's going to happen now?" His voice was pure sin. "I'm going to jerk your panties down and find your pussy's soaking wet."

Holy shit.

I could stand up, shove my skirt back down in place, and walk out of his office. I could unleash the full force of my temper on him and make sure he never attempted to talk to me again.

But I couldn't move. My elbows were glued to his desk. My ankles stayed locked together, encouraging him to carry out his indecent plan. My back arched subtly without thinking, and my heart beat a thousand times a second.

He didn't wait for me to protest or agree.

I stared straight ahead as his fingers hooked around the thong, and then the fabric was yanked down with such force, it had an edge of pain. I bit down on my bottom lip to hold in the gasp at his aggression. He wasn't soft or sweet; he was so much better. Would I burst into flames right here on his desk?

The underwear fell to my ankles and then his fingers were there, delving between my legs, rubbing my dampness. I hung my head as the moan erupted from my throat, low and deep.

"You're going to sign," he said. His hand stirred over my clit, one small circle and then gone. He grabbed my hair by the top knot, yanking my head back with a sharp tug. It was so he could smear the moisture he'd collected on his fingertips all over my mouth. Over my parted lips and pushing inside. "Here's the goddamn proof."

Who the hell was this man?

I was thankful for the support of the desk. Lust had turned my knees to rubber, my insides to jelly. I had to struggle to breathe over the aching fire he'd started. Everything burned, and burned for him.

He released my hair and my head lolled to hang down between my shoulders. I could barely hear over the rush of blood in my ears, but he'd moved. Kyle dropped behind me onto a knee and gripped my ankle, urging the panties over my heels one by one. I was too overwhelmed with desire to resist.

As soon as I was free from my underwear, his grip was back on my waist, forcing me to turn around once again.

I wobbled on my heels, both unsure of what he was doing, yet also filled with jittery excitement, and my backside slammed against the edge of the desk.

He was on his knees in his two-thousand-dollar suit, staring up at me, but there was no doubt he was the one in charge. His palm flattened on my belly over the skirt bunched up there, and he pressed me back until I was seated on the desktop, my bare ass cold against the smooth wood. I moved like a puppet under his command, my body doing whatever he ordered it to.

"Get those legs open," he demanded, but didn't give me time to comprehend. His palms clasped my knees and shoved them apart, putting my wet pussy on full display. With him on his knees, it was right at his eye-level, and he moved in for the kill. I had to thread a hand through his thick hair and hold on as he hooked my knees over his shoulders.

I froze with anxiety and desire, both wanting what was about to happen and terrified of it. This was a really bad idea, not just because we were in his office during work hours, but he'd broken my heart. I shouldn't let him get close, even just for sex. Mind-blowing, toe curling, everything-I-ever-wanted sex.

"Kyle . . ."

Too late. He dragged his tongue steadily along the inside of my thigh, not stopping until he'd found his intended target. His tongue was furious, lashing at my clit, and making my whole body jerk.

Oh.

Oh, wow.

I gripped the edge of the desk under my ass with one hand and yanked on his hair with my other, desperate for more and hating how quickly he'd gotten me to fold. *In over your head with him, Ruby. You knew that already.*

He paused only to utter the phrase, "Sign it."

And he went right back to work.

I stared at the top of his head which was buried between my spread legs and my vision blurred from the pleasure. "You son of a bitch."

His dark laugh only made more heat fill my belly. Before, I'd loved it when he didn't fight fair, because I didn't either. He'd get his way, and he knew it.

Maybe I had, too, right from the beginning. But I wasn't going to blatantly agree to his terms. My mind scrambled to find something to negotiate. He'd taken emotion out of the equation, yet there was something else I desired, which just happened to make him uneasy. *Perfect.*

"A line needs to be amended," I said. "Total honesty between partners."

He slowed as he considered it, and when he stopped altogether, he must have grasped the full extent. No hiding behind half-truths or deflecting questions, as he liked to do. Getting information out of him was no easy thing.

My belly did a flip-flop as he grabbed a pen and scrawled the line of text after the final paragraph. Like it was easy to give this up. Shit. I thought I'd been so clever, and now I had the suspicion my term was going to come back around to bite me.

The pen clattered to the wood, and Kyle refocused on me. "Done." He slid two fingers deep inside me, hard and fast. "Now say yes."

"Fuck." My eyes wanted to roll back in my head. I half-expected to come away with a fistful of his hair, I was tugging on it that hard. Like everything else he'd done today, his tempo wasn't slow. His thick fingers moved roughly, fucking me with a blissful burn.

It was impossible to restrain my moans. How sound-proof were the offices? Was anyone still around to hear if I lost control? "Someone's," I panted, "going to hear me."

"Not if you stay quiet." His mouth was a volcano, causing mini eruptions of pleasure, and threatening a big finish.

"I can't . . . when you're doing that."

"Sure you can. I believe in you."

His tempo was blistering. My legs were trembling on his shoulders. God, he was going to have to stop, or at least slow down, or I was going to lose my mind. My inhibitions were likely to go right along with it.

My tone had a fair amount of warning. "You're going to make me come."

"Not until you tell me what I want to hear."

There was no point fighting any longer. We both knew I would agree, whether I put my signature on the non-binding document or not. "Yes. Yes, Kyle." How could I say no? At this point, all I wanted was . . . "More."

I collapsed backward so I was propped on my bent elbows, and surrendering set me free. I gazed at him as his tongue stroked my clit and his fingers slammed in and out. They'd grown slick and glossy with my arousal. He'd set a demanding pace, and it was probably taking a toll on him physically, but he didn't slow down.

Not even as a third finger joined his first two. His palm was turned toward the ceiling, allowing him to slide right in to the perfect spot.

"Your fingers," I said between two gulps of air. "Fucking magic."

His mouth worked in conjunction with his hand,

hurtling me so close to the edge of orgasm, I could barely tolerate it. I picked at the buttons of my blouse, undoing them as fast as I could with one hand, and yanked the shirt open when I had enough done so I could expose my bra. I needed a hand on my breast, pinching my nipple. Didn't matter if it was my touch or his.

I jammed my fingers inside the cup, searching, and my eyes lidded with desire as I found the tight, painful bud of flesh. My pinch stung in a delicious, perfect way. It all looked so good, his determined gaze watching me while his jaw worked, and it felt a million times better than it looked. And he obviously liked how I was touching myself—his eyes hooded further.

But it was difficult to keep unwanted emotion from slipping in. I'd loved him and hated him, and now I was stuck somewhere between. We'd both changed over the years. Would the new version of myself be able to survive the new version of him?

He nuzzled and used suction, focusing the sensation all on my center. When he made a soft noise of contentment, like he was enjoying tasting and fucking me with his fingers almost as much as I was enjoying him doing it, I lost the ability to breathe. He was wild, yet powerful, and the look in his eyes said he wanted to consume me. Eat me up, one lick at a time.

I'd let him. I'd love every second of it.

The orgasm crashed like a wave. It stormed through my bloodstream, sweeping along my body first with pinpricks of pleasure, then followed with fire. The muscles in my thighs tensed and clamped down on his head, holding his face to me as I rode, bucking with ecstasy.

I tried to stay quiet, I really did.

He might have told me to keep it down, but I'd successfully muzzled him with my pussy. If anything, it served him right. In this moment, I didn't give a shit who heard as Kyle delivered an orgasm so great, my body went boneless. The moans poured from my mouth and I rocked against his face, enjoying every drop of my climax.

The thud as I banged flat on the desk was loud enough to be heard over my cries as they began to ebb. I fell slower back to the present, coming down off my high, and it barely registered my legs had released their vise-like grip on him.

He climbed to his feet and wiped a hand over his short beard, removing the evidence of what he'd just done. I couldn't do anything but lie on the desk and heave breath into my lungs while he towered over me. His gaze wandered along my skin, tracing the curves of my body appreciatively.

"Oh my God, Kyle," I whispered.

The thrilled smile that swept across his face was beautiful, and my heart swelled.

No, I warned myself. *Stop that.*

He leaned over and planted a kiss on my lips, and when he straightened, his fingers went to the buttons of my blouse. Not to finish undoing them, but to refasten. I peered at him and the magnificent wood he was sporting, and grasped his hands, causing him to stop.

"What are you doing?" I asked softly.

He stepped back, fished my underwear off the floor, and put my foot through one of the leg holes.

"What the hell are you doing?" I kicked the panties off, glared up at him, and was surprised when his jaw was set. "Aren't you going to fuck me?"

His victorious expression only lasted a moment. "No."

"I'm sorry, *no*?" I propped myself up on an elbow and reached for his belt. "Per our agreement, I thought you didn't get to say no."

He turned his hips away from me. "The agreement you haven't signed?"

"Oh my God, you already have my verbal. When did you get so annoying about the details?" I launched upright, plucked a pen from his desk, and scrawled my signature at the bottom of the page, followed by the date. "Done. Fuck me."

His gaze followed the stroke of my pen, and dark satisfaction streaked his face when I dropped the paper on the desktop. But then his expression turned down. "No."

I'd come to his office today not wanting to see him again, and now I was throwing myself at him. Practically begging. My eyes narrowed into slits. "What the fuck is this game?"

His movements slowed. "It's not a game. We can say no if we have a valid reason, which I do. I'm at work."

My vision hazed into red, but I walked myself back from the edge. "Wasn't a problem a minute ago. You know, when you had me coming all over your face."

"Yeah, coming *loudly*. Imagine what you sound like when it's my dick."

Asshole, even if he had a point. This was supposed to be a partnership, though, and I didn't want him holding anything over me, including orgasms. "That issue is easy enough to solve. I won't come."

Had I just told him I'd murdered someone? Kyle's face twisted with horror. "Not possible."

My vision went red again. "You think you're that good, huh? News flash, your dick doesn't have superpowers. It's possible to have sex with you and not come."

He let loose a laugh like I was talking utter nonsense. "Superpowers? No, probably not. But we both know my dick's even more *magical* than my fingers."

I wanted to punch him in his smug face as he used my own words against me. Unfair. Like an interrogation under duress, anything I said during sex and foreplay should be inadmissible.

I stood up so quickly and was still lightheaded from the orgasm; tiny spots danced in the edges of my vision. I shoved my skirt down and hurried to do up the last button on my blouse, trying to get my head on straight. What was I really upset about? He'd given me an amazing orgasm. It was stupid to be pouting about not having sex, and I was smarter than this.

The new idea formed. I drew in a deep, cleansing breath, and peeled my lips back into a bright smile. It was so wide, it froze him in place.

Chapter
SEVENTEEN

KYLE

Ruby's shit-eating grin made a red flag spring up so hard, it nearly knocked me to the ground. She had two different stages of anger. One was your standard fare. Her face would flush, her words would heat, and she'd tense up like she was locking down the fire doors to contain the worst of it.

But the other stage I was less familiar with. She appeared quiet and calm, while I was aware she was nothing but below the surface. That was when she was the most unpredictable.

She finished smoothing her clothes back into place, and gave a tug to the sides of her loopy ponytail, cinching it tighter to her head. The loose tendrils of hair at her temples were tucked behind her ears, and she lowered gracefully to sit in the client chair. She crossed her legs, folded her hands together, and pressed them into her lap. So prim and proper, like she hadn't begged me to fuck her thirty seconds ago.

I was sweating under my collar, and my dick ached with need, but I'd meant what I'd said. Chances were the back offices were empty and no one had heard Ruby's throaty moans, but I wasn't that big of a risk taker. She was always louder when we had sex.

Her back was ramrod straight, and her chin jutted out, giving her an air of power and control. Everything about her body language screamed she held the upper hand.

"Okay," she said. "Tell me about New York."

Clever girl. She knew I didn't want to talk about it.

I sat in the matching chair beside her, adjusting my uncomfortable hard-on. The taste of her was still on my tongue, and her smell lingered in my nose. Making her come always got me hot, and my body threatened to riot when I'd shot down the offer to fuck her right there on my desk.

"New York is a state on the east coast. It's next to New Jersey."

There was no reaction to my wiseass comment. Ruby didn't miss a beat. "Why did you leave?"

The moment she'd asked me to add the addendum about honesty, I figured she'd go digging, but I didn't expect it quite so soon. Maybe over dinner sometime, or after we'd thoroughly fucked our brains out.

But I'd been willing to sacrifice a little information to get her on board. Joseph's crazy plan had worked. I drafted the agreement, and used the willing list he'd sent me. There was no doubt it had come from the blindfold club.

When she'd asked to see mine, I knew I had her. Her eyes had sparkled with curiosity, and she was too interested to walk without getting a peek at my fantasies.

I could understand. I couldn't fucking wait to see which boxes she marked. *Dear God, please check anal.*

"I was in a relationship," I said. "It ended badly. She was a partner at the firm."

What were the battling emotions on Ruby's face? Surprise and . . . jealousy? I shouldn't have liked the concept of her being jealous, but the irritation ringing her eyes was hot.

This ridiculous partnership agreement was a means to an end. It bought us time to work toward forgiveness, and when Ruby eventually broke the policy about discussing love, because she'd be the one to do it, hopefully we'd both be ready for more.

"Did you leave her without saying goodbye, too?" Ruby asked casually.

I didn't rise to the bait. "No, but if it helps, she made it clear she didn't want to see me again."

Her eyebrow curved into an arch. "What did you do?"

I shifted in my seat. My dick was unable to downshift around Ruby, even when talking about Sharon. "She wanted more. I did not."

"Come on, there's a helluva lot more to your story."

"Yeah, but that's as far as I'm going to tell it." When she opened her mouth to object, I added, "We said we'd be honest, and I have been. I did not agree to full discovery."

She shrugged. "Guess you should have chosen the sex, then, counselor." Her expression was firm. "So, this woman was one of the three since me."

I knew exactly where her line of questioning was going to go, because if the roles were reversed, I would have done the same. "If that's a question, it feels rhetorical." I didn't have high hopes of being able to derail her. One of the many things I'd admired about Ruby was her tenacity. But I could try, or at least stall her. "And your number is? You never actually answered me."

Pink highlighted the apples of her cheeks. It was rare, but cute when I could make her blush. A filthy freak hid beneath her deceptive, good girl front. Shit, she was beautiful.

Ruby didn't answer, and my suspicion grew as she

rose to her feet, her determined gaze fixed on mine. My pulse kicked when she stood between my parted legs and bent over to set her palms on my knees.

"I know what you're doing," I said.

She folded one knee under herself, then the other, so she was kneeling before me. Her hands glided up over the suit pants covering my thighs. Her tone faked innocence. "What am I doing?"

Any chance of losing my erection died as her hands stroked me through the fabric. I didn't stop her as she inched her way toward my belt. Everything inside was humming with anticipation as she tugged the leather end free. I reached for her, tracing fingertips over her cheekbone, and curled my hand to cup her face. I swiped my thumb over her lips and pressed down softly, stilling the tremble there.

As my thumb brushed away, I demanded her answer with one word. "Ruby."

Her eyes were so big and clear as she sighed. "Three point five."

My mind was chaos. Which did I focus on first? The fact that her number was similar to mine, or the bizarre point five? "What?"

She used the distraction to drop my zipper and tug open the fly of my pants. This time, my cock was only sheathed from her touch by my thin boxers, and the heat of her palm was searing. *Jesus, don't stop.*

I exhaled as she drew down the waistband of my boxers, so only the head of my dick was exposed. I stopped breathing as she leaned forward. Her soft tongue swiped over the sensitive underside, toying with the ridge at the tip, and I jerked in response. It felt so good, just her feather-light caress.

Yet my brain wouldn't be quiet and let me enjoy. "What constitutes as half of a fuck?"

Ruby sat back on her heels and took her mouth away from me. Why couldn't I keep mine shut? I didn't want her to stop. The memories of her lips wrapped around me were awesome, but I didn't want memories right now. I needed the real fucking thing.

Her hands were still on my thighs, but she turned her gaze away and stared blankly at the floor. "He had whiskey dick. Neither of us came, and it lasted all of thirty seconds."

Oh.

"I wouldn't even count that one, then." Without thought, my hand was in her hair, turning her gaze back to me. I didn't like it when she broke our connection. "Who was Whiskey Dick, besides being a fucking idiot?"

Because drinking too much and ruining her night was the dumbest thing I'd ever heard. But I wasn't sure why I'd asked. Did I really want to know? Did I want to think about her with other guys?

"I don't remember. I was pretty loaded, too." She made a face. "It was the first time after . . . I don't want to talk about it." She leaned forward, and her hot breath rolled over my exposed, damp skin. "I'd rather suck your cock."

She wanted to deflect, and my lips threatened a smile. "You'll get no objection from me."

The tip of her pink tongue traced patterns on the head of my dick, and with her hair pulled back, I could watch every sexy lick. The muscles in my thighs contracted against the waves of pleasure. I still had one hand resting on the back of her head, and balled my other into a fist to prevent myself from doing something foolish, because I was throbbing and hungry.

She worked the waistband lower, easing it over my hips until all of me was available to her. Just the brush of her fingers was enough sensation to feel goddamn amazing, and I clenched my jaw.

It was impossible to hold back. "Fuck, get that hot mouth on me."

She lifted her head—and then she fucking *grinned*. Was she aware she was the sexiest thing ever? I was about to tell her, but her lips descended on me and sucked my words away.

Motherfucking shit, it felt so good. Hot silk poured over my flesh, and tightened until it was snug. Ruby's fingers dug gently into the meaty parts of my thighs, stabilizing herself as she began to move. Was my cock sinking deeper into her mouth with every pass? Because it sure the hell seemed like it.

"Mmmm," she moaned as she retracted my dick from her mouth and wrapped her fingers around the base, gripping me tightly. "I've missed this—"

She jolted and froze, panic etching her face. It made something foreign inside me hurt. I hated that she felt like she'd revealed too much. And, hell. She'd said my same thought out loud, so my voice was heavy with sincerity. "God, Ruby. Me, too."

We were already skirting on dangerous ground. How long would it be before she crossed the line and voided the agreement? I'd just gotten her to sign, and I wasn't ready for it to be over. So I wrapped my fist around the knot of her hair and guided her to take me back inside.

The sexy noises she made were insane. Soft, throaty moans, where I could feel every vibration rattling up my spine. It was as if she genuinely enjoyed pleasuring me. I loved how she made it seem like it was a treat for her versus a chore.

"You're so goddamn good at that." I groaned and pushed down a little, testing her response. Did she like when I controlled? Or would she merely tolerate it?

The fingers ringing my cock squeezed tighter, and she went with it. Unbelievable. I exhaled loudly. Her tongue swirled, showering me with sparks of pleasure, and a heavy moan rumbled from my chest.

"Yeah," I whispered on a struggling breath. "Just like that."

Watching my dick slide in and out of her rose colored lips was erotic. Her eyes fluttered closed as if savoring me, and she hollowed out her cheeks, sucking hard. It focused all the sensation, and I pulsed in the heated bliss of her mouth. I wasn't going to last long. Her relaxed tempo gave me time to enjoy each stroke and every pass of her wicked tongue.

The head of my cock touched the back of her throat. Ruby couldn't get all of me in her mouth, but her fist pumped on the base, working me in time with her lips. I slumped in the chair, gripped the armrests for leverage, and thrust upward, pushing deeper.

There was a soft pop as she released me from her mouth, smiling as she pressed the tip against her lips and stroked her hand along my full length. Jesus, this woman. My fingers clenched the chair so hard, I was sure the wood was going to splinter in my hands.

"Dinner," I barked. "Tonight."

She continued to pump, sliding her palm over my damp skin, but her expression was skeptical. "Like, a date?"

It was absolutely a date, but she didn't need to know that. "No. We have business to discuss."

Her skepticism shifted into a dubious look. "What business?"

"Our willing lists."

Her tempo slowed, just for a moment, and she tried to play it off like she wasn't excited, but I caught it. Ruby had enough emotion for both of us, too much to contain, and it made her an easy read.

"I have plans," she said.

My voice was dark and commanding. "Break them."

Were my words so powerful, she felt she couldn't refuse? Her grip tightened as her eyebrows tugged together. She nodded slightly, as if confused by her own approval. Her submission was an injection of fresh lust, and she delivered sweet relief when her lips parted, enveloping me again.

I lost all sense of time as she brought me close to the edge of coming, and then backed off.

"Fucking tease," I said in a low, playful voice.

"Who's the fucking tease?" Her smile was evil. "You did it first."

Then she got serious. My hips bucked upward, encouraging her to go faster, and everything grew intense. My mind narrowed in on the singular goal of coming. Need was hot as fire, burning me up from the inside, begging for release.

"Oh, shit. Oh, *fuck,* I'm coming," I said in a rush.

It poured from me in spurts, every wave a blast of acute pleasure. She slowed her movement so she wouldn't overwhelm me. The tingling explosion rolled down my legs and up my back, a sensation that cut off my breath and fucked with my heartbeat.

When she came to a stop, the muscles of her throat constricted as she swallowed, and I jerked with an aftershock. My ears were ringing, and as I struggled to recover, I locked my gaze on her.

"You're so fucking sexy," I whispered.

There was a shy smile from her.

Ruby drew away and wiped her lips with a single finger, and I chewed back another groan. I had to be careful and not say anything else. I could inadvertently prompt her too far, or accidentally break the policy myself.

And I was determined not to fuck things up with her a second time.

It wasn't awkward between us afterward, unlike New Year's Eve. I stayed silent, watching her as she stood, retrieved her underwear from the floor, and stepped into it. My gaze was glued to her legs as the fabric rose and disappeared beneath her skirt. Once it was done, I lifted my focus to her flushed face. Was she . . . glowing?

Okay, get dressed as quick as possible and get a fucking hold of yourself.

I did up my pants and came to my feet, feeling marginally in control. Pulling out my phone helped as well. I punched in her name as a new contact. "I was thinking dinner at seven thirty. What's your number?"

The glow I thought I saw disappeared. "It's the same one I've always had."

Well, shit. The awkwardness hit us like a surprise subpoena.

She snatched the phone from my hand and thumbed out the numbers, then passed it back with a plain look. "Okay, there you go, partner."

"Thanks." I pocketed it, and then my hands moved of their own volition. Inaction wasn't going to be a problem today. I slipped an arm around her, pulling her against me, and kissed her. It allowed me to feel the jolt of surprise that ran through her, but she softened in my embrace, molding her body to mine.

I'd just had satisfaction, and yet I couldn't wait until there were no clothes between us, and a bed was beneath our bodies. Couldn't get enough of her.

Pace yourself. I pulled back, enjoying the affected look in her dazed eyes. "Let me get you your copy of the agreement."

I left her standing there and went behind my desk, pulled out the staple from the pages, and shoved them in the top tray of my all-in-one printer.

Ruby shifted her weight from one foot to the other, and didn't seem to know what to do with her hands. Visibly anxious. The scanner warmed up and pages rolled through the machine with a mechanical whine.

"Why have you only slept with three women since me?" she said.

I drew in a breath, grabbed the warm copies, and held the pages out to her. "Why have you only slept with three guys since me?"

She took the papers. "I asked first."

"You did, but I'm not going to discuss it."

Her tone was innocuous, feigning confusion. "Hey, what is this, right here?" She pointed to the line I'd hand-written about honesty. "I can't seem to read it."

"I understand what you're saying, but I can't talk about it." I gave her a stern look before I went to the door and put my hand on the doorknob. Her clothes were back in place. The cute ball of hair at the crown of her head was undamaged, other than a few lose strands that framed her face. Unless someone had heard, no one would know what we'd been up to in here.

"We had a deal—"

"We *have* a deal," I corrected. When I opened my door, it forced her to grab her briefcase and shove the agreement inside. "I'm sorry I can't answer your question."

"Why not?"

The muscle along my jaw flexed. "Because it's a violation of the final paragraph."

Her eyes went wide. "What?"

I ignored her shock and pressed on. "Thanks so much for *coming*, Ms. Carter." Did she enjoy the innuendo as much as I did? "I'm looking forward to our next meeting. Until then."

Chapter

EIGHTEEN

RUBY

I'd lied when I told Kyle I had plans tonight. Well, kind of. A new five-pound sack of almond flour was waiting for me on my doorstep, packaged in a box from Costco. I'd ordered it yesterday, sure I was going to need it after my mystery meeting with him. And then my sister had called and asked if I'd be willing to make her three batches for her coworkers.

I left the box unopened on my counter.

Holy shit. I'd signed the agreement with my ex for on-demand sex, but not love. I needed to shower and shave all the things, and while I dragged the razor over my legs, I tried to think about how stupid I was being, or how ridiculously fast I'd caved.

His text message came as I was flat-ironing my hair. He wanted to pick me up, but needed my address, and I used the opportunity to ask if the dress for our 'meeting' was business casual.

> Wear whatever you think is appropriate.

> And preferably easy for me to take off.

Did he have any qualms about sending the message? Probably not. I tried to draft a sassy response, but couldn't do it easily and didn't have time. I had to tackle the willing list, and there were several items on there that required Googling.

Later, I was down on my hands and knees, digging through my hall closet for my one missing ankle boot, when a knock came from my front door. It sent my stomach plummeting and soaring all at once.

It'd only been a few hours since I'd seen him, so it'd been forever and yet not enough time when I opened the door and gazed at him. He had on dark, inky jeans and an olive green sweater, covered with a tailored and expensive-looking leather jacket. My mouth wanted to water at the sight of my new partner.

His gaze drifted downward, noting my ivory oversized sweater with a cowl neckline that I wore over shiny black leggings. He seemed to approve of my outfit until he reached my feet, and saw how I was standing on an angle.

"Hi. You forgot something."

"I know." I motioned for him to come in and limped awkwardly back to my hall closet on one shoe, digging through the clutter. When I finally was victorious, I glanced up at him. "Are you staring at my ass?"

His tone was matter-of-fact. "Your ass is outstanding."

I laughed softly and pushed away the flutters his heated gaze gave me, while struggling to get the other boot on. When I took my *outstanding* ass away from his view, he moved on to look at the rest of the space. The kitchen was straight back, and to the right was the living room. My left wall was covered in a mishmash of colorful frames.

It was pictures of my family, my friends, my time at college and law school. It'd taken me over a week to arrange and hang all thirty of them, and I loved how it came out. Yet Kyle peered at it critically. His focus lingered on the picture of me with Grant at my graduation.

"Where are we going?" I asked, yanking my coat down from a hanger and slipping it on.

"The Bedford. Have you been?"

"No." I grabbed my purse. "But I'm ready when you are."

My apartment was on the third floor over a shoe store, and the street was always busy during the day with shoppers, and at night with bar-goers. I followed Kyle down the stairs in the narrow hallway and out the main door, where we were violated with frigid winter air and the hum of cars traveling the street.

"I had to park a few blocks down," he said, leading me along the sidewalk where our shoes crunched over rock salt. I banded my arms tight over my stomach as if I could hold the warmth inside my coat better, even though it was already buttoned up.

We crossed two intersections, and the headlights flicked on and off on the SUV parked at the curb. "This is me."

Of course it was. The beautiful black Range Rover looked practically new. Street lights gleamed off its pristine body, defying the salt covered asphalt around us. Like his luxury vehicle was too nice to get dirty, immune to the snow plow sludge.

"What happened to the Acura?" We'd had some fun together in the back seat of his car during our year together.

"I sold it when I moved back." He opened the passenger door for me, but I didn't move to get in. "What's wrong?"

"No. No romance."

He glanced from me, to the open door, and back again, his expression broadcasting disbelief. But I held my ground, firm. This wasn't supposed to be a date.

"Why don't you get in and we can discuss where it's warmer than ten degrees."

He had a point. Why did he have to have so many perfect points? I got into the passenger seat and grumbled to myself as he shut the door and hurried around the front of the Rover. Dammit, his SUV was nice. All sexy leather and luxury, and probably a bigger back seat than his old Acura . . .

"Okay." He climbed into the driver's seat and started the engine, which purred instead of roared. "Explain why me being a gentleman has you upset."

"No dates, no flowers, no opening doors. This," I motioned between us, "is just sex." I needed to keep him firmly compartmentalized, or my feelings would stray into a muddy, gray area of emotion.

His expression was smug. "Please point out to me where in our agreement it says I can't do anything you label as romantic."

My face twisted as I tried to recall the exact wording he'd used in the text. Surely it was in the non-negotiable final paragraph.

But, was it?

Oh, shit. No. It wasn't.

His tone was evil, yet attractive. "If I want to open doors for you, Ruby, I'm fucking going to."

And with that, we were off.

For the first few minutes, we were quiet. I stared out the window and settled into the seat. Should I have been surprised I felt comfortable? Like no time had passed between us? I frowned. So much had changed.

I studied him as the stop lights and glowing neon of

shop signs strobed colors over his face. One hand was perched at the top of the steering wheel and the other was on his thigh, fingers splayed out. He looked at ease, yet in command. His brown hair was perfectly styled, and when I drew in a deep breath, I caught a hint of his sexy cologne.

His head was fixed forward, but the corner of his mouth curled into a half smile.

"What?" I asked.

"You're looking at me."

"And?"

He braked slowly as we hit a yellow light, and his gaze turned my direction. His voice was smooth as velvet. "I like having your attention."

Uh oh. I turned away from him so fast I risked getting whiplash. I didn't want him to see the effect his words held. After what we'd done this afternoon in his office, anticipation was thick between us. It clung to my skin like a matte coating. It couldn't be seen, but it could certainly be felt.

"How is it," he asked, "over at Sterns and Clifford?"

"It's all right." My voice went quiet. "I thought I'd be out of the junior pool by now." He made a noise of agreement, and when he didn't say anything else, it prompted me to ask him, "What about you? How is it working for your parents?"

It was so subtle, the way his shoulders tensed and his grip increased on the steering wheel. "It's fine."

Yeah, that was convincing. I wasn't going to press him, though. Kyle had always been closed off, and perhaps it was good to keep distance. "Sounds like they keep you busy. Today was the only spot I could get. Your assistant said you were booked solid."

He grinned, and before he said anything, I knew.

"Shit," I groaned. "You set me up."

"I wasn't sure how much convincing you were going to take." He shot me a quick look and his eyes were full of mischief. "Or how loud you'd be while I was persuading you."

"Asshole." But was I mad about his manipulation? No, I wasn't. I liked to think I could dish it out as well as I could take it.

The turn signal on his car ticked as we waited to make a left. Traffic was cooperating for once, and I wasn't sure if that was a good thing or not. Being in this quiet, confined space with him was overpowering.

His voice dipped low. "Did you fill out your list?"

My heart beat faster. "Yes."

"Did you bring it with you?"

Of course I did. This was supposed to be a business meeting, and I wasn't going to show up for one unprepared. The fucking list was burning a hole in the purse sitting on my lap, and I'd swear I could feel the heat of it on my legs. Most definitely *between* them. It fried the ability to be anything but serious.

"Yes," I whispered.

"Keeping with our honesty policy, I can tell you, I'm very, very interested to see what you put down."

I raked a hand through my hair, forcing my voice to stay level. "It's the same for me."

"The stuff I checked . . . I just want to add, no judgement, okay?" He looked almost stricken for a moment. "Just because I'm interested in something doesn't mean I need to have it, or that I've done it before."

It was strange to see him unsure, and I couldn't stop grinning. "Whatever you put down, I'm sure I can handle it. There'll be no judgement from me."

"Good." He said it like he was only trying to be polite. "The same for me."

Did he think he was going to out-freak me? Unlikely. I squeezed the handle on my purse. What if none of our desires aligned? I shook my head in response to my internal question. The sex on New Year's Eve proved how compatible we were. We'd fuck each other out of our systems, and then move on.

We parked in the parking garage, rode down to the street level in the freezing elevator, which smelled like someone lived in it, and then strolled toward the restaurant.

Glowing candles flickered in the windowsill and gold lettering arched on the glass, announcing The Bedford. We were ushered into the main dining area, where the lighting was subdued. Flames lapped at wood in the two-sided fireplaces encased in glass, but the focal point of the room was at the back.

"It used to be a bank," Kyle said when we reached our table.

The room had once been the bank lobby, but now it was occupied with tables. Beyond the old teller windows near the back, an enormous vault was open, its round mouth wide and welcoming. There were couches in there, where people from the bar mingled, and the walls were lined with safety deposit boxes.

Who would have thought a bank would be sexy? Because that was exactly what this restaurant was.

I'd been too busy gaping to realize Kyle was helping me take off my coat.

"Stop that." I jerked away.

He seemed to enjoy my irritation. "I'm going to pull your chair out next, and you're going to deal with it, Ruby."

The waiter arrived and listened to us bickering with a puzzled expression. In the end, I submitted, just so we could get this show on the road. The sooner dinner was over, the sooner the weird sensation that this was a date would pass.

"Wine?" Kyle asked, staring at the menu. "You still into cabernet?"

Dammit. Would I get used to this? He hadn't been around the last five years, but he knew me better than any other man. Once I showed him my list, hell, it'd solidify that title.

"Sure," I choked out. "That's fine."

We made small talk until our order was placed and the waiter arrived with the bottle of wine. Kyle hadn't even hinted at the willing list. He must have sensed I was going to need some liquid courage before handing over my darkest fantasies in easy-to-read text.

"You can fill 'er up to the top," I said to the waiter who poured my wine. I wasn't even joking.

My breath became shallow when the man slinked away, leaving the two of us to get down to business. Kyle's fingers disappeared inside the leather jacket he'd hung on the back of his chair, and he produced a folded sheet of paper.

Oh my God, it was really happening. It was an asinine thought, as this was specifically why we'd come here. Hopefully he couldn't see how nervous I was as I dug my list out of my purse. I clutched the paper tightly. "I, uh, have a few things I wasn't sure about."

He blinked. "You're not sure if you want to do them?"

"No, like, there are things on here that I don't know what they mean."

"Oh." He looked somewhat relieved. "An example?"

I unfolded the paper, keeping it close, even though no one would be able to read the small print unless they were right beside me. "DVP?"

His face went totally blank, disguising the thoughts beneath. He kept his voice quiet. "That's . . . two P's in the V."

I didn't get it. My voice went so low he probably couldn't understand me, but I mouthed the words. "Two pussies in the . . .?"

He gave a weird, choked off laugh and matched my near silence. "Two penises in the vagina."

My mouth rounded into an *"Oh."* Christ. I stared down at the list.

"What else?" he asked.

"That's it," I lied, folding the paper slowly. Hopefully nothing he had checked was stuff I didn't understand. My belief was if I didn't know what it was, chances were I wasn't going to be interested.

"All right." Kyle set his paper down on the table, but his fingers lingered. "To reiterate, no judgement."

"You're making me a little nervous."

He pushed with his fingertips, gliding the folded paper along the tabletop. I passed mine to him, and my heart launched into my throat. Every unfold he made was like peeling back a layer of my clothes until I was fully exposed and naked in the room crowded with strangers.

My face burned as I unfolded his paper and looked at Kyle's desires, the ones he'd been so nervous to reveal and worried I'd judge him. I scanned the checkmarks beside the items and my mouth went dry.

Holy.

Fucking.

Shit.

I'd marked almost twice as many boxes as he had.

KYLE

It was a miracle my jaw didn't hit the table with an audible thump. I stared at the columns of text and her perfectly ticked checkmarks beside them, and my dick hardened at the speed of light.

"Jesus," I breathed.

I'd made a colossal mistake.

Her face turned bright red, and she folded my list back in two, setting it before her and ripped her gaze from mine. Embarrassed and ashamed, and I couldn't fucking stand it.

"Fuck, Ruby. Give that back to me, I need to add to it." I'd been so stupid. This had been my chance to communicate whatever I wanted, and I'd blown it.

"This was a mistake," she said, still refusing to meet my gaze.

"No, no, the only mistake was mine." I leaned across the table, grabbed the paper, and dug a pen out of my jacket as fast as humanly possible. "I thought I'd scare you away, and I played it safe. I'm sorry I underestimated you."

She sat completely still as I marked off all the boxes I really wanted to. Her posture was stiff. "You were supposed to be honest."

"You're right, and I'm sorry." I didn't want to start this thing off with a lie, but the idea of losing her before we even began had made me second-guess myself. At least my genuine apology seemed to soften her. "Look at me," I ordered when I'd finished. "You're fucking amazing, you know that?"

Her reluctant gaze trailed over the table, up my chest, and finally reached my eyes.

"I'd forgotten how perfect we are together. I won't forget again." It was skirting the line of our agreement, but fuck it. I thrust my willing list back toward her. "This time, it's one hundred percent."

She took it from me, looking reluctant.

I hadn't gotten a chance to examine her list before. I had opened it, saw the high number of answers, and my brain went haywire. This time, I savored each ticked box.

Everything I wanted to try was here, and to get a chance to do it with Ruby? "I feel like the luckiest fucking guy in the world."

She still hadn't looked at my revised answers, and I scrambled to salvage. My priority was her not walking away. If she did, I was certain we'd be done for, and I wasn't going to allow it. She was back in my life now; I wouldn't tolerate the alternative.

"Please," I said. "I'll give you whatever you want. Anything. I'm so excited about your answers, I'm harder than I've ever been in my goddamn life. Just look under the table."

Her lips twitched, threatening a smile, but it didn't break.

"Or look at my list," I added, "and see how much fun we're going to have together."

She latched a hand on the bell of her wine glass, brought it to her lips, and drained the entire glass. When it was done, she set it down, her fingertips pausing on the rim as if deciding our fate right then and there.

I exhaled as she unfolded my paper, and her blue eyes scanned downward. My expressive girl tried to maintain indifference, but she failed when she licked her lips, and her gaze focused with interest.

"Your list is impressive," I said, full of appreciation. The spankings weren't a surprise, and neither was the girl-on-girl action. But there were several items on there I wouldn't have guessed, and I was fucking thrilled. "Have you done much of the stuff—"

"No." Her eyes widened a degree. "Like, not any of it." She turned her empty wine glass on the table, as if needing something to occupy her hands. "But . . . I'm all for trying new things."

"Me, too."

How fast could I rush her through dinner and get her back to my place? Tomorrow I'd talk to Joseph and get his advice on how to proceed in the areas I didn't have experience. It'd be awkward for me, but I could deal. Joseph had admitted during his time running the club, he'd trained several men who wanted to become Doms.

Which was appealing. In court, I was used to persuading the jury, controlling the way they interpreted the facts. In my personal life, I controlled my emotions. So it wasn't a leap that I craved controlling pleasure, both hers and mine.

The waiter appeared tableside, his attention on Ruby. "Would you care for more wine, miss?"

"Yes," we answered at the same time.

She seemed to loosen up after her glass was refilled. She wasn't drunk by any means, but the wine took the edge off, and I hoped my enthusiasm played a role as well. When she seemed comfortable and confident again,

I made my move.

"You'll come home with me tonight."

Her movements slowed to a halt. "Oh, will I?"

Under the table, I ran my palm over my dick, smoothing out my discomfort. It had to be my place. From the limited amount of hers that I'd seen, it was too . . . *comfortable*. My apartment was an advantage.

And there was the fucking wall of photos at her place which had dug under my skin. Her whole life was up there, including a picture with some burly guy, who I'd never met, when she'd graduated from Randhurst law school. I hadn't made it on her wall, which of course I didn't deserve to, but he had. Was he one of the three since me?

Focus.

"You think I can wait after reading your list? I can't." My tone was rich and deep. "I'm going to be like a kid in a freaking candy store when I've got you in my bed. I don't even know where to start."

A blush crawled across her face in the firelit room, and the gleam in her eyes was unmistakable. She'd marked bondage. She'd marked edging. Fuck, she'd said she was interested in not only anal play, but anal sex. She wanted what I did, at least as badly.

Maybe even more.

Her expression turned playful. "What are you thinking for tonight?"

"Yeah, that's not how this is going to go." Unlike her, I didn't need any alcohol in my system to feel ballsy. "You like it when I'm in charge. I do, too. A whole, fucking, lot." She sucked in a sharp breath, but didn't deny my statement. "Will you do everything I tell you to, Ruby?" I leaned forward over the small table, which made the space between us feel secluded and intimate. "Starting right this very second?"

Her bottom lip was snagged between her teeth and, Jesus, she looked incredible. All turned on just at the idea of my control.

Her single word was breathy, but her eyes lidded heavy. "Perhaps."

This wasn't helping the dire situation in my pants, but I ignored it. "Are you wearing underwear?"

The large sweater she had on couldn't hide how her breathing picked up. Her tone was concerned. "Yes."

"I don't like that. Take them off."

Her gaze flitted around to the other tables. She whispered it with fear. "Right here?"

A smile warmed my lips. "I'm sure this place has a restroom."

It drove me insane how quickly she shot to her feet, as if eager to follow my command.

"Wait," I added. "Before you go, I'm going to need proof you've done as told."

Her gaze shift upward as she considered my statement. Something was decided, she grabbed her purse, and then her boots clomped away.

I used the alone time to get a grip. I had to come up with a game plan for this evening, but my mind was racing with different scenarios. I didn't want to do too much, too quickly. And I didn't have any of the heavier BDSM things at my place.

Julius would.

I shook my head, pushing the thought away. Giving Ruby the willing list was as close to the blindfold club as I wanted her to get. If things progressed between us as I hoped they would, I didn't want her to know my sister's secret. It wasn't mine to tell, and I didn't want it to color Ruby's perception of Payton if they ever met.

Time dragged while Ruby was gone and I only had her list to keep me company. Should I text Joseph? I could send him a picture of her answers, but even though he didn't know her, doing that felt like a violation of her trust, which was the whole point of this thing.

As if the universe knew I was thinking about using my phone, it vibrated with an incoming message.

Fuck me! It was the lower half of Ruby's body, her pants bunched around her knees, exposing her gorgeous-ly bare pussy at the delta of her thighs. Her plum colored panties dangled on her finger.

"The, uh, grilled Bavette steak?" A male voice interrupted.

I nearly dropped the phone as the waiter auctioned off my plate of food, his gaze flicking over my screen. I slammed my phone in my lap and glared up at him. "I had the steak."

He slid the plate before me and gave me smile that said, "You lucky fucker."

I shot him back one that said, "Your tip is in jeopardy."

He was gone by the time Ruby returned from the re-stroom. She dropped down into her chair, her expression pleased, as if thrilled she'd met my challenge.

"Looks good enough to eat," I said. Then I picked up my fork and knife and cut into my steak. Her gaze dropped down to her own food, and I left her to wonder which one I was talking about, her dinner or the image she'd sent of her amazing body.

Eating dinner with her tonight was a new kind of foreplay. The activities on the agenda for this evening hung overhead, pressing anticipation and desire down on us until it was all we could talk about. It was all I could *think* about.

But discussing it at the table was an exercise in frustration. It was hard to keep our excited voices low and the language from becoming too explicit. Occasionally, she would glance around to check if anyone was listening in. Did she want to be caught? Would that bring the same rush to her as it did to me? She'd been a bit of an exhibitionist in law school, so I assumed that interest had grown with her other tastes.

She practically vibrated on the drive back to my apartment, twisting in her seat to face me. "Were you into all this stuff back when we were together?"

I shook my head. "I mean, I was interested, but . . . I wasn't comfortable yet with being that guy."

Although my eyes were on the road, I pictured surprise on her gorgeous face. "You are now?"

"Yeah. At least, I think so." I put as much seduction into my tone as I could manage. "I guess we'll see, won't we?"

Out of my peripheral vision, I watched her body tighten, and I enjoyed her response. It all turned me on so much. How she matched me. The potential to become these new versions of ourselves and to go down that path together. Sharing our desires so candidly seemed to interrupt our issue of communication, and I hoped it wasn't temporary.

"And you?" I asked. "Were you into this at Randhurst?"

She pressed her lips together. "I was interested."

That's all she'd say about it, and we were quiet the rest of the short drive.

I eased my Range Rover into my parking spot. I hustled around the car, but of course she beat me on getting her own door open, and she smiled brilliantly. So pleased with her accomplishment.

"You should let me be a gentleman now." My tone verged on sinister. "Because I won't be when we get upstairs."

We strolled into the elevator, and when I slapped the button for my floor, she stared at the glowing circle intently. "Penthouse, huh?"

I rubbed a hand on the back of my neck. "Yeah."

It wasn't like my place was amazing, but it was pretty sweet. A one-bedroom, one-bath luxury apartment in the River North district. Nine hundred square feet which cost me over three grand a month in rent.

On top of Sharon's hush money, my father's firm had offered me an enticing salary, followed by a nice acceptance bonus when I'd taken their offer.

Coming back to Chicago wasn't supposed to happen. Every decision my parents made was driven by the almighty dollar, and I'd sworn for years I wouldn't become them. Yet, here I was, working for them, back under their thumb.

Ruby followed closely as I strode to the end of the hall, her boots thumping along swiftly on the hard floor. We moved with eager purpose. Her breathing was rushed as I slid my key into the deadbolt, turned the lock, and pushed the door open.

When she went to step inside, I threw my arm out and

grabbed the doorframe on the other side, blocking her entry. "Maybe I want to fuck you right here in the doorway so the neighbors can see."

A female voice rang out from inside my darkened apartment. "Guess I'll just be going, then."

What the fuck? I fumbled a hand over the light switch, clicking it on, and took in the situation as Ruby stifled a gasp. Was the cause my apartment, or the woman curled up on my couch?

"What are you doing here?" I demanded.

Payton blinked against the sudden light and looked sheepish as she threw the blanket off her lap. She stood, pressed a button on the remote, and an image froze on my flat screen. "Dominic's in Helsinki until Tuesday, and our internet went out as I was binging on *Stranger Things*. I didn't think you'd mind if I came over since you didn't answer any of my texts."

"What texts?" I dug out my phone. Shit, there they were. I must have missed them during dinner, too distracted by Ruby and our discussion. "Oh. It was loud at the restaurant."

The women eyed each other with interest as I led Ruby inside and the door shut behind us. Payton had a pleasant smile, trying to play it cool, but she seemed thrilled at my progress on the New Year's resolution. "Since my brother's not going to introduce me, I'm—"

"Payton," Ruby said. "It's nice to meet you. I'm Ruby."

Payton's gaze swung to me, curious. "You used to know a girl named Ruby."

"Yes," I said. "This is her."

My sister's curiosity was replaced with surprise. As we'd become closer over the last year, I'd mentioned my past relationship with Ruby, and Payton had seized on it. Although I didn't confess how exactly things ended, she knew it hadn't been good.

"It's nice to meet you, too." Payton's voice was even, but gone was her typical warmth. Which knocked me back a little. I'd never seen my sister protective of me. She moved toward us, then swung to her right, where my washer and dryer shared a little room with my coat closet. "I'll grab my coat and let you two get to the fucking."

"Oh, God," Ruby whispered so quietly, I barely heard it. Her face was pure mortification.

"She didn't say it to embarrass you, I promise. That's just how she is."

Payton reappeared, cinching the belt closed on her long coat. "Have fun." Her gaze locked onto mine. "Call me tomorrow? We can grab lunch."

It sounded far more like an order than a request, but I let it slide with a nod. She wanted details on what was happening between Ruby and me, and her sisterly concern was kind of nice. Her attention moved to Ruby, critical and evaluating, but Ruby was either unaware, or taking it in stride.

"Should I leave the door open?" my sister teased.

"You'll have to ask your brother," Ruby fired back. "It was his suggestion."

Something dangerously close to respect flashed in Payton's eyes. My sister could be an intimidating woman, but Ruby held her ground.

"Closed would be fine," I said. "Hope your internet's working when you get home."

She waved the comment off. "I'll swing by Evie and Logan's place and see what they're up to. Now that they have the baby, they never go anywhere."

She was avoiding going home to an empty apartment. "Aw, did the big bad TV show scare you?"

Her face said she'd been busted. "Watching it in the dark was a bad idea," she muttered. Then she nodded goodbye and left.

My sister's presence had completely derailed my plans and I struggled with how to get back on track. Ruby peered up at me, her expression echoing my thoughts. I helped her out of her coat, and went into the laundry room to hang both of ours up, leaving her to wander further into my place.

She stood in my living room, surveying the cobalt blue couch Payton had been occupying.

"It's a bit much, huh?" I asked. The room was whites, chrome, and grays, with the large couch a gigantic punch of color. It wasn't what I would have picked, but I could live with it. "The place came furnished."

"Oh." She surveyed the room.

The space was modern and clean, and had been renovated just prior to my move in date. I wasn't sure about the couch, but the rest of the apartment was cool and somewhat sexy. The view of the Chicago River snaking below wasn't bad either. Under the orange-yellow hue of city lights, one of the bridges was rising to allow a boat to pass beneath.

"Your sister's really pretty." Her voice was hushed. "I thought you weren't close with her."

"We weren't. When I moved back, I started hanging out with her and her husband."

"That's nice."

"Want something to drink?" I asked as I turned off the

television Payton had left on.

Ruby's gaze didn't leave the windows. "No, thank you."

Okay, now what? I went to a cabinet, pulled down a bottle of bourbon and a glass, got some ice, and poured myself two fingers' worth. Normally, I drank my bourbon neat, but tonight I wanted my drink cold to contrast the hot woman before me.

"This is awkward," she said, turning just enough to give me her profile. "Like, I know we're supposed to get naked, but I'm suddenly not sure how to do that."

As I sipped my whiskey, I gave a silent *thank you*. It was the 'in' I needed. My voice firmed up. "You let me worry about the how. Take off your boots."

My command was a match being dragged against the striker strip of a matchbox, igniting the desire in us. Her eyes heated. Lust flared wildly.

She leaned over, grabbed a heel in a hand, and tugged the black boot off, followed by the other. I stood there, sipping my bourbon, but drinking her in more. She padded on her sock-covered feet to the laundry room and set her shoes inside, then looked at me expectantly, awaiting further instructions. *Jesus.* How did something so simple have such an impact on me?

I cast one long finger down the hall toward my bedroom, keeping my expression authoritative, and I watched her throat as she swallowed hard. Her brown hair swayed gently down her back as she went.

My bedroom wasn't large, and the bed took up the majority of the space. I left the lights off, but the shades were open, so plenty of light from outside filtered in through the wall of windows to our right. It cast a large block of pale shadows over the wood floor and the thick white rug the bed was set on.

I'd thought this room was sexy before, but knowing what was going to happen here made it infinitely more so.

I rested my tumbler of bourbon on the dresser as Ruby turned in place to face me. When her lips parted to say something, I placed my finger over her mouth, stilling them. Her eyes were inquisitive and beautiful. I'd swear on a stack of Bibles she'd grown more stunning in the last five years.

I dragged my finger over her chin, drawing a slow line down her neck. She took in a deep breath, her gaze locked onto mine, and when I reached the neckline of her sweater, I splayed my fingers out, pressing my hand over the swell of her breasts.

Down my hand continued. It trailed painfully slow, inching toward her waist.

Her eyes flared with lust and she sighed when I slipped my fingertips beneath the hem of her top and skated them over her bare skin. Then I followed the path I'd drawn down her body, only this time in reverse, lifting her sweater as I went up.

Her arms rose without a command from me, and the bulky top was peeled away, revealing her plum colored bra. Her nipples strained against the lace, already begging for me to touch her. I cast her sweater aside, took in the sight of her in a bra and her skinny black pants for an appreciative moment, and then dipped my head down to bring our lips together. Her eyes fluttered shut for the impending kiss.

Oh, not yet, Ruby. I wanted to keep her guessing. Whatever we did tonight would set the tone for our partnership going forward.

I grasped her elbow abruptly and pulled her stumbling along, until we reached the window and I had her flattened to the glass with a loud bang. She gasped against it, and the sharp noise of surprise from her was a surge of adrenaline. I hooked my arm under her elbows, pulling her arms back and forcing her to arch into the glass. It left my other hand free to grab the back waistband of her pants and stretch them over her ass, yanking them down.

It took a second jerk until I was satisfied and the pants were left wadded at her knees, exposing her naked lower body. Excitement lit me up as I mentally prepared for what I was about to do.

I slapped my palm against her left cheek, and I didn't hold back either. There was a loud crack, and she jolted with a grunt. A sweet mixture of discomfort and satisfaction.

"This fucking ass," I said, striking her other cheek with the same intensity. "You want me to spank it raw?"

"Yes," she breathed.

I pulled her elbows together tighter, hard and high, which had to be uncomfortable, but she didn't ask me to stop. Her shallow, hurried breaths were wordless pleas to continue. I crushed my chest to her back, bringing my mouth beside her ear. "Yes, *what*?"

I traced the tip of my tongue over her neck and up, licking her all the way along the edge of her ear.

Did her whole body shudder? "Yes, *please*."

I rewarded her with another spanking, only this time I left my hand against her heated skin. I pushed down, sliding my fingers between her legs and finding her pussy wet and hot.

"Oh, God," she groaned. Her hips pushed back into my hand so she could grind on my fingers, but I wouldn't have it. Her pleasure was mine to control. Mine to give.

I released her with a shove toward the floor, and my tone was dark. "On your hands and knees."

She couldn't seem to get to the floor fast enough, encumbered by her half-down pants, but her knees thudded to the rug, and she launched forward onto her hands. I bent and gripped the ankles of her leggings and yanked them off, leaving her naked except her delicate bra. She was all smooth, pale skin, pink between her legs, and my gaze swept over the exaggerated curves of her hourglass figure.

"Goddamn, Ruby," I said when I leaned over and rubbed a circle on her damp clit.

She was so fucking wet, and it was like my touch was sending sparks along her body. She twitched and bowed. I half-expected her to purr with satisfaction. It was so hot, I began to sweat and reached for my drink.

The oaky bourbon slid down my throat, and I took a knee beside her hip. She was trembling, and worry stopped my heart. Oh, shit, had I been too harsh? Had I fucked this up? "You okay?"

Her head hung down until her chin was buried in her chest, and her long curtain of hair draped to the floor. "Yes. God, yes. I don't know why I'm shaking."

Relief poured through me, followed by a strange sensation. Not warmth, or strength, and it took a long moment to place. It was power.

And it felt really fucking good.

She was a vision like this. Sex on display. Waiting for me.

There was a flinch when I set my glass on the flat spot of her lower back, directly centered between her hips.

"Oh shit, that's cold!"

"Quiet. That bottle of bourbon was expensive," I said. "I'm trusting you to stay still as I do this, and not waste any of it."

She seemed to solidify, eager to meet my challenge.

I anchored myself by putting my left hand on her hip. "Are you ready?"

Of course I didn't leave Ruby any time to answer my question. I brought my hand crashing against her, and the slap of my palm against her skin was loud. The sound seemed to register to her before the sting, and the amber liquid sloshed inside the glass, sending the ice cubes rattling noisily.

The next spanking I approached from the side. I slapped so that I swatted across the cheek, and quickly swung back the direction I'd just come, gripping a handful of her pink skin to keep her hips from rocking away from the blow and tipping my drink. The sight of my fingers clenching the perfect, round globe of her ass was sexy.

"Fuck," she whispered. Her palms were flat against the ground, but her fingers were bent, as if trying to dig into the rug. She wasn't shaking anymore. She held perfectly still.

"Good girl," I said, picking up the drink and taking a sip. Condensation had begun to form on the sides, so it left a glistening water ring on her skin. I made sure to set my drink back in the same place. Breath left her in a quiet hiss at the cold.

I spanked her again. And again.

We made a song with our sounds. My hand would smack, the ice would clatter in the glass, and sighs of satisfaction came from her. I didn't let up until her skin was flushed red and moans fell from her mouth like a waterfall.

I'd stop occasionally to savor my bourbon along with

her reaction. I was in awe of how she enjoyed it. Thrilled at how much I liked giving her what she hadn't experience before. She'd been too afraid to ask for it, but always craved this. If she could trust me to take command of her desires, how long would it take for her to trust me with her heart?

The thought was so distracting, I brought my hand down on her too low, and my fingertips connected with her swollen clit. She yelped with surprise and jolted, making the glass tip forward onto its side. As it rolled off and dropped to the carpet with a thud, ice and the last sip of bourbon dribbled on her back. It snaked glistening lines over her curves and dripped off her sides.

"Fuck, that's cold!" She pushed back so she was sitting on her heels, sending the ice speeding down her back like a luge. The cubes bounced on the rug and skittered across the hardwood.

I put my hand between her shoulder blades and wiped downward, smearing away the wetness of my drink. She was silent as I collected the ice cubes in the glass, but her head turned to watch me. As I met her gaze, her head snapped forward, as if unsure she had permission to even look at me. Her hands rested on her thighs, and once again, she simply waited for my next directive.

Did she even know she'd assumed the perfect submissive pose?

"Stay exactly like that." It came out gruff, not because of her, but at my annoyance of having to leave her for a single second.

My feet pounded the floor into my kitchen, and I moved with precision. The glass was abandoned in the sink. New tumbler pulled down. More ice. Three fingers of bourbon this time.

I hadn't wanted to leave, but coming back to her waiting like this made it all worth it. Her tiny toes peeked out from beneath her pink stained bottom. The length of her spine called my gaze upward. I could easily undo the bra band and set her magnificent tits free, but I liked teasing both of us.

Ice tinkled in my glass, alerting her to my presence, and her posture straightened.

"You're going to play with yourself," I said, "while I watch and finish my drink."

Ruby put a hand on the floor and tried to stand, but I was ready to stop her with a firm grip on her shoulder. She peered up at me, stunned. "Here?" Her gaze flitted to the bed. "I thought—"

"No." My tone was strict. "You think you've earned the privilege of getting in my bed, after spilling my drink?"

Tonight was as much of a performance as closing arguments in a jury trial could be.

There was a battle going on in her head. The war between the lawyer who wanted to argue the spilled drink was not her fault but mine, and the submissive who wanted to be good and please. Her chest lifted as she sucked in a breath, and she slowly pressed her hand between her legs.

Fuck, yes.

"On your back," I ordered. "Your head toward me."

Even the way she moved was sexy. Her hands slipped under her hair and she spread it out like a puddle of silk around her. I stood with my feet parallel to her shoulders, peering down at her as she stared up at me. Her knees were up and together, her feet flat on the carpet.

I put my glass to my lips and drew the cold liquid

in, letting it linger on my taste buds before swallowing it down. Then I demanded it in a voice which only seemed to come out with her. Dark, and absolute. "Spread."

Her back bowed upward as she stepped her feet apart. My gaze didn't waver from hers, and although I couldn't see everything she was doing to herself, it didn't matter. Her expressive face gave it all away. Pleasure turned her eyes a darker shade of blue.

My command was to play with herself, but I didn't say where specifically, and it pleased me she understood the distinction. One of Ruby's hands slid down her stomach and between her legs, while the other rubbed over her lace-covered breasts. She teased and plucked at her nipples while the hand below her waist stirred, and I enjoyed from my high vantage point. How sharp the points of her nipples were, and how wet and ready her pussy was for me.

It was crazy how powerful I felt with her lying at my feet, writhing before me. How did I get this lucky?

The plan was to finish my drink, but when her fingers slipped inside her bra to grip her breast, I couldn't wait any longer. I set my glass down with a loud bang and reached out, offering to help her up. "Fuck, come here."

She grasped my arm and let me haul her to her feet, and I descended on her. I groped, dove my hands under her bra straps and tore them down over her shoulders as my mouth sealed over hers. Our tongues tangled with each other.

She was greedy for the kiss I'd denied her before, and I matched her urgency. Our lips moved together, fucking each other's mouth. Our kiss was hot, wet, and dirty. But I needed my mouth on her flesh that I'd kept hidden from myself.

I missed the taste of her skin.

She'd barely unhooked her bra before I hurled her onto the bed, receiving a sound from her like *"omphf."* She scrambled backward, making room for me to join her or climb on top of her naked body. Being fully clothed while she was completely bare was a way for her to see my domination. She was exposed and vulnerable, in theory. However, in actual practice, her gorgeous naked body made me weak.

My shoes came off in a hurry, thudding to the floor, followed immediately by my socks.

I placed one hand on the bed beside her, a knee between her parted legs, and leaned down so I could bury my face in her tits. So soft, warm, and delicious. She smelled like sugar and vanilla. I circled my tongue over her hard nipple then flicked it back and forth.

Soft cries echoed in my ears when I squeezed her breast with a firm hand, bit down, and drew away, pulling her nipple with my teeth. Ruby's fingers were in my hair, raking gently down my neck, tugging at my sweater.

"Kyle," she whined with so much need, it was like she was aching. Desperate for me.

I reached behind my back, grabbed a fistful of wool, and yanked both the sweater and undershirt off in one swift move, hurling them to the floor. Then I was right back on her, sucking, licking, and nibbling. I nipped a line from one breast to the other while she squirmed and tried to grind her lower body against my stomach, determined to get friction against her pussy.

Wedging my hand between our bodies, I moved my fingers down until I made contact with her clit. A bolt of lightning must have gone through her. She arched up violently, her head flung back, and she nearly knocked my teeth together.

"Oh!"

I grinned to myself and put the hard bud between two fingers. She was slick and trembling, and her moans swelled as I forked my fingers back and forth. Giving her *some* pleasure, but not *all* of it.

"I want your fingers inside me." It was so rushed, it was a blur of words.

"What?" I teased. This time I circled the pads of my fingertips, delivering maximum sensation and unleashing an enormous sigh from her. My tone was evil. "These fingers?"

"Yes," she hissed. Her nails clawed into my back.

As I speared my middle two deep inside her pussy, I clamped my lips tight around her nipple and sucked hard enough to hollow my cheeks.

"Fuck, *fuck!*" Her hands flew over her head and she gripped fistfuls of the comforter while her hips lifted off the bed. "Oh, God, yes."

It rang out like a sob of relief and shot straight to my dick. Lust for her clouded my thoughts, and pent-up tension tightened my muscles until they were cords pulled taut. I pumped once, then twice, curious how high up off the bed she'd go to try to keep my fingers inside her. Her face twisted like she was in agony, but it clearly wasn't.

I had no choice but to leave her dangling on the cusp of orgasm. I wasn't trying to be cruel, but I wanted us to find that moment of pleasure together. It was a partnership, after all. When I withdrew my fingers, she collapsed on the comforter and glared daggers at me.

The bed rocked gently as I backed off and put my

hands on my belt.

Ruby's anger shifted to delight as I unlatched the buckle, and her delight froze as I pulled the belt free from the loops with a sliding noise. In a heartbeat, she had her knees closed and was propped up on her elbows, anxiety painting her face.

I raised an eyebrow. "You marked this on your list."

She swallowed a breath and seemed to falter. "I did."

Her apprehension was obvious as I folded the belt in half, but I steeled my voice. "On your stomach."

Could she see in my eyes what I was trying to communicate? *Trust me, Ruby. I'm not going to hurt you.* She hesitated for a moment, then slowly rolled over. Her arms stretched out before her as she pressed her face against the comforter, bracing for a lashing.

I undid the button of my jeans, unzipped, and tugged everything down, stepping out of my pants while holding the belt. My dick bounced painfully free, so hard I didn't even want to stroke it. I stared at her lying across my bed, her body parallel to my headboard, and I let the end of the belt drop free from my grip.

My goal tonight wasn't to check this box off her list, but to keep her guessing. "Your ass is starting to lose the color I put on it. Can't have that."

She took in a shuddering breath, but didn't protest. Her willingness was crazy, and I was dizzy from the level of trust and power she handed to me. It almost made me break.

For the second time, I ordered myself to focus.

I slapped my hand on her ass, and even though this one was less intense than any of the others I'd given her, she jolted more than ever, expecting the bite of leather.

She pulled her elbows toward her shoulders and pushed up on her bent arms, turning over her shoulder to look at me with surprise.

I glided my palm down from where I'd spanked her, over her thigh, and cupped the back of her knee. Then I pushed up. She misunderstood, and tried to get up on all fours, but I spanked her again. She fell back down on her stomach as I forced her to bend her knee and separate her legs, all the way until her knee was by her elbow.

Now it was time for the belt.

I pushed the end under her bent knee and elbow, threaded it through the buckle, and pulled the loop closed, binding her leg to her arm with a jerk.

"Oh my God." She seemed to approve.

I rolled my fist on the belt, keeping it tight, and climbed onto the bed. As I straddled her straight leg, she excitedly gulped for air, and gazed at me with big eyes. I shifted on my knees, bringing the tip of my cock right against her slit, and I teased both of us with two long passes between her folds.

Jesus. Her soft skin on mine was heaven.

"Do you feel how wet I am?" she said. "Shit, Kyle. You turn me on so, fucking, *much.*"

And I was done for.

I thrust my hips forward, sliding straight and true until I was all the way inside her.

RUBY

Sweet relief took over as Kyle filled me. There was no way it had been just this afternoon when he'd had me coming all over his desk. It felt like I'd been waiting a lifetime for this moment.

Fuuuuuck.

His thick cock pressed in, and it pushed away my ability to think. I couldn't do anything but lie there, take it, and love every second. The skin on my ass seared like a hundred sunburns when his warm hips flattened against it, but I groaned in enjoyment.

His expression was raw, but his movements were deliberate. His pace crawled as he watched his dick's slippery slide in and out of me.

"Mmmm," I moaned. I had to breathe in and out through my clenched teeth. It felt so good—

No, don't come yet! It was way too soon.

He tugged on the belt in his hold, tightening the strap around my thigh and arm. "No coming yet."

Good lord, could he read my mind? I panted as he worked his thick cock deep inside me. No, I realized. He couldn't read my thoughts; he could read my signals. He knew exactly what I sounded like when I got close. We'd had so much practice together, but it hadn't been anything like tonight.

Those had been mock trials. Tonight was the real

fucking deal.

He exhaled loudly as he moved faster, and I curled my hands into fists. The bed beneath us didn't make a sound, but I made up for it. I cried out with bliss as he established the perfect tempo to undo me. I couldn't keep my shit together.

"Oh, yeah," I gasped. "Oh, fuck, I love your dick."

There was a deep chuckle from him, and his hand cracked against my ass as a reward. He didn't drop his rhythm, either. Just kept plowing into me.

"Yeah," I babbled. "Give it to me."

Before him, I'd been silent during sex. I'd let the naughty words run in my head, but never dared to speak them. The first night we'd been together, I had been shy, but Kyle had come into my bed like a freight train. Unstoppable, loud, and dirty.

I'd probably cringe if a transcriptionist read back to me all the things I said during sex with him. I was aware I sounded like a porn star, but it wasn't rehearsed. I meant whatever I said. And strangely, the dirty talk went mute *after* him, too. I didn't realize how much I'd missed it until it came roaring back on New Year's Eve.

Kyle's hand gripped the nape of my neck and eased me down so my cheekbone was flat against the bed. His dominance was . . . amazing. Spectacular. I'd always thought I'd be into it, but this was so beyond what I'd expected.

And it was only the first night.

What would he do to me with a week? A month? Even a year—

Don't get stupid, my heart warned. This would be over in a few sessions. I could avoid getting attached if we had a limited run, but long term would be impossible. He'd spelled it out in concise language how this wasn't a relationship, and he wasn't going to offer more. Goddamn him. I wasn't interested in that either, not until he took the option away from me.

His hand on the back of my neck drifted over my shoulder and along my arm that wasn't tethered under his belt. Soft skin, damp with sweat, pressed against my back as Kyle leaned over me. His fingers continued their path along my forearm and curled around my wrist.

Shackling me.

God, I loved it. The shift in position allowed him to put his lips to my ear and fill it with the sound of his rasping breath. The stubble of his short beard tickled across my sensitive skin.

I shivered.

Goosebumps rose on my legs, even though I was hot.

His thrusts weren't as quick now, but it allowed him to move much deeper. Heat spiraled up my legs and built like an inferno in my core. There was more contact, more pleasure. If I had use of either hand, I would have pushed one between the bed and my body, and touched myself until I came. I was so greedy for release.

"Yeah, you like that?" he said in a low voice, and I could feel his lips moving against the shell of my ear. "When my cock's so hard and deep inside you?"

"Yes," I sobbed, my eyes slamming shut.

"Me, too." He left a damp trail as he licked the side of my face, and then sucked on my neck. It focused my need into a sharp, white-hot point between my legs, right where he was pumping into me.

Time suspended.

His hand clasping my wrist began to move. It worked

upward and he laced his fingers through mine. Still holding me down, but more as a partnership. He couldn't get his hand back now unless I released him, too.

I turned my head into his kiss, and everything tilted on its side. Lust morphed into passion, so thick we were doomed. Even when I had to break the kiss to gasp for breath, he was there, dropping kisses on my cheeks or the corner of my mouth.

"God, Ruby," he whispered.

My body clenched and shuddered at the sound of my name in his sexy voice. It was hopeless, I couldn't hold off any longer. "Can I come?"

"Mm hmm," he mumbled, still kissing me.

My orgasms were like running down a steep hill. They started off slow, but as they picked up speed, control fell away and I had no choice but to surrender to what was happening. I was just along for the ride, a passenger in my own body, and it was exhilarating.

"Oh, God, oh, God, oh, God . . ."

Pleasure burst through me, making everything tingle like pins and needles, but in a good way. I convulsed, flinching and contracting with each powerful wave. The ecstasy wiped from the top of my head down to the tips of my toes at the speed of light, and then it lingered.

"Fuck, I can feel you coming." His voice was hurried and excited.

I let out an inaudible scream. He'd built the orgasm up in me so much, it went next-level. My legs were trembling. My lungs wouldn't work. I struggled against my bonds, one leather and one made of flesh, trying to find something to cling to. I squeezed our fingers together so tightly, it had to hurt.

Kyle's thrusts were erratic.

His chest, pressed to my back, hardened right along with his grip on my hand. Even the muscles in his forearm flexed and strained. My orgasm's hold began to release me right as he seemed to find his.

He let out a deep, loud groan. Then came the slew of swear words as he climaxed. Most of the time he chant-ed *fuck*, but tonight he added in a *Goddamnit*. His move-ments jerked to a stop, and he pulsed. Each throb inside me filled me with heat and a pleasurable sensation I want-ed to go on and on.

It didn't, though.

His eruption faded and, as he softened into me, his grip on the belt relaxed. He let me free there, but his hand remained clasping mine. I was still trapped under him, but nowhere was I more captive than I was by his mouth. His languid kiss was a prison I'd willingly stepped into and pulled the door closed behind me. I was eager to be his.

Just sexually, my mind pointed out. *You won't be his again.*

His persuasive mouth, not his crushing weight, got me to stay beneath him. Even though our lust had been sated, I wanted to keep kissing him. He showed no desire to leave me, either. His lips pressed against mine. Slow and gentle.

It sent my head spinning.

Remaining like this was dangerous. When the kiss ended, I squirmed, showing him I needed up. He slid out of me and rolled onto his side, taking his heat away, and instantly I regretted the decision. My dumb heart wanted him close.

Fuck, all the more reason to get out of his bed

and go home.

"Everything okay?" he whispered.

"Yeah." I freed myself completely from the belt, climbed off the bed, and shuffled through the dark doorway I assumed was the bathroom.

It was.

When I was done, I leaned against the doorframe and gazed at him. Kyle was sitting back against the headboard, the covers over his lap.

"Let's try this again. Everything okay?" His tone was light, but his eyes couldn't hide he was concerned. I'd been in the restroom a while, spending a little time examining the interesting marks he'd left on me, and a lot of time mentally preparing myself. I needed to put distance between us, like, yesterday.

"It's fine," I said.

He treated me to his blank expression, disguising the thoughts going on in his head. "Mind bringing me my drink when you come to bed?"

I crossed my arms under my breasts. "I don't think that's a good idea."

"And why's that?"

How could I tell him? He was the only man I'd ever loved. I couldn't have amazing sex and cuddle with him afterward, no matter how much I wanted to, and expect to stay immune.

I frowned. "It's just not, okay?"

He flung the covers off and was up out of the bed so fast, it was stunning. His palms were warm as he held my arms and pulled us chest to chest.

"Remind me," he demanded. "What was the line you made me add to our agreement?"

I sighed and stared up into his eyes. Why did he look worried? "Fine, you want honesty? Your agreement doesn't say shit about getting into bed with you after we've . . ." Did he understand what I was trying to say? "I can't shut off my emotions completely. You put in the final paragraph, so if you want this to work, I'm going to need distance after we're together."

He blinked slowly, and then had the fucking nerve to laugh. It was a warm, deep sound.

"What the hell is so funny?"

His palms coursed down my arms so he could pick them up and sling them over his shoulders, forcing me to hang them around his neck. His smile was brilliant.

"I thought you were pissed about what we did. What I did."

"What? No, I—" He distracted me by planting his lips on mine, and I turned to the side. He didn't seem to care. His mouth continued to find places to kiss me. My voice was hushed. "I liked it a lot."

His words dripped with seduction. With persuasion. To emphasize his request, his hands trapped my waist. "So, stay."

"I just told you, I can't." Yet I made no effort to escape from him.

His eyes gleamed with arrogance. "If you feel like you can't handle it, that's fine."

The asshole was challenging me on purpose, and his words made my face grow hot. I bit back my knee-jerk reaction, which would have been telling him I could handle anything he threw at me.

It was good I didn't say it. It would have been a lie.

I centered myself and plastered on a smile. "Okay,

thanks for understanding."

He so rarely gave himself away, it was a treat when his expression turned into a scowl. I hadn't given him the answer he expected. Would he try to talk his way into getting what he wanted?

I'd do everything to make that impossible. I moved quickly to my pants and retrieved them from the floor. "Thank you for dinner."

"Stop."

He used the same tone from before, the absolute one which made me want to do anything he said. Since my back was turned, he didn't see my eyes fall shut, but he had to have seen my shudder.

"You don't want to spend the night," he continued, "that's fine. But you'll have a conversation with me first. Don't just fuck me and leave."

Holy shit. My eyes went wide and I spun to face Kyle. He looked pissed at himself that he'd said it, because it revealed a lot. Did he still believe the lies I'd left on his voicemail, saying he was just a good fuck and he'd been nothing more to me?

"I wasn't—" I tried to defend myself, but his angry eyes accused.

Wait a minute. What was he playing at here? Why tell me we couldn't have a relationship and then demand I act like we were in one?

"You don't make any sense," I said, more to myself.

He stormed over, wrapped his arms around my waist once again, and lifted me. "That's your fault. You cause it."

Was he drunk? This was the most he'd ever let his guard down with me. And . . . oh my God. Was this because of the scene we'd just done? I'd given him my trust tonight. Was he attempting to do the same now?

I wrapped my legs around his hips and held on as he laid me down on the bed. If I was going to curl up beside him in his bed, he needed to concede something as well. At least it seemed like now was the perfect time to get what I wanted.

I waited until he had us positioned with our heads on the pillows, the sheets over us, and his arm around me like he used to do when we were together. "What happened in New York?"

His shoulders tensed.

"Hey," I said. "You wanted to have a conversation. Seems fair I get to pick the topic."

He was silent for ages. He didn't look at me, he just stared vacantly over my shoulder, as if he could wait me out.

"This conversation is fascinating, counselor," I said, "but I think I better get going."

He locked his arm tight, preventing me from leaving his side, and his focus came back to me. "Sharon wanted a ring."

"Ah," I said. "She gave you an ultimatum." Was this Sharon an idiot? Kyle wouldn't like that. And why would anyone want to force a proposal, anyway?

"I don't know how to talk about this with you," he said.

"Why?" I kept my tone light. "I thought we were partners."

He sat up, scooting back in the bed, so I rested my head on the comforter covering his thigh. His hand slipped into my hair. "She pretended she wanted me to spank her."

I hesitated. "Pretended?"

"It was a tactic. When she realized we weren't going to be more, she changed her story." His fingers toyed with my hair, absently combing through it, even as his tone changed to a frustrated one. "She used what I'd done against me, and took all my options away. That's why I came crawling back to Chicago."

Well. This explained his worried expression when I'd come out of the bathroom. He'd been concerned I was freaking out.

The rule was never to ask a question you didn't already know the answer to, but I did it anyway, my heart lodged in my throat. This wasn't violating our agreement, either. It only specified we couldn't talk about feelings for each other. "Did you love her?"

I shouldn't care if he had, but logic didn't work when it came to him.

His answer was immediate. "No."

Tightness eased in my chest. Damn, that had been one dangerous fucking question. We'd been together ten months, and not once had Kyle said, *"I love you."* I had convinced myself that was okay. Even though he didn't say it, he'd shown it to me in plenty of other ways. I'd repeated the mantra relentlessly to myself how actions spoke louder than words.

So, if he'd said yes, he'd fallen in love with this Sharon chick, I might have broken down in tears. Thank God.

Skip this line of questioning, Ruby. "Do you miss it? New York?"

"Not really. Big cities are a lot alike. It wasn't that different from Chicago." He looked relieved I wasn't going to press him further about Sharon. "It's crowded. Filled with rude people. Lonely."

His voice tightened on the last word. I pushed upright, bringing my eyes level with his. Once again, he seemed upset with what he'd revealed. Was this why he asked me to stay? Was Kyle lonely?

"You had plenty of friends at Randhurst. You didn't keep in touch with any of them? I think Clarissa and Justin live here in River North."

His expression said I was missing the obvious. The realization took shape. *Oh, no.*

"I got all of our friends in the divorce." It was meant to be a joke, but it fell flat.

"You did." He said it casually and free of blame, but wasn't it mine? When word got out to our circle of friends what had happened, they'd rallied behind me.

I felt like dirt. "I'm sorry."

"How are they?" he asked. "Did Greg ever grow a pair and break up with . . . what was her name?"

"Christina, and sort of. He got another girl pregnant."

"No shit, really?"

"Yeah. I don't know when he found time to cheat on Christina with how controlling she was. Not that I condone that sort of thing, but that girl was a fucking psycho."

Kyle chuckled. "Truth. And . . . what about Leslie?"

"Oh, she's a lesbian now."

His eyes went enormous. "Really?"

"No, not really." I laughed. "Actually, I have no idea what she's up to now. After that night, we didn't talk much, and I guess she wasn't doing well in school, because she didn't come back the following year."

"Oh." He gazed at me, and his eyes seemed to sharpen with curiosity. "We never talked about that night."

My tone was playful sarcasm. "But we're such great communicators."

"Any regrets?"

I swallowed a breath, and felt brave. "Just that she fell asleep on us before we got to the good part."

He grinned and shook his head with pleasant disbelief. "You're something else, you know that?" He skimmed his fingertips over my cheek, curled his hand in my hair, and dragged me into his lap. We were naked, only the covers on his lap between us, as his lips found mine.

His closed mouth pressed tight but he adjusted the angle, and the kiss began to gather steam. His lips parted. His sweet, soft tongue sought mine, encouraging me. I fell deeper into him. What had started out as a simple meeting of mouths escalated into something fiery and passionate.

Oh, holy motherfucking hell.

I clasped the sides of his face, swept up in our desire. His hands were all over me. They caressed down my back, banded around me, and pulled me tight to him. We were breathless from the heat generated between us.

Inside my head I was rejoicing, and screaming at myself. This kiss was a beautiful nightmare, because it felt like it was filled with love. Was what we were doing right now breaching our agreement?

He must have had a similar thought, because abruptly the kiss was over. Kyle turned his head and cast his gaze to the edge of the bed, his chest rising and falling with his hurried breaths. "Okay, time to go."

"Yup." I scrambled off him in total agreement. Every second I remained with him was more dangerous than the last.

It was twenty-five degrees outside, but my kitchen was sweltering. My oven had poor circulation, so to cook the macarons evenly, I had to prop the door open with a wooden spoon. It had driven Grant from the room, which was a help. He was a big guy and took up a lot of room in my tiny workspace.

"How is it now," I yelled around the corner to where he was sitting in my living room, "at work with Morgan?"

He paused whatever he was watching on my television. "She's kept it professional."

"What do you feel like ordering for dinner? Thai? Pizza?"

"Pizza, hey?"

I smiled knowingly. Grant would eat pizza for every meal if he could. The plan was to eat dinner while I baked, and then meet some of our friends for drinks. We were going to celebrate his re-release into the wild as a single male. As I was the only other single in our group, I joked I'd be his wingman and show him the ropes.

Only . . . I wasn't single now, was I?

I sifted the dry ingredients into the meringue and began to fold the batter. "Go ahead and order it. I'm going to be piping these in a few minutes, and then they need to rest."

I didn't allow myself to think about last night, because when I did, my thoughts skipped right over the scorching hot sex and straight to the conversation afterward. To the kiss which had sent us both into a panic.

He used to kiss me like that, and I'd used those kisses as proof he loved me when he didn't speak the words.

Last night Kyle had offered to drive me home, but he'd had two glasses of bourbon, so I took an Uber and collapsed into my bed feeling like a confused mess.

"Pizza's been ordered."

I lifted the rubber spatula and watched the tails slowly melt back into the batter, signaling I was done mixing. Another turn of my spatula could overdo it and ruin the cookie shells.

My phone chimed with a text message. I hadn't heard from him all day, but why would I? This was supposed to be about sex only. He wasn't going to ask me to a movie or fucking brunch.

> What are you up
> to right now?

> I'm making macarons.

> Those are cookies,
> right?

> Yes.

> I'm coming over.

My heartbeat picked up and my breath went shallow.

> You can't. I have plans.

> Baking cookies
> is not plans.

> I'm getting in my car.

"Who are you texting?" A curious voice floated from around the corner.

Shit. "Uh . . . McAsshole."

Heavy footsteps pounded closer until Grant came into view. "What the bloody hell? You gave him your number?"

"Yeah, like six years ago."

Concern etched my friend's face. "He's decided to use it now, yeah? What's that dickhead saying?"

"He wants to come over."

Poor Grant. He stared at me like I'd just confessed I was an alien. "What's this?"

I rolled down the sides of my piping bag and picked up the bowl, spooning the batter inside the bag, mostly so I didn't have to watch his face as I dropped the bombshell.

"I slept with him last night."

All I got from Grant was silence.

I twisted the bag closed, went to my baking trays already lined with the silicone template sheets, and began to pipe the circles.

"And also on New Year's Eve," I added. The quiet was unnerving. "It's just sex."

"Just sex." His tone was dubious.

"Yeah. We've come to a mutually beneficial arrangement."

Grant gave a humorless laugh. "Oh? What's that about?"

I squeezed the bag with too much force and the blob of batter overran the template. "Shit," I muttered. "We're, like, fuck buddies. Whenever one of us wants to bang, we bang."

I risked a glance at him. His expression was unease. "So, he wants to come over and *bang*."

"Yeah." I felt his judgement and frowned. "I'm a big girl."

"Hey, sure. I'm not telling you what to do, or how I think it's a bloody awful idea. It isn't my place, is it?"

I pressed my lips into a thin line. "Nope."

"Though I'm remembering what you were like when we met, Rube. Right after he'd left you." Grant was the only one who used the nickname, and I liked it, but his words now cut through all my bullshit.

He was right. I'd been a mess. It was a miracle I'd made it through my first semester my final year of law school, with all the drinking and stupid partying I'd done. Grant had even helped my sister scrape me off the bathroom floor the night I'd been with Whiskey Dick. The first guy I'd brought home, some random from the bars I was going to use, determined to fuck Kyle out of my thoughts.

It hadn't worked, but it did take me on the express elevator down to rock bottom, and from that moment on, things improved. I also went celibate for the next two years, choosing to focus on my career.

"Like I said," I aimed for a firm tone and failed, "it's just sex. I'm not going to get attached." I couldn't have sounded less convincing if I'd tried. One night with Kyle and I was already in serious trouble.

My phone chimed again.

I swallowed hard. What would happen when he got here and discovered I had company? Male company? I lied to myself that I was curious to see how Kyle would react, but deep down the truth was there. I was desperate to see him again.

KYLE

I knocked on Ruby's door, and as I waited for her to answer, I shifted the messenger bag on my shoulder. The door swung open, and the funny feeling in my chest was back as I set my gaze on her.

Her hair was pulled up into a high ponytail. She looked casual in jeans and a deep orange cable-knit sweater, and beautiful as hell. A slight smile bowed on her lips as she let me inside her apartment, where it was excessively warm.

"Hey," I said.

"Hi. What's with the bag?"

I unslung it from my shoulder and handed it to her to hold while I took off my coat. "Don't worry about it, it's for later."

Her eyes narrowed playfully like I was a shady character, but she didn't peek inside. Her gaze swept over my dark jeans and the oatmeal colored sweater I wore over a blue button-down, the shirttails hanging out beneath.

"I wasn't kidding when I said I had plans," she announced. I hung my coat in her closet and set the bag on the floor, propped up against the wall. "After I finished the macarons, I was supposed to go out for drinks with my friends."

"That *was* a real reason. You didn't have to blow them off for me." But inside, I was thrilled. Did she want to see me as badly as I wanted to see her?

Ruby snorted. "I didn't blow them off. When I told my friend you were coming over, he bailed."

I hesitated. "He?"

"Yes." Her expression was plain. "He."

A timer beeped in the kitchen and she pivoted on her heel, leaving me to follow. I ignored the wall of pictures to my left, not wanting to see all the people good enough to earn a place there, and the reminder I wasn't one of them.

This was no small cookie-making project.

Every available surface was occupied with something baking related. The eat-in kitchen table had two trays on it with yellow circles. There were bowls, a mixer, various other things I didn't know but assumed were tools, and sacks of flour and sugar.

She touched her finger to one of the yellow circles on the tray and seemed satisfied with the results. I watched her pick up the cookie sheet, march it over to the oven, and slide it inside. Only she wedged a wooden spoon in the door when she closed it.

"You know, the heat is supposed to stay in the oven."

"Oh my God, is *that* how it works?"

I ignored her attempt to play dumb. "Can I ask why you're making enough cookies to feed a small army?"

"My sister's a high school vice principal. Monday they have a teachers' in-service day, and she wanted to reward her staff."

"And she demanded you make her cookies?"

Ruby shrugged as she set the timer. "I like making macarons. It's kind of my thing."

It hadn't been *her thing* in law school; this was something she'd gotten into after. I disliked not being in the know about her new hobby. I stood in the center of the kitchen, in her way, as she unwrapped a stick of butter, dropped it into the bowl beneath the mixer, and set the machine running.

She washed bowls in the sink, paying no attention to me as I surveyed the room. Her fridge had two tickets stuck to it under a magnet, and I stepped closer to read the small print. Huh.

"I wouldn't have pegged you for an orchestra lover," I said loudly over the hum of the mixer and the running faucet.

"My friend Grant plays cello. It's their season finale." She shut off the water and stacked the bowl in the drying rack. "They're just a community orchestra, but they're good."

There was an abrupt knock on her front door, drawing both of our attention.

"Oh, crap, I forgot about that." She dug some cash out of her pocket and went to the door, revealing a scrawny guy holding a flat, white box.

"You ordered pizza?" I asked when she returned to the kitchen and set it on the table.

"Grant did, before you hijacked our plans."

I frowned. "I didn't know I was hijacking. You didn't tell me."

She waved my statement away and gave a smile. "I know, I'm just teasing. It's fine." She lifted the lid and the delicious scent slapped me in the face. "Are you hungry?"

I'd barely eaten today. I'd worked out way too long this morning in a desperate attempt not to call her. I'd skipped lunch to meet Joseph, scarfing down a protein bar on the drive out to the suburbs.

My scheme of showing up at her place, getting her to

the brink of orgasm, and then begging she let me take her out to dinner, fell by the wayside. She'd said no dates, but fuck that. Even if we didn't leave her apartment, I could still make it feel that way. I could be romantic, plus I had backup plans B and C in my bag.

"Yeah," I said, dropping my voice low at the same moment I moved in on her. "I'm *hungry*." I suppressed her quiet gasp with my kiss, and she melted beneath me.

I had to hold myself back. Our final kiss last night had unleashed so much longing, and I was determined not to let that happen again. The kiss had been a collision. My head had twisted, choked with thoughts and emotions I wasn't ready for. Maybe after a few more 'not dates' we would be.

"Okay." She eased me back, her expression dazed. "Plates are in the cabinet next to the fridge."

I sat at the table and ate while she continued to work on the frosting in the mixer, stopping every now and again to either check her recipe on her iPad, or take a bite of her pizza. We talked about different things. How long she'd lived in the apartment, her job, and how her wild, party animal sister had ended up a vice-principal. Then the conversation turned to my family.

I told her the version of how Dominic and Payton had met at a bar, the story I'd believed until the night my sister had called me from the Federal building. Ruby listened with interest as I explained how Payton had gone on a whim to Japan where Dominic worked, and wound up falling in love.

"Sounds like he's a nice guy," Ruby said.

"He is. He makes my sister very happy." I finished my piece of pizza and grabbed another. "It's worth mentioning I'm better looking than he is, in case he ever brings it up. We have a bet—"

Her stirring strokes slowed. "When would he bring it up? We're not dating."

Fuck. I couldn't believe I'd walked right into that. My *girlfriend* might meet family, but she wasn't that. She was my partner. "I meant, in case he decides to pop in on my place unannounced like Payton did. Let's just hope it's not when I'm fucking you against the window in my living room." I grinned. "Although you'd probably like that, wouldn't you?"

A half smile was her only answer as she resumed her stirring.

I'd made a huge misstep and was grateful I'd been able to correct it.

The conversation was easier after that. I listened as she explained what she was doing and the detailed process of making the macarons, and enjoyed watching her enthusiasm. I liked her pride when she sandwiched the lemon frosting between two yellow cookie shells and presented it to me.

"I get the first one?"

She nodded.

The macaron was more delicate than it looked. I took a bite, surprised at how soft and chewy it—*Oh my God.*

"Shit, that's good," I said, my mouth still half full. "This is really, really good."

She laughed. "Thanks. I'm glad you like it. Now is when I break the news to you I have one more batch to make."

Disappointment flashed through me, and was gone just as quickly. I could make that work. "All right. What can I do to help?"

Doing dishes wasn't the sexiest job ever, but she had

opened a bottle of cabernet, fed me pizza and two of her lemon macarons. If having clean bowls ready for her would speed the process along, I was all for it.

When the dishes were done, she was still whipping egg whites in her stand mixer and measuring out sugar on a scale. She didn't seem to notice when I slipped from the room and grabbed my bag. I went on a self-guided tour of her apartment and discovered the bathroom across the hall from her bedroom.

As I changed, I glanced around the small room. The clutter of makeup and hair products was contained neatly in a wire mesh basket. Otherwise, her bathroom was clean. What a change from her time at school. She'd been kind of sloppy then. She wasn't quite that girl anymore. Ruby seemed more pulled together these days. More focused, and with a harder edge.

Was it self-centered to wonder if I had anything to do with that?

I left my clothes folded on the side of her bathroom counter and returned to the kitchen, where she was sifting the flour into a bowl. She didn't seem to notice my reappearance until I set my bag on the chair. She glanced over her shoulder at me, and then did a double-take. Amusement froze on her face as she stopped what she was doing and gave me her full attention.

"What. Are. You. Wearing?"

"I thought I'd help with the baking."

Surely she'd never smiled so big in her life. "What happened to your clothes?"

"I didn't want to get anything on them."

"Isn't that what the apron's for? Oh my God, I'm dying. I can barely look at you." She giggled. "That's amazing."

I'd checked myself out in the mirror before leaving the bathroom, wearing the lobster apron and claw shaped oven mitts, and nothing else. It was funny to me, and her reaction was even better. And at least the kitchen was hot from the oven, so my bare ass wasn't cold.

"Where did you get that?"

"A white elephant game at my sister's Christmas party."

She bit her bottom lip as her gaze dipped down to where the apron stopped. It was just long enough to cover my junk. "You naked under there?"

"Why? You want to see my lobster roll?"

The noise from her was a half-laugh, half-snort. "I'm sorry, your *lobster roll*?"

I closed the distance between us and took her face between my two lobster claw mitts. "Not my best, I admit."

"No, it wasn't—"

I pressed my lips to hers. Soft and sweet at first, just our mouths meeting. But then I felt her warm hand on my ass.

Her forehead leaned against mine. "You *are* naked."

I went in for another kiss, this time more serious. I couldn't touch her with the mitts on, couldn't do shit. I flung one aggressively to the floor, followed by the other.

"Uh, oh," she whispered. "The gloves are coming off."

A devilish grin widened on my face. She had no idea.

I grasped Ruby's hips and dropped a final kiss on her mouth. "Turn around," I said, using the most seductive voice I had. "Finish what you were doing."

She rotated slowly in my hold until her back was to me. Then she picked up the sifter with one hand, and turned the crank on the side with her other. *Perfect.* I skated my fingers along the waistline of her jeans, moving steadily toward the front, putting my arms around her.

Her voice was all-knowing. "What are you doing?"

"Don't worry about it." I popped the button free at the top of her fly, and nuzzled my way into the crook of her neck. The loose hairs that had slipped out of her ponytail tickled my nose. She shivered when my mouth connected with her soft skin. Did she smell like vanilla because of her baking, or because she was just fucking delicious?

"Oh," she sighed, and the sifter slowed to a distracted crawl.

I nibbled the curve of her neck while inching down her zipper. My voice was sinful. "We haven't even gotten to the good part yet, and you're already losing focus."

The crank resumed its noisy turning, but she tilted her head to the side, granting me more access to feast on her neck. Every little shudder and sigh she gave was so fucking sexy. I wanted to devour her.

When her task appeared to be done, I slid my hand down the front of her undone jeans and eased my fingers inside her panties. Jesus, she was wet already, and my cock hardened. I pressed it against the flat of her ass, letting her feel what she did to me.

"Oh, God," she jerked when I twitched my fingers. The metal sifter clattered on the counter so she could brace herself with her hands. I sucked hard on her neck, not caring if I gave her a hickey like I was a goddamn teenage boy.

I wasn't above marking her as mine. That was what she'd be after tonight. I was already hooked on her, so it only seemed fair.

Her hands gripped the counter's edge so furiously, they went white as I traced my fingers over her damp clit. Her head tilted and lolled backward until it was heavy on my shoulder. Ruby's eyes were closed and her mouth open so she could suck in labored breaths.

"What's next?" I asked. "You need to add the flour to the eggs?"

She nodded, not even opening her eyes, although she made a face. Like my question was annoying and had disturbed her contentment.

"Then get to it." I withdrew my hand and gripped the sides of her jeans and panties. I jerked them down her long legs, revealing her beautiful, creamy skin.

We were right beside the mixer and it meant she didn't have to walk anywhere, which was good. Her jeans and underwear were wadded around her ankles. She looked amazing like this. The long sweater stopped just where her cheeks did, and it teased me with flashes of the bottom of her ass whenever she moved.

I grabbed the oven mitts I'd thrown off, put them on the floor behind her, and knelt on them, giving me a much better view of her perfect ass.

There was noise from the counter above. She'd pulled

a clean rubber spatula from the dish rack and, in her haste, she'd nearly dumped the whole thing over. I fanned my hands around the globes of her bottom and squeezed, causing her to jolt once again.

She was so cute. Flustered and sexy, but she was standing up straight. "Bend over a little. I need to see that pussy, sweetheart."

Whoa.

A rush of memories came flooding back. When we'd been together, I'd called her *sweetheart* occasionally. It slipped out now before I could stop it. A habit that wouldn't die, or something more? She followed my command, leaning over, and it caused the sweater to lift and expose more of her nakedness.

She was all pink, and lush, and mine.

"Oh, fuck." She gasped the words as I bent forward and buried my face in the seam of her legs. "Kyle. I can't do anything when you're doing that."

"You can, and you will. Finish," I gave her a playful bite on a cheek, "or you don't get to."

She groaned, both in satisfaction and frustration as I resumed teasing her with my tongue. She tasted so good. Sweet. Perfect. A taste I couldn't get enough of.

I lifted and separated her ass cheeks so I could get at her clit more, while listening to her soft cries of pleasure and sounds of her struggling to mix her batter.

She muttered it between big breaths. "I'm going to fuck this batch up."

"Why?"

"*Why?* Because I'm riding your face when I'm supposed to be counting strokes. It usually takes me thirty-five to get it just right."

"How many have you done so far?"

She turned her upper body halfway around so she could look down at me, and her expression was tortured. "I dunno, three?"

I shoved my tongue between her legs, swiping it over her clit, getting her to flinch with pleasure. I sat back on my heels and peered up at her. "Four."

The realization dawned on her. She swooped the spatula through the bowl, and looked at me. I grinned, and repeated the long lick, loving the way she felt on my tongue.

"Five," I said.

The spatula turned the sticky batter.

Ruby's legs were trembling when we made it to twenty-five, and I figured now was the time to take it to the next level. My tongue started at her clit, but wandered backward . . . all the way back, and up. She jolted and there was a loud bang as her hips crashed into the counter top.

"Twenty-six," I said. I didn't hesitate, I just repeated the same motion. "Twenty-seven."

"Christ," she moaned.

I'd never rimmed before, and after our discussion of our lists, I'd learned she had never received it, either. Her reaction seemed to be enjoyment, but . . . "Do you like it?"

"It feels so wrong," she whispered, "and so fucking good."

Lust bubbled through my veins. She moaned, loud and long, as I delivered another. "Twenty-eight."

By the time we made it to thirty-five, she could barely stand. She was hunched over the counter, one hand holding the lip of the bowl and the other the spatula. Her legs were quaking, and goosebumps dotted her thighs. I wanted a picture of this moment. Me sporting a huge erection under the ridiculous apron, my hands on her ass, holding her pinned to the counter while I licked her from front to back.

"Are you finished?"

Her voice was almost as shaky as her legs. "I have to put it, uh, in the bag and pipe them."

"Do it." I stood up, and since it was bare and calling to me, I slapped my palm against her ass. The skin gave a nice ripple, and she yelped with surprise.

She needed to walk, so I helped her step out of her pants and tossed them onto a chair in the living room. She hurried to do her final task, moving as if she was being timed. I undid the knot at the back of my apron, took it off, and dropped it to the floor.

Ruby was concentrating too much to notice me as she went on filling the sheets with perfect circles of batter. I watched as she did the last one, tossed the pastry bag into the sink, and picked up the cookie sheet. The final step, she'd told me earlier, was to tap the sheet and let out any air pockets. Then, the shells would need to rest for a while before going into the oven.

So when she banged the last sheet against the counter, I knew she was ready to surrender full command to me, eager to get the pleasure my tongue had promised with more than thirty licks.

Her gaze swept over my naked body, lingering on my dick that was so fucking hard for her. I took the trays from her and set them on the kitchen table, clearing space on the counter while she followed my command of "Get naked."

She stretched the sweater up over her head and flung it away. Her bra was a simple white one, more for her comfort than to impress me, but it didn't matter. She looked enticing in anything, and nothing at all. Her arms twisted behind her back, the bra was undone, and it fell to the laminate floor.

Her unblinking gaze was on me the whole time, silently commanding me to come and get her, and I was happy to oblige. I descended, once again pinning her hips roughly to the edge of the countertop. I fumbled my palms over her warm, full breasts, squeezing and pinching as she squirmed. Then I urged her to bend over, only this time there was plenty of room for her to rest on her elbows.

I traced my tongue down the length of her spine as I sank to my knees, and she shivered. Her back bowed toward me, so I set my palm in the center and shoved it back straight. Not that it mattered what her posture was, but one of the things Joseph had said during his crash-course this afternoon was to utilize constant correction.

Every adjustment I made to her body would keep her focused on what she was doing. *How* she was doing. The more we both concentrated on our goals, the deeper the level of bond we could form.

I was greedy. I wanted the deepest one possible.

She cried out as I pulled her cheeks apart and focused my mouth on the tight ring of muscles between them. I spun my tongue in a circle, teasing her, and the shakes were instantly back in her legs. As I paused for a moment, I watched them shimmer across her skin.

Having that kind of effect on her was intoxicating.

Her hand reached back and gripped my hair, tugging at me. I took her hand and placed it on her cheek, showing her how I wanted her to hold herself open to me. I needed my right hand free. One stroke of my palm down the side of her thigh pumped more lust into my system. Feeling her tremble was a new level of satisfaction. Of power.

From the back of her knee, I crept my hand upward,

sliding over her goosebumped skin. I sank my index finger deep inside her pussy, all the way until my knuckles were pressed firmly against her clit.

"Oh!" Her back rounded, her focus abandoned for pleasure.

I kept my finger still, buried inside where she was hot as fire. I cracked my other hand hard on her ass before reaching up to shove her back straight once more. The forearm she used to support herself squealed against the countertop.

"Pay attention to *me*, Ruby. Not just how you feel."

She exhaled loudly and made it somehow sound like a promise to do better. It was the sweetest music. Her pussy clenched on my finger, and I rewarded her, drawing it slowly out, only to plunge back in.

She whimpered with enjoyment, but held her position this time.

I returned to my task, lashing my tongue wildly against her asshole, and her fingers clenched hard on her own cheek, as if trying to pull it further open. Allowing me more room. Should I order her to put a knee up on the counter? No. She was shaking too much already. I didn't want her to lose her balance, especially with what I had planned.

Would she be able to maintain her posture with what I was about to do? My finger was drenched, her pussy soaking. I withdrew slowly, and made sure she was damp enough where my mouth was, preparing her for a new experience.

Her muscles tensed subtly. She seemed to figure out immediately what I intended when I replaced my tongue with the pad of my index finger. I swirled once, half expecting her to stop me. But she didn't. She sucked in a shuddering breath and stepped her feet wider apart. Inviting me to try.

I began to intrude, one deliberate centimeter at a time, watching for any signal she didn't want to continue.

"Oh…" Her tiny sigh sounded curious. Interested, even.

I pressed further, until the second knuckle was squeezed tight by her muscles. She mewled. It was a soft cry of pleasure, but she might as well have screamed it. Ruby seemed to enjoy the slow, gentle glide of my finger, and I eased it deeper with a rocking movement.

Until I was full-out fucking her with it. Her pants for breath were loud, and she collapsed forward, resting her upper body on the counter.

"I'm going to put my dick here," I said. "Not right now, but tonight. I'm going to slide it right inside this tight, little ass." I worked my finger faster, and her hips moved subtly in response, as if trying to find maximum pleasure. "Do you like my finger inside you?"

"Yes," she whispered.

"Do you want to come?"

It was a sob from her. "Yes."

I withdrew slowly and eased back from her, using the dark tone she brought out in me. "Then get on your knees."

RUBY

Need was humming through my body. It buzzed in every cell, clamoring for release. Whatever Kyle's plan was for me, I was on board. If he was going to ask me to put on the lobster apron and oven mitts while we fucked . . . of course. No problem.

As I lowered myself onto my knees, he stood. Was he wanting me to go down on him? I liked when he told me what to do, and he seemed to as well. So, I knelt on my kitchen floor and awaited further instructions. To say I was eager was a gross understatement.

He ran the faucet and scrubbed his hands clean quickly with dish soap, and shook the water off. He grabbed a paper towel and dried them, and . . . reached for my plastic bag of powdered sugar?

"What are you doing?"

He ignored my question, and instead scooped two heaping spoonfuls into the sifter. If that wasn't confusing enough, he just left it sitting on the counter, like it was forgotten, as he knelt on the floor in front of me.

Kyle's hands were cool and damp from where he'd washed them, but his mouth against my neck was hot. He pressed the length of his body against mine, and although it felt great, I wanted what was poking against my hip. Hard, and thick, and very ready for me.

How long would he draw this out? From the very

second I'd opened my apartment door to him this evening, I'd been in a heightened state of arousal. Maybe longer. Perhaps it had started when he'd presented me with the agreement, and never really gone away.

I gasped when he curled both hands under my ass and lifted me into his arms. My knees parted around his hips. Anticipatory fire swept through me. Just inches away from sliding down on his cock, any second now—

Nope. One of his hands moved up, holding tightly around my back to support me as he lowered me down. The flooring was icy cold against my back, and I held both my breath and my tongue. Need clawed at me, and if he wasn't careful, impatience was going to have me clawing at him.

He had me settled on my back, him over me like we were going to start fucking missionary style, but he rose onto his knees, peered down at me, and wiped a hand over his mouth. Like he was looking at a mouthwatering meal. Okay, I couldn't deny that was kind of hot. His expression was pure lust.

I reached for him. "I want you inside me."

He grasped both of my wrists in one firm hold. "This isn't about giving you what you want." He leaned over me, lifting my arms up. "It's about giving you what you *need*." He pressed my wrists over my head and pinned them to the floor. "These stay here."

I sighed in both frustration and excitement. "Okay, I *need* your cock inside me."

As his hand slid away from my wrists, I felt his hold whether it was physical or not. He smiled confidently. "Do as I tell you, and you'll get it."

His palms coursed down my extended arms and

brushed over my breasts. Then they were gone as he reached up onto the counter.

"Sorry about the mess," he said.

"The mess?"

The metal sifter was in his hand, and as he shook it gently, it sent clouds of powdered sugar raining down on me. Over my breasts, my stomach, and between my thighs. The swirling fog of sugar had barely settled when he set aside the sifter and admired his work.

God, I couldn't think over how hot he made me. Kyle slid his hands up the sides of my rib cage, his thumbs collecting powder as they brushed up over my breasts. I arched up into his touch, sending some of the excess powder to the floor.

My bottom lip quivered as he locked his thumbs and forefingers around each nipple and began to tug. The ache was sharp and wonderful. I wanted more. No, wait, I *needed* more. Before I could even ask, he knew. He pulled harder, and I drew in a deep breath through my nose. His pinch hurt, but in a good way.

And then he released me, causing a small puff of dust as the sugar was flung free of my skin. My hands itched to touch him. My arms ached to be around him. But I wasn't going to disobey his command. I was so fucking curious how much more he'd do, and a little bit in love with this new version of Kyle.

Well, not *in love*. That was totally the wrong phrase to use. I enjoyed this new version. That was all, I told myself.

He supported himself over me, his hands slippery with the powdered sugar, and lowered until his lips grazed over my hardened nipple. He'd told me I couldn't move my arms, but he hadn't said shit about my lower body. I hooked my leg around his and tried to bring us together, but he locked a hand on my hip and pressed me against the floor. His expression was stern and scolding.

I closed my eyes as he licked the sugar from my skin in unhurried, teasing strokes. He was torturing me, that had to be it. Was he trying to get me to break and move my arms? I was going to die of need here on this dusty, sugar-coated kitchen floor.

I swallowed hard as he moved lower. "You're going to go into sugar coma."

His voice rang out from between my legs. "Worth it."

"Then I'll take advantage of you. Ride you exactly how I want to."

He laughed like I was being ridiculous. "Please." His tongue swiped between my folds, sending heat blasting up my spine. "I already told you. Not what you want, but what you need." He licked me again. "And what you need is for me to make you come."

Oh, yes. He was right about that. "Okay, then, fucking do it already."

It was beyond difficult to stay still as he pleased me with his wicked tongue, especially when he made comments about how my sweet pussy tasted better the longer he went down on me. Fuck, his dirty mouth was incredible, both in what it said and how it teased me without words.

Desire spiraled up my legs as he sucked on my clit, pulling it into his mouth. His fingers were inside my pussy, fucking me deeply. I climbed the hill toward orgasm, beyond ready for it, when his fingers retreated and shifted down, between my cheeks.

"Oh, fuck yes," I moaned.

Kyle's fingers pressed in, and my body yielded

hesitantly to the intrusion. The stretch was uncomfortable and foreign, but strangely addicting. So dirty and wrong, and hotter than the surface of the sun.

His mouth was relentless. His tongue flicked and fluttered. If I'd had use of my hands, I'd have held his head at the perfect spot, but I couldn't. He kept moving, so I lifted my lower body, grinding against his lips. That, in combination with the dirty thrusts of his fingers, sent me sprinting wildly down into my orgasm. I fell out of control as ecstasy pulled me into oblivion like gravity.

"Oh, God, *oh, God*!" My cry as I came was so loud, it verged on a scream. He didn't let up, either. His tongue continued to move, wringing more pleasure from my body. Sparks shot through me, followed by aftershocks of bliss. I convulsed, everything shaking like a massive earthquake.

The orgasm wasn't as long as I was used to, but it was fucking intense. I collapsed on the floor, shaking in the aftermath, unable to catch my breath. Kyle dropped soft kisses on the spot where my leg met my body as he gently removed his fingers from me.

My ears were ringing, and blood pounded in my head. The orgasm had done a number and left me hazy. At one point, he put the sifter back up on the counter, stood, and went to the sink. Water ran from the faucet. He washed the powdered sugar from his hands and grabbed paper towels, wetting them.

"Mmmm," I moaned as he dragged the warm, damp towels over my skin, scrubbing it clean. "That feels nice." I smiled at him when he gave extra attention to my boobs. He'd been practically obsessed with them when we'd been together.

"Better?" There was a gleam in his eyes, telling me he

wasn't just asking about the powdered sugar.

"Yes, much." I sat up and continued to recover as he used the paper towels to mop up any of the remaining mess on the floor. "That orgasm was pretty spectacular."

He looked pleased with himself as he tossed the towels in the garbage. "Sounded like it."

When he'd risen to his feet, he held out his hand, offering to help me, but I pushed it away. I moved onto my knees and clenched a hand around his hard dick. He didn't fight me. He leaned back against the counter and gripped the edge with his hands, making his arms flex and show off his tone.

"You look really good," I blurted out as I pumped my fist on him. "I mean, you've always been hot, but . . . Damn, Kyle." My gaze drifted over his chest and down his trim torso, then up to meet his blue eyes.

He blinked with what seemed to be surprise. Which . . . come again? He oozed confidence. There was no way he didn't already know this, yet his voice was unsure. "Thanks."

I smiled more to myself than him, and leaned in, setting the tip of his cock against my lips. His head was tipped down and he stared at me intently as I opened my mouth and took him inside. Our gazes held each other's, and it was . . . *hot*. His eyes were full of longing, but his eyebrows pulled together and his hands seized my jaw.

His tone was light and soft. "And just what do you think you're doing?"

I said it with a mouth full of dick. "Returning the favor?" I backed off him. "Is this a problem?"

He chuckled. "No, just don't get carried away." He brushed the bangs out of my eyes so he could look at me better. "I believe I mentioned I have plans for you tonight.

Don't go ruining them."

His soft, unspoken threat made desire pool inside me. What would he do if I did? Would he spank me so hard the marks would stay on my body until tomorrow? The idea made me shudder with desire.

I wrapped my lips around the head of his cock and swirled my tongue over his velvet skin. I loved going down on him. All the noises he made. Feeling him twitch as I licked a long pass on the underside. Sometimes giving him pleasure was better than receiving it. And when our gazes were connected, like they were right now, and his eyes brimmed with want? That was when he looked the absolute best.

No other man compared to Kyle McCreary.

Shit. I was pissed the thought had snuck into my mind. This was about sex. *Sex, and not one goddamn thing else, Ruby!*

I swallowed him up in my mouth as best I could, and my tongue cartwheeled over him, eliciting a sigh from above. It was somewhat awkward kneeling on the hard floor, but it was worth it when his breath hitched. I liked the sensation when his fist curled around my ponytail and guided me along.

It didn't make sense how I trusted him so completely in the bedroom, but not outside of it. Every night since learning the truth, I'd wondered what would have happened if I hadn't made the wrong assumption, left him the angry voicemail, or lied about the night he'd left.

Would we have still ended up here, me happily sucking his cock after he'd given me a mind-blowing orgasm on the kitchen floor?

More thoughts I shouldn't be having. I poured my

frustration into my task, letting my annoyance with myself fuel my desire. I bobbed faster on him, sliding my fist along until it was wet with my saliva, and Kyle was panting.

"Okay, enough," he said.

Only I didn't stop. Maybe it was a last-ditch effort to curb my feelings for him. If I disobeyed, it stood to reason he'd punish me. Would he go deep into my willing list and try one of the darker things there?

Of course, I wasn't supposed to enjoy punishment, but I worried I would.

What if it was already too late for me? Goddamn him for telling me we couldn't have anything more. I fucked him with my mouth, ignoring his second command to stop. He was close. So close.

He jerked me back off him using my ponytail, and although it didn't hurt, the action got my attention. Kyle leaned over, gripped my face in his hand, and squeezed my cheeks as he lifted, using both that and the hold on my ponytail to pull me to my feet.

He stared down at me, his eyes flaring with irritation, and something . . . intriguing. Perhaps he was a little excited I'd pushed. Did he like my willful disobedience? His expression said I was about to find out.

"When you're begging later," his voice was steady but low, "I want you to remember this moment." He released me, only to bring his mouth crashing against mine. His kiss branded across my lips, all urgent and furious, and I submitted to it. Surrendered.

His kiss, his *fucking* kiss. It wasn't playing fair.

KYLE

I couldn't decide if I was pleased or not with what Ruby had tried to do. On one hand, I was thrilled, as it played perfectly into my plans, but on the other, it meant going longer before sinking my dick inside her. Longer before we could try something neither one of us had done before.

When I finished kissing her, I turned to look at the cookie sheets on the table. "How much longer before they can go in the oven?"

She took a breath, went to the cookies, and tested them. Was she nervous about how I'd respond? Her tone was hushed, as if anxious. "They can go in now."

I made sure there was no emotion in my voice or on my face. "And they take how long to bake?"

"Fifteen minutes."

That would work. "Meet me in your bedroom in fifteen minutes, then."

I grabbed my bag off the chair and exited down the hall, turning left into her bedroom and flipped on the light.

I froze.

When I'd moved to New York, I hadn't taken my shitty college furniture with me, and I'd sold most of the stuff I'd bought while there so I didn't have to deal with the headache of moving it back home. Part of me wasn't sure how permanent my time in Chicago would be, which was why I rented my place furnished.

Ruby didn't have that issue. Some of the stuff was new, and the bedding was different, but the bones of her apartment during law school were still here, and it was like stepping back in time. I remembered the white dresser with chipped paint and glass knobs, because one time I'd fucked her up against it. The desk was the same, too, although now she was using it as intended instead of as a place to discard worn clothes.

Jesus, even the bed. Was this the same one we'd spent countless hours in together? Or had she only kept the headboard? It sent me reeling when it shouldn't have. What difference did it make if it was? I needed to focus on the future, not the past.

I frowned as I stared critically at it. My issue was with its placement. The bed was in the corner, making one side of it hard to get at. I dropped my bag onto the edge and dug around to find the four-piece restraint system I'd bought this afternoon.

"What the fuck are you doing in there?" she yelled from the kitchen, after I'd grabbed the foot and dragged it squealing away from the corner.

"Mind your fucking business," I volleyed back.

Installing the four clip-in points wasn't difficult, and when it was done, I shoved the bed back into place and got to work on the rest.

I finished well before the timer in the kitchen buzzed and took a seat on the end of the mattress, waiting. There was the sound of the oven opening and closing, followed by pans being set down. Then, a light switch snapped off and footsteps, muffled by her hallway carpet, approached.

Ruby stepped into her bedroom and looked around, letting her eyes adjust to the low light, before locating me. She'd had a few candles in the room already, and I'd brought more with me, just in case. The candlelight flickered and cast warm, amber light up onto the walls.

Her expression soured, and she crossed her arms over her chest, which plumped up her tits. Her tone was patronizing. "Anal by candlelight?"

I gave her only half a smile. "We'll see. Lay down on your back in the center of the bed. Now."

Her breath caught and her arms unfolded. It was crazy how my dominating tone could change her attitude from snarky to submissive in a heartbeat. I stood as she sauntered to the bed, her head held high but her shoulders relaxed. There didn't seem to be a drop of apprehension in her. It was interesting how she grew more confident in direct proportion to my dominance.

She freed her hair of the ponytail as she crawled onto the bed and lay down, turning her gaze up to the ceiling and spreading her hair over the pillow like a splash of dark silk. Her nipples were already erect.

"Are you cold?" I asked.

"I'm okay."

"Good." I reached into my bag, pulled out the four black cuffs with Velcro straps and metal clasps, and studied her face as she examined them. I dropped three of the cuffs to the bed, and took one of her wrists in my hand. She said nothing as I wrapped it in nylon and Velcro. Ruby just watched me.

"Still okay?" I clipped the clasp around the ring that was secured to the bed frame.

She nodded, like I hadn't given her permission to communicate verbally.

I took my time, drawing it out as I took away her

freedom to move. When it was done, I gave each strap a tug, tightening to make sure she didn't have any slack. She was secured spread-eagle in the center of the bed. The only thing moving was her chest with her hurried, uneven breathing. Yet she was excited. It was written all over her expressive face.

"I like this." I stood at the side of the bed and ran a hand over her body. In its wake, goosebumps pebbled on her skin. "I can do anything I want to you."

It was true. Everything I'd marked on my willing list, she had, too. Having that freedom was a gift. Last night had shown us there wasn't likely to be regret or shame, and now I was eager to try more.

There was one other thing I wanted to limit tonight to give Ruby the full experience. I produced the black blindfold from my bag and crawled onto the bed. I straddled her belly, letting my semi-hard dick rest between her breasts. My erection had faded while I installed the bondage system, but the sight of a nude Ruby, tied down to the bed, had it perking up quick.

I dangled the blindfold on a finger in front of her face. "Yes?"

She smiled and nodded, and it was sexy. She lifted her head so I could slip the bands behind as I settled the fabric over her eyes. I checked to make sure it was positioned so she couldn't see, and then rose off of her.

Fuck me. I hadn't seen anything sexier or more inviting in my life. I studied the picture of her bound and blindfolded for a long moment, trying to commit it to memory, right along with the feeling of control flooding me. She was totally at my mercy.

Since she couldn't see, I emptied out the rest of my

bag and set the items on the nightstand so they'd be easily in reach when I was ready for them. The black, cordless vibrator was up first.

She flinched when I turned it on, the soft buzzing noise startling her. Her lips curled into a smile, asking when she already knew the answer. "What's that?"

It was a small wand massager, but it packed a powerful punch, according to Joseph. I set the speed on low, picked the first vibration pattern it had, and placed the head of the wand against her pussy.

"Oh," she said as she inhaled sharply.

The hum of the vibrator rang out. Short. Short. Short. Looooong.

Her hips squirmed and she moaned. I used my fingers to spread her open, and pressed the vibrator against her clit as the pattern continued.

"Oh!"

I didn't need to ask if she liked it. Her body was showing me exactly how much she did. The wand cycled through the pattern only a few times, and she was panting. If I kept it where I was, she'd come quickly, so I took it away.

She sighed. "Did you just have all this stuff at the ready?"

"No. I have a friend who . . ." I wasn't sure how much to tell her. "He's into the lifestyle. He's a Dominant. So we, uh, went shopping this afternoon."

Even with half her face hidden by the blindfold, I could see her wide grin and pictured her bright eyes. "Oh my God, really? Tell me everything."

Instead, I moved onto the bed. I used the vibrator on her, touching it against her beautifully pink pussy as I got comfortable, sitting between her open legs. She grew serious in one cycle of the pattern, and another moan slipped from her parted lips.

"Or just do that," she whispered.

I'd been sure my shopping excursion was going to be painfully awkward, but I'd been wrong. Joseph was professional and business-like about the matter, and had a few free hours to help. If anything, he'd seemed to enjoy it. Perhaps he missed his role at the club. He seemed eager to share his knowledge with me of being a Dom, and interested in training me as a side project.

The idea had appeal.

"My friend, he's a private man." Which was true. Although Joseph didn't have ties to the blindfold club anymore, he was not a fan of the spotlight. News had broken of his engagement soon after Payton's wedding, and the tabloids had seized on it. They'd tried to build up a scandal, since the daughter of the richest man in Chicago wanted to marry a man fifteen years her senior.

There was certainly scandal involving Joseph, but thankfully the real one hadn't come out.

Ruby's jaw clenched for a moment as she drew in a breath. The vibrator against her center made her voice tight with pleasure. "How'd you meet him?"

Not only was I hesitant to talk about Joseph, I wanted Ruby focused on what we were doing right now. I knew she wouldn't ask any further questions when I answered, "He was a client."

The vibrator continued to sing its song between her legs. Short, short, short, *long*.

"Mmm," she groaned. Her back arched up toward the ceiling and her hands balled into fists. I took the head of the vibrator away, and she slid back down to rest on the bed, exhaling loudly, loaded with frustration.

"We're going to work on our communication," I said. When she seemed to have cooled down enough, I returned the vibrator to its home, grinding it on her clit. She whimpered and shifted, and I grinned. "You're going to tell me how close you are."

It didn't take long. Two rounds and her chest was heaving. "I'm going to come."

"No, you're not." I shut the wand off and set it aside while I leaned forward, scooping my hands underneath her legs.

She jerked as my mouth made contact with her swollen clit. I licked up and down, side to side, tormenting her. I started slow, and built up until she gasped for air and her legs shook.

"Tell me," I ordered.

"I'm close." Her moan was half of a sob. "Kyle, I'm so close."

I didn't stop my tongue, but I slowed my movements. I worked it over her bundle of nerves in unhurried strokes, all while Ruby whined. The goal was to take her right to the edge then back her down from it, over and over again, until she was begging.

I dipped my tongue all the way inside and fucked her with it, before I licked upward and nuzzled.

"Fuck," she gasped. "I'm gonna come!"

"Don't you dare," I ordered, lifting my mouth away. I ran my hands sensually over her body, massaging and touching.

She shivered as she reluctantly stepped back from her orgasm. Her word was almost silent, a ghost. "Please."

"No." I turned the vibrator back on, set it between her breasts, and slowly traced it downward. She knew where it was going, but I wasn't in a rush to get there. I wanted every inch I got closer to fill her with more nervous anticipation. "Give me a safe word."

She swallowed a breath as the vibrator crossed over her belly button. "I need a safe word?"

"*No* might come out of you soon when you don't mean it. Humor me."

"I can't think." The vibrating head of the wand was only a few inches from its destination. It crept lower, lower still, until . . . "Oh, God. Michael Bublé."

The laugh halted in my lungs. "Michael Bublé," I repeated. "Where the hell did that come from?"

"New Year's Eve," she hissed, enduring the pleasure I was inflicting on her.

My free hand was resting on her knee, and it clenched instinctively. The slow dance and the kiss. This was a good sign.

"Okay." Hopefully she couldn't hear my excitement over the hum of the machine. "I'll stop if you say *stop*. Or Michael Bublé."

Her breathy word was sarcastic. "Great."

"Getting close again?" I changed the pattern to a steady pulse, and she groaned. "Tell me when you're about to come."

She said nothing, but her body betrayed her. The muscles low on her stomach flinched and quivered, so I spread her folds open with my fingers, exposing her clit, and tapped the vibrator against it.

Her frustrated whimpers got me hot. Even though her ankles were cuffed, she could still move her knees inward, and she tried to close herself off to me. I put a hand on the inside of her thigh and pushed it open, giving her correction.

"Shit," she blurted out. "Fuck, make me come."

"No, no, no, Ruby." I kept tapping at her, giving her a hit of pleasure and then pulling it away. "We're just getting started."

Was her expression horror?

For the next twenty minutes, I mixed it up. I used the vibrator, my tongue, and my hand, or any combination of the three, to edge her. She stopped communicating with words after the first ten, devolving into grunts and moans. Some were pleasure, but most were frustration.

It wasn't like I enjoyed watching her suffer, but I'd be

lying to myself if I said I didn't like the power trip. I had two fingers inside her pussy and the vibrator against her clit when I brought her dangerously close. I could feel her internal walls trying to milk my fingers for enough satisfaction to push her over, so I pulled out swiftly and shut off the vibrator, dropping it beside her hip.

"No!" she cried. I slapped those same damp fingers against her pussy, getting her to jerk against her restraints. Her voice was broken. "Fuck you."

I threw myself over her, attempted to kiss her, but she turned her head away, running from my lips as soon as she realized what I wanted to do. Her head swivel back and forth, jerking in a violent shake of her head. *No*, she said with every cell of her body.

Nerves turned into a stone in the pit of my stomach. Shit. I'd pushed her too far. Joseph had said to take her as far as I thought she could handle, and then add another five minutes to it. It was normal to underestimate. "Ruby—"

"Please. *Please*," she whined. "Please just let me come. Please, Kyle. I'll be good. So, so good."

Oh, sweet Jesus. If I'd been standing, her begging would have brought me to my knees. I swallowed hard and did my best to sound stern. "You're begging. Do you remember what I said?"

"Yes, fuck. I'll do whatever you say from now on, I promise. Just . . . *please*."

I closed my eyes. Her words were so powerful I had to hold still for a moment to endure them. Then I settled over her, slipped my hand between our bodies, and gripped my cock. "Yes," I said. "I'm about to fuck you so good, you'll get wet tomorrow just thinking about it."

Her sob was coated in relief, and as I pushed inside

her, it only got louder. The restraints protested as she tried to move her arms, maybe in an attempt to touch me. I sank deeper and deeper into her wetness, my mind blanking with pleasure.

"Can I come?" she gasped in my ear.

I drove into her, just one single thrust. "Yes."

Her body bucked upward with tremendous energy. Her mouth dropped wide open, but nothing came out. The explosion stored up inside her was so epic, she seemed to lose the ability to breathe.

"Tell me every time you're coming," I ordered, rising on my balled fists as I drove into her. The contractions of her pussy squeezed me, making my vision haze. *Don't come. It feels really good, but don't.*

"Fuck, *fuck!*" she screamed, finally finding air. "I'm . . ."

The orgasm went on and on. She was wild beneath me, thrashing against her bonds. I picked up the vibrator and switched it on as I wedged it between us. "Don't fucking stop coming."

I didn't really expect her to be able to, but holy shit, she obeyed. Her convulsions were accompanied by guttural moans. Her body jerked as I continued to pump into her. She couldn't touch me, couldn't move, and it all seemed to add to her orgasm.

It was uncomfortable with the vibrator digging into my stomach, and I focused on that rather than how good it felt. Because it felt way too fucking good. Her rasping, struggling breath seemed to slow as the pulsing inside her died down, and I lifted the vibrator away for a moment to give her a reprieve.

Ruby had been more of a one and done kind of girl when it came to sex, but I'd also never edged her or demanded more. Was it possible?

I forced the black wand between us again, the vibrations reverberating against me. "Come again, right now."

"Oh, God," she moaned, arching up and crying out. "Fuck, I'm coming."

Fucking hell! I stopped moving and rode out her orgasm, stunned and determined not to follow her into her release. Giving her orgasms back-to-back made me greedy. "Good girl," I moaned over her soft cries, encouraging her. "Again. You're going to give me one more."

"No," she whined. She tried to move away from the vibrator, but couldn't. "No, it's too much."

She'd said *no*, but not *stop*. She hadn't safed out. I fought against my programming to stop when I heard her *no*. I pressed the toy harder against her and pounded my cock deep, going as fast as I could in the less than ideal position. My voice was pure domination. "Yes, again. Do it now."

"No, no . . ." Only her words seemed mindless, as if talking to herself.

The shift happened faster than the snap of my fingers. She threw her head back and her body locked up, seized with euphoria. Her lips moved, mouthing out inaudible obscene words. The final orgasm seemed to detonate in her, leveling all in its path.

I shut off the vibrator and dropped it to the mattress, focusing only on her. I framed her face in my hands and kissed her gently, guiding her back to me after sending her so far down into pleasure, she seemed lost. Her body was quaking uncontrollably, so I smothered her with my warmth and put as much of my skin on her as possible. I wanted her to feel our connection and how I was right here with her.

Our mouths fit together so perfectly.

I gently pressed my tongue against the seam of her lips, asking for more, and she welcomed me inside, her tongue brushing against mine. Like last night, our kiss started innocently enough, and quickly flared out of control. Even though I was lodged deep inside her, it wasn't enough.

I wanted part of me buried inside her, and for it to stay forever.

Since I was on top, my arms wrapped so tight around her, I no longer knew if she was the one shaking, or if it was me. We remained, kissing passionately, as Ruby gradually returned to normal. With our chests pressed together, I could feel her heartrate calm and her ragged breath slow.

"You all right?" I set my lips against the side of her neck.

"Yeah. Yes. Holy shit." Her voice was hoarse. "I'm still shaking. God, that was insane."

I reached up and fumbled a hand over the clasp at her left wrist, freeing her. As soon as I moved to release her other wrist, her hand tangled in my hair and yanked me into her brutal kiss. She was a feral animal, pawing at me to come back as I undid her ankles.

Ruby didn't bother to remove her cuffs, and the clasps swung when she moved her arms to embrace me. The cold metal kissed my skin as she brought her knees up, her legs wrapping snug around my waist. It felt . . . right.

After giving her such an intense orgasm, I shut off my thoughts for a while. There was no need to think about what I wanted to do to her next. She was wild enough for the two of us, and I enjoyed giving Ruby her freedom back. She seemed to be making up for lost time.

"It feels so good," I mumbled with my face between her

tits, "fucking you."

She sighed and squeezed me tighter.

I fucked her until our bodies were sticky with sweat and I worried one of us would overheat if I didn't put space between us. She frowned, her face pouting and announcing she was disappointed I had pulled away, but when I sat up and cooled off, the craving for control returned.

"On your stomach," I said, my tone firm.

Gone was her pouting expression. I only got a flash of her excited look before she rolled over and arched up, presenting her flawless ass to me.

"Hands behind your back." My words were spoken softly, but carried weight. She complied, crossing her wrists in the small of her back. The black cuffs looked good against her pale skin. I grabbed one of the clasps and snapped it around the ring on the other, turning them into handcuffs. "Fuck, you look amazing."

I snatched up the bottle of lube I'd placed on the nightstand, along with the trainer plug Joseph had encouraged me to buy. When I'd mentioned how neither of us had tried anal before, he'd said the best chance for success was *"lots of prep, and lots of lube."*

The silky lube was thick and cold as I spread it over the toy. She had one side of her face flat against the mattress and watched me over her shoulder.

I laid my free hand on her ass. "Ready?"

She nodded.

There was a sharp intake of breath from her as I eased the plug inside. Once I had it all the way to the base, I squeezed her thigh. "Okay?"

"Yeah. It feels . . . weird."

I moved to kneel between her legs and guided her to

lift her hips. Since her arms were bound behind her back, she supported herself on her chest. I teased the tip of my cock against her entrance, and she wiggled, trying to line us up so I would slide inside.

"Fuck," we said at the same time. With the plug in her ass, her pussy was even tighter, and I groaned. One thrust. Another. Ruby moaned and pressed her face deeper into the bed.

"It feels good," she said.

I couldn't agree more. I was aching to drive harder and find my release. My cock had been uncomfortably hard most of the night, and was reaching the limit on not being a selfish prick. My body threatened mutiny. Every molecule in me craved to come.

She rocked her hips, pumping on me like she needed control. "I want it." She moved faster, beating against me. She amended and clarified. "I *need* it . . . in my ass. Please. Give it to me."

I exhaled like someone squeezed all the air from my lungs. She was so unbelievably hot. I slowed my tempo to a stop and pulled out of her. She seemed anxious, and the position she was in didn't look all that comfortable, so I leaned over the edge of the bed and grabbed two pillows. I wedged them beneath her hips and stomach, giving her more support.

The plug thumped to the floor after I slowly extracted it from her. More lube. First, I squeezed a good amount onto her, and then I smeared a handful over myself. The smooth, slick glide of my fingers over my dick felt good, but I had a dirtier desire.

No woman I'd ever been with had been up for anal, and maybe that was part of the appeal. It was forbidden, and like a stereotypical male, that made me curious and interested. This same reverse psychology was another reason I'd put the final paragraph into our partnership agreement. I was hopeful by taking a normal relationship off the table, it'd make Ruby hungry for it.

I peeled her backside apart and prodded, letting my dick slide around in the liquid. It wasn't sticky, but thick and slippery, and it felt almost luxurious.

Her breathing was short and rapid, her shoulders tense. I had to be feeling some of her same nerves, just the flip side. I didn't want to hurt her. If she didn't enjoy it, I wasn't going to either.

I clamped a hand around the base of my dick and found where I wanted to go, and slowly began to press at the tight spot. The lube made me slide the head inside, but her fingers reached out for me, touching my stomach and asking me to wait.

"Oh, fuck," she cried. "Go slow."

I moved at a snail's pace, focusing in on every stuttering breath she took and each tiny movement she made. Jesus Fucking Christ, her body gripped me like a tourniquet. It was so tight, I clenched my teeth together.

I barely moved as a bead of sweat rolled down my back. Her hands relaxed a little as I drew backward, and then eased forward. In. Out. A tiny bit more on each pass. Her eyes were closed, at least the one I could see, and her face was pure concentration. Perhaps I could distract her as she got used to the sensation.

"Where's my cock right now, Ruby?"

She shuddered around me, but it seemed to be a good one. "Oh my God."

"Tell me. Where is it?"

"It's in my ass, fucking me."

I throbbed and my balls tightened. *Not yet, just wait.* I gazed down and watched as my glistening cock disappeared inside her. So, very, hot. It was a tiny miracle I didn't come just at the sight of it.

I was almost all the way in, and it seemed that every gentle thrust I gave her loosened her up and allowed me to push further. "That's it," I whispered. "Take it deep."

She moaned softly, and it was my undoing. I needed to come, and I needed to do it now, but I wanted her with me. I scanned the bed until I found the vibrator, turned it on, and leaned over.

I shoved it between her and the pillows, positioning it so she could grind on the pulsating head while I fucked her from behind. As soon as the vibe made contact, she moaned again, only this time it wasn't quiet. It was loud, and long, and full of satisfaction.

My hands fell to her waist as I straightened and widened the stance of my knees so I was at the right angle. Ruby's moans picked up in frequency and intensity as my pace increased. My thoughts were a blur, overridden by sensation and the primal need that ripped through me.

Come. Come. Come.

My body chanted it and I had no idea if it was talking to me, her, or both of us. I wanted to hold out but I wasn't sure if I could, and if she even had anything left after the multiple orgasms I'd given her before. But as she moved on the vibrator and panted for air, I began to believe.

"I'm close," she gasped. "Can I come?"

I couldn't even form words, but grunted something I desperately want to sound like approval, because her question had pushed me past the point of no return. My chest tightened and I dug my fingers into her waist, holding on as the pleasure descended like an avalanche.

The ecstasy blasted out of my core, one hot torrent after another, all while Ruby began to come as well. Her body shook with tremors while she cried out, and her fingers clawed at my skin. The pulsating contractions from her prolonged the sensation, wringing extra pleasure from me until I felt like there was nothing left.

I didn't exist anymore; there was only her heat, and soft skin, and the intoxicating smell of vanilla.

Autopilot took over. I lay down beside her, unhooked her cuffs, and trailed my fingertips over her back, tracing the line of her spine. She remained still, allowing it, and although her eyes were closed, she looked peaceful. Maybe even happy.

"Going to sleep on me?" I whispered.

Her eyes popped open and her mouth curved into a lazy smile. "No. Just . . . trying to come back to Earth."

"So, it's safe to say you didn't hate it?"

She laughed softly. "Yes, I certainly didn't hate it."

There was a ripping sound as she pulled off the cuffs at her wrists, so I sat up and undid her ankles, then kept my gaze on her as she crawled off the bed and disappeared across the hall into the bathroom.

The vibrator was dumped to the floor, and as I straightened the pillows, I scrubbed a hand over my face, letting my palm bristle over my five o'clock shadow. Last night she'd tried to flee immediately after the sex. It was because her defenses were down. I was hopeful it was the same tonight, and I'd do everything I could to avoid her booting me out of her bed. I'd have to handle the next few minutes with her carefully.

I made it easy on her at first. When the door swung open and she came into the bedroom, I got off the bed and left her to lie down while I moved to clean up in the bathroom. When I returned, she seemed to still be naked, although I couldn't tell for sure. She was under the covers, lying in the center of the bed.

It made me smile. "You think if you take up enough of the bed, I won't join you?"

Her expression hardened. "We talked about this last night. I need distance after."

"Wrong, you *want* distance." I strode to the edge of the bed and peered down at her. "What did I tell you tonight was going to be about?"

She launched upright, the sheets shifting around her waist, exposing her magnificent breasts, and her face filled with fire. "I told you, if this is going to work—"

"I'm getting in that bed, sweetheart." My voice was final, but I attempted to soften it with a smile. "I'm not above tying you back down to do it, either."

Chapter
TWENTY-NINE

RUBY

Kyle McCreary slept in my bed three nights this week, that asshole.

And I loved it.

Well, I *begrudgingly* loved it. I told him I merely tolerated his presence, and he'd smiled like the Cheshire Cat. After all we'd done on Saturday night, I was a little relieved he'd fought to get into bed with me. I'd ordered him to stay on his side and said I'd kick his ass out if he started snoring, but I was glad when he peeled back the covers and climbed in.

We stayed up late, finishing the bottle of wine and talking. When we avoided our past, conversation was easy and, good God, it was like no time had passed at all. We still liked the same things, and still liked to argue about the things we didn't. We still . . . clicked.

It had been a long time since I'd slept beside Kyle, and a lump welled in my throat. Fuck, why did he have to make my feelings so complicated? My anger at him over the years had rolled into a big ball that time polished down, making it smaller and easier to ignore. It lingered, though, weighing me down.

And now, who was there to blame? We'd both made mistakes, which I believed we wanted to move past.

I climbed into my bed and curled up beside the man who I'd once loved with everything I had. Was I foolish to go to him? Probably. But I was impulsive and willing to risk it. How much of my heart was there left to break, anyway?

At the end of the week, I returned to the dry cleaner, who was a fucking miracle worker and saved Morgan's dress. I dropped it off at Grant's place, had a beer with him, and spilled my guts about the whole messed-up situation with Kyle, partnership agreement and all.

"Don't judge me," I said. "I know it's stupid. I'm stupid."

"Rube." Grant's expression was serious. "You're not stupid. You loved McAsshole."

"More than anything." The only upside to my terrible temper was that I loved just as fiercely.

His dark brown eyes were warm and unassuming. "Love like that is powerful."

Of course Grant understood. I stared at the bottle of beer in my hands. "Before that final day, the only reason we were breaking up was because Kyle was moving across the country." I took my last sip and set the beer on the table. "Now he's back, so the obstacle's gone, but . . . he says he doesn't want anything more. And I'm not sure if I do either."

Grant gave me a plain look. "You don't, hey? Need me to fill you in?"

"Fuck." I set my elbows on the table and my face in my hands. I had to stop kidding myself. I knew exactly what I wanted. I'd been in the partnership with Kyle for a week, but it'd taken me far less time to realize I was going to want more. "What do I do?"

"Talk to him?"

"I can't. It'll mess everything up."

He picked up my empty bottle and dropped both of ours into the recycling bin with a loud clack. "Just my opinion, yeah? Better to know now." Grant leaned back in his chair and crossed his thick arms over his chest. "If McAsshole's only in it to sleep with you, then don't waste any more time on him."

"And if he's not?"

"Then don't waste time pretending it's just sex."

I left Grant's apartment feeling anxious, and nerves itched under my skin. He was right. I wanted more from Kyle, but I was terrified to lose what we had. It felt like I'd just gotten him back.

On the walk to the El station, I pulled out my phone and texted him, my fingers numb in the cold.

> Do you have
> plans tonight?

> Yes, we're having dinner.

My walk slowed and my lips curled into a smile.

> Oh, are we?

> I'm picking you
> up at seven.

I climbed the metal grate steps up to the station and placed my pass on the turnstile, which was so loud I almost missed the next chime of a text message.

> It's not a date. We have
> business to discuss.

> But, you know. Wear
> something sexy.

The noise of the approaching train covered my laugh.

Kyle took me to *Celeste*, a three-floor restaurant in his neighborhood. The host escorted us up the stairs to the deco room with warm tones and buttery light, most likely from the gold coated ceiling. It was a narrow space, small tables on one side and the bar on the other. It was also crowded and loud, yet still felt intimate as we slipped into our seats at the small, round table.

"What are your motivations, counselor?" I ran the pad of my finger along the rim of my martini.

"My motivations?"

"You always hold your business meetings in romantic restaurants?"

"This place is romantic? I hadn't even thought about it."

So obviously a lie.

"Business," I reminded, my tone pointed. We'd had plenty of small talk on the drive over here, and I still didn't get what game he was playing. *If you want to date me, just fucking date me already.*

Kyle took a sip of his Old Fashioned, and leaned forward so he didn't have to speak too loudly over the din of the crowd. "The man I went shopping with last week, he's asked to meet you."

My finger stopped its path on the rim and my brain went haywire. The mystery Dominant wanted to meet me? For what? Before I could come up with anything, Kyle spoke again.

"Let me rephrase. He and his fiancée are interested in

getting to know us better. Maybe even . . . playing with us."

Holy hell.

Something like unexpected excitement fluttered through me. Not just the thought of another couple, but the way the word had rolled so casually out of Kyle's mouth. *Us.*

But I instantly had so many questions. "Meaning what, exactly?"

"That's up to you. If you're interested, we'd discuss our boundaries, and I'd take those back to him. He and I would go over what everyone's comfortable with."

My heartbeat picked up, galloping along almost as fast as my thoughts. The word *play* could encompass so much. What was I comfortable with? What about Kyle? "How do you feel about the idea?"

His smile was soft and seductive. "It has appeal." His blue eyes scanned my face. "And you?"

It was like negotiations, neither of us wanting to completely tip our hand. "Yes." My tone mocked his professional one. "I also find the idea appealing."

He leaned back in his seat, his hand wrapped around his drink, and his fingertips played with the condensation there. It was impossible not to think about the night he'd put his glass of bourbon on me, and I shuddered with flashback pleasure. Did he know what he was doing to me?

"Can I ask a shallow question?" I felt guilty, but I needed to know. "Have you met the fiancée? Are they attractive?"

"Yeah, I have, and it's not shallow of you to ask. He asked the same about you." Kyle's expression was serious. "Attraction is important."

Don't hold out on me, Kyle. "Okay, so . . .?"

"I think most women would say he's attractive, and

she's very pretty."

I didn't mean it to sound jealous or vain, it was more out of curiosity. "Is she better looking than me?"

"I don't think so. I've always preferred brunettes, and she's younger than us—" His hand darted into his sport coat and pulled out a folded sheet of paper, followed by a pen. "I'm getting ahead of myself."

"What's that?" My heart fell into my stomach. I didn't want another partnership agreement, and certainly not one that included strangers.

"I mentioned my friend likes his privacy." The paper was unfolded, set on the table, and slid toward me. "It's an NDA."

Relief washed calm through my system.

I reviewed the non-disclosure agreement quickly, seeing it was pretty standard, but who was this guy? Or how kinky did he anticipate it getting that he needed an NDA? I scribbled out my signature and the date, folded it up, and handed it over. I said it like a joke although it wasn't. "Is he famous?"

"No. Joseph is just a cautious businessman who likes to keep a low profile."

It made sense. If he was successful, his extra-curricular activities getting out could have a negative impact on potential clients.

"Well, now that that's out of the way, let's talk specifics." Kyle's expression flared with desire, silently challenging me to go first.

I glanced around. There were tables on both sides of us, and close, too. My voice was skeptical. "Here?"

"No one's paying attention to us."

I chuckled. "You're wrong. There's a woman at the

end of the bar who seems plenty interested in you." His head turned. "Shit, don't look at her!"

He ignored me. The woman was sitting with two girlfriends, laughing and appearing to have a good time, but every now and again her gaze would wander over our direction. More specifically, Kyle's.

Not that I could fault her; he looked gorgeous. He wore a navy blue sport coat over a simple white dress shirt, a few buttons undone, and blue jeans. His hair was parted on one side with just a hint of unruliness, and there was his delicious few-days-old beard.

When he caught her looking, the woman's head snapped forward and she stared at her drink like it was the most exciting thing she'd ever seen. We were too far away to see if she was blushing, but her posture suggested she was embarrassed.

"You should go get her number," I said. What the fuck was I doing? "She's cute."

Kyle's attention jerked back to me, his face blank. "I'll pass." What was he thinking about? "That wouldn't bother you?"

Yes, of course it would. I absolutely hated the idea, but I'd painted myself into a corner with my teasing and his dumb requirement of not talking about feelings. I shrugged. Was it still a lie when it was done with body language?

His expression didn't change at all. A lifetime passed.

"All right, then I guess I will." He turned in his seat to face her, preparing to stand.

What the fuck? Impulse took over when the woman's gaze connected with Kyle's.

No. He was mine.

I was dimly aware I was acting like a child, but couldn't stop myself. I launched over the table, grabbed the back of his head, and jerked him into my kiss.

It seared over my lips and I loved the familiar taste. Bourbon, and lust, and the flavor that was distinctly him. It was like he was ready for it. He'd called my bluff, and this kiss was his victory. *Oh, hell. Let's just make it a victory lap, then.* His hand pushed my hair out of its way and cupped my cheek, deepening the kiss until I was burning from the inside.

When we finally drew away from each other, I was short of breath and his mouth pulled into a dazzling smile.

"I lied," I choked out. "It'd bother me."

He looked pleased as he swiveled in his seat, returning his full attention to me. "Good. If the roles were reversed, I know it'd fucking bother me."

I settled back down into my own seat, adjusting the cloth napkin. "Then, full disclosure, I had a client hit on me today."

"Yeah?" Up went Kyle's shields, and his eyes shuttered. "How'd that go?"

"Since the guy's currently going through a divorce?" I grimaced. "Yeah, no thanks."

Naturally, I left out the part where the client was Tariq

Crawford.

The enormous football player had finished up his appointment with Henry at the same moment I was coming back from filling my bottle at the water cooler. He'd flashed a disarming smile and struck up a conversation. From his easy-going attitude, you never would have guessed he'd just come from a meeting regarding his divorce.

It all seemed pleasant and without purpose until he'd moved to stand a little too close. His voice had dropped low as he asked if he could have my number. You know, just in case he couldn't get in touch with Henry. I pasted on a smile, not wanting to make such a huge client feel uncomfortable, and politely reminded him I was no longer involved with his divorce.

"Is that your only reason for turning him down?" Kyle asked, pulling me from my memory. His face was emotionless, but he seemed stiff.

"No," I said. "I had other reasons."

Was it excitement he was trying to disguise? His voice was hurried. "Which are?"

"Unimportant." I took a sip of my martini and set it down, keeping my gaze locked on his. "I want to talk about Joseph. Was this your idea or his?"

For a moment, it seemed like Kyle wasn't going to let it go, but he appeared to relax. "It was his. He's offered to help me."

"With what?"

I'd swear the temperature in the room climbed a thousand degrees. He was so handsome in the golden light of the room. "He's offered to train me to become like him. A Dom."

"Holy shit." Beneath the table, I crossed my legs. It

wasn't that much of a stretch, was it? Kyle already took command in the bedroom, but from what I understood, there was more to it than just that.

"Is that what you want?" I asked. "Would you like being responsible for someone else?"

"The right person?" His voice was like gravel, and I felt it all the way down to my toes. "Yes."

I couldn't breathe. His gaze drilled into me and a noise sounded in my head. It could have been an airhorn celebrating, or the warning sound a submarine makes when it dives. Either worked. I felt elated and anxious at the same instance.

His expression was unreadable. "Does that scare you?"

"No, I . . ." I wasn't sure how to feel about it. If I was honest with myself, I liked when he told me what to do. He'd always had a dominant personality, starting years ago with him demanding my phone number at the university bookstore. Even tonight, he'd taken command, and there'd been a freedom in that. "I'm interested in why it appeals to you."

He considered his answer but seemed to go with something simple. "I like being in charge." He knocked back his drink and set it on the table. "Pushing you to new limits is exciting."

My mouth went dry. "So, I'd be your submissive?"

He went wooden, not realizing his mistake until it was pointed out. He didn't even seem to be breathing.

I didn't want to watch him suffer needlessly, and tried to be brave. "I'm not sure I'd say no to the idea."

Okay, he definitely wasn't breathing now. His eyes were as big as the appetizer plates the server set down before us. Kyle waited until the guy was gone before blinking, and then gradually return to life. "Say that again?"

"Why? You heard me the first time."

Putting it out there was shockingly liberating. I'd spent a lot of nights wondering what it'd be like to be a submissive. To have another person focused on me, and push me to explore new things. To improve. And the thought of Kyle being my Dom? It was so hot, my skin felt like it was sunburned.

"Ruby." His voice was heavy, yet filled with hope. "Tell me you're serious."

It was madness, but it was certainly one way to move past our current arrangement. "I am."

The air shifted around us and everything in the restaurant faded away. It was just us. Could he hear the heart pounding in my chest?

Kyle reached across the table and trapped my hand beneath his large one, his fingers curling around my palm. It was a simple touch, but felt more sexual than anything else. Like his hand was wrapped completely around my naked body. Touching me everywhere. Owning me.

It made me weak with desire.

My voice stumbled through the thick fog of lust. "W-W-We need to talk—"

His hand tightened and surprise painted his expression.

I'd had a stutter growing up. Always the first consonant, worst on the W, but sometimes it would also present on a long S. I'd worked hard to correct it, and by the time I hit college, it was virtually gone. Only stressful situations brought it out.

Public speaking was one, which was an enormous hurdle to overcome. Being a full-time trial lawyer was never in the cards for me, but I still had to get over my fear so the stutter wouldn't be an issue if I had a case that went before a jury.

Kyle knew all about my stutter, because he'd helped me get through it.

There'd been times where we'd be eating lunch in the union hall between our classes, and he'd force me to go up to a table of strangers. I could talk about anything, even how I thought it was stupid what he was making me do. He didn't care, as long as I spoke.

It turned into a game after the initial rocky attempts, and then the game became fun. Sometimes I made up elaborate stories about Kyle just to embarrass him. The first time I'd talked to a table of strangers for five minutes without a single stumble, he'd grinned so wide I thought his face was going to explode. No, fuck that. I'd worried I was going to explode. It may have been the moment I realized I was in love with him.

I hadn't stuttered in years.

Kyle's face skewed with concern and his voice was soothing. "It's okay. There's nothing to be nervous about."

"I'm not." I shook my head, frustrated with myself. The worst part was speaking after the stutter. Worrying it would continue almost always made it happen, so I forced myself not to overthink. "I don't know where that came from."

He searched my face, and hesitated before proceeding. "All right. You were saying?"

"We need to talk about," I said, pleased the stutter was gone, "how this will change our partnership."

"I don't think it would change much. We're already exclusive, discussed limits, and agreed to be honest with each other."

His casual avoidance struck a nerve and my excitement flagged. "Don't think," I said coolly, "I don't know what you're doing."

"What am I doing?"

"Avoiding discussion of the terms you laid down in the last paragraph."

His arrogant look was infuriating. "Which terms are those?"

"Don't." My voice was filled with so much warning, it sobered him. "Just because you don't have any, doesn't mean you get to treat my feelings like they're a game."

It was a bit unfair, but how I felt. He looked offended. "I have feelings."

"Yeah?" I tossed his words back at him. *"Prove it."*

His shoulders straightened and his expression fell until he looked like he might be ill.

As I waited for him to find a response, my annoyance grew to dangerous levels. He thought I'd give him my submission and expect nothing in return? And he was typically quick with words. Why was it so hard for him to just say what he wanted? It made me suspect everything he said was calculated.

"I'm willing to talk about how I feel," he said finally, "but I'm going to need you to do it first."

Seriously? More evidence this was a game to him, and I wasn't going to play it.

"Okay, fine. I already apologized for the lies I left on the voicemail message. And I'm sorry for whatever I said when I was so drunk I didn't even realize I was sleeping on a bunch of coat hangers on my sister's floor." Anger threatened to overtake me, but I shoved it down. "You knew I was wasted, and yet you never called me back. Do

I wish we'd both done things differently? Sure. But what do you expect me to do other than say I'm sorry and try to move forward?"

This was his opening to now apologize for his mistakes.

Instead, he stared at me like he was trying to decide if he should select me from a jury pool.

I'd done my part, and his silence was infuriating. I shot to my feet so fast, I bumped the table and our silverware rattled. "Forget it. I just remembered I have plans to be somewhere else."

"Sit down."

It was the dark tone and my knees went soft, but the rest of me stayed strong. "No. I can't do this anymore if it's not leading somewhere."

He stood, bringing us face to face. "You want it to?"

Hadn't I just told him I did? He'd trapped me. Forced and manipulated me into revealing my feelings and breaching his stupid agreement. I thought I wanted his dominance, but not if it was going to be like this.

"Yes," I said. Of course I wanted more. At least, I had until fifteen seconds ago. Anger burned up my throat as I pushed the question at him. "W-W-Why the hell don't you?"

His mouth dropped open. No sound came out at all.

Oh, fuck this. I couldn't deal with more of his silence when I needed him to not leave me hanging. I ripped my coat off the back of my chair, grabbed my purse, and fled from him, wishing I could hurry away from the stuttered sentence just as easily.

Kyle's voice called after me, asking me to wait, but I tugged my jacket on as I went down the stairs. It was crowded in the bar on the first floor, and I weaved my way through to the entrance.

My emotions were a swirling disaster. This week with him had been amazing. Not just the sex and the new experiences, but the everyday moments, too. The quiet discussions post-sex. Waking up beside him and stealing sips of his coffee.

The temperature outside was above freezing, but it was still offensively cold. I skittered across the gritty pavement in my heels, heading up the sidewalk. I could try for an Uber, but a cab would be faster . . . assuming I could find one.

I had to take careful, deliberate steps as I headed for the end of the block. Had I known *Celeste* was only a few blocks from his apartment, I would have worn different shoes. After picking me up this evening, he'd parked in his building's garage and we'd walked over.

There weren't any cabs on this street right now. Should I head toward the shopping center? I glanced back the way I came, only to see Kyle barreling out of the restaurant, still putting one arm into the sleeve of his long coat.

"Ruby," he yelled. "Just wait a minute."

I stood on the sidewalk, shivering in the cold as he hurried toward me. My first thought was to flee, but as I'd technically already done that, I'd stand and fight. His expression was pure determination, and my pulse quickened with every step he took. He came like a guided missile, and when he reached me, his hands closed around my waist, locking me in place.

He used the weapon of his mouth, slamming his over mine, taking without permission. I tried to squirm away. "No."

"I'm sorry," he whispered. "I'm so fucking sorry I took off after the voicemail." His lips were firm and urgent, and there was a hint of tongue. Just enough to drug me into letting the kiss continue. "I'm sorry I didn't call you the next morning. I know I should have." It was as if he needed to keep kissing me to get his words out. "I'm sorry I was five years late telling you the truth."

His apology leveled me. His strong arms were the only thing keeping me upright.

"And I'm sorry I struggle to put how I feel into words. I've never been good at that." He mumbled it against my lips. "But I want what you want."

The world was spinning so fast, it was going to fling me off. "You want more? A relationship?"

"I want all of it."

There was a sharp pain in my chest, as if my broken heart was trying to put itself back together.

"I promise," he said, "this thing between us is going somewhere." His kiss migrated across my jawline, heading toward my ear. When it reached its destination, he uttered it with his breath hot on my neck. "Right now, it's going back to my place."

I was too distracted to protest when his arm looped through mine and he urged me down the sidewalk toward his building. I had to hang on tightly, because my legs turned to rubber bands. His statement how he wanted *all of it* buzzed in my ears.

Yet this was more communicating than we'd ever done, and I worried the magic was going to wear off the second we stepped inside his apartment.

"I should have known," I blurted out, "you weren't the kind of guy who'd run out on me like that."

He pulled to a stop. The tip of his nose and the edges of his ears had turned pink from the cold, and his hair fluttered in the wind, but he didn't seem to notice any of it. His intense gaze went straight into my core.

"And I should have known you were lying about the guy." His breath was visible in the cold and danced in the wind. "It wasn't news to me that when you get upset, you sometimes lose your head." His deep voice echoed down the empty street. "If you'll let me, I'd like to help."

I gave a tight laugh. "You're going to try to control the part of me that's uncontrollable? Good luck."

"I'm serious."

"So am I. You think I haven't tried to get my shit under control?"

We went on the move again and hustled through a crosswalk. It felt like as we got closer to his apartment, the faster he went.

"Kyle. Where's the fire?" *Besides the one in my pants.* "Some of us are wearing shoes that prohibit jogging."

He ignored my question. We flew into the lobby of his building, onto the elevator, and then we were headed up. He stared at our reflection in the dull chrome doors, not saying a word, his expression blank.

What was he plotting in that brain of his? "What are you thinking about?"

"How quickly I can get inside you."

I couldn't hold back the smile. Why did his place have to be all the way at the end of the building? We raced down the hall, and as soon as we were inside his apartment, we tore at each other's clothes. The coats and shoes came off first, discarded by the door. I pushed his sport coat off and tossed it onto a chair as we moved toward his bedroom, our kiss only breaking when he tugged off my top in one clean jerk.

We left our clothes like a trail of breadcrumbs, ending with our underwear beside the bed. Our mouths crashed together as we fell on top of the mattress, a tangle of limbs and naked skin.

We both seemed eager to act on our feelings. I was pulled on top of him, straddling his lap. Kyle's mouth found my breasts and sucked, while his fingers stroked between my legs. His dick was hard, and nudged where I was damp and aching.

"Fuck me," I said. "I need you."

He groaned in approval, and pushed his hips up, sliding inside me while his hands guided me down, all the way until our connection was complete.

I sat up on him, enjoying the sensation when he was fully seated inside me. "Oh . . . God, I love your dick."

"You've mentioned that."

I echoed our conversation from New Year's Eve. "I feel strongly about it. It bears repeating."

He grinned and grabbed my hips as he began to move, thrusting into me. I was on top, but even in this position, he wanted to be the one in charge.

I rocked back and forth, and then pounded my body down on him. God, it felt so good. His palms worked up to my breasts, and his lust-heavy gaze alternated between his hands and my eyes. He stared at me as if I were unbelievable, and I understood.

I couldn't believe it, either. He was mine again. We were together. It was like I'd tucked my volatile emotions for him away into cold storage, but a single spark was all that was needed to send the whole thing up in flames.

It burst from me as a passionate wave. I launched forward, clasping my hands on his face, and poured everything I had into my kiss. His arms banded tight around my back. Behind my eyelids, my eyes were wet with tears, but I refused to let them escape.

We were drowning in each other, gasping for air, yet I moved faster on him. Need swelled and consumed, forcing everything else away. All that remained was the desire to lose control. To give it over to this man, and trust him to take care of it.

We moved so fast, the bed squeaked and shook. The headboard knocked against the wall, and our loud moans competed with the sound. My thighs burned from the exertion, and my breasts crushed against his hard chest, but I couldn't stop. Never wanted to.

He slid a hand between our bodies, searching. When the pads of his fingers found my clit, it was a white-hot shock of pleasure.

"Oh, oh, *oh* . . ." The crescendo built, the song of my approaching orgasm so loud, it was deafening.

Bliss rocketed through me. It fired along every nerve ending, catapulting me into oblivion. Kyle gasped as my body tightened on him, and then he followed me. The muscles of his chest hardened and shook, and we rocked together in our mutual climax, fusing our mouths together.

It was . . . intense.

I was shattered and whole at the same time, loving the way his strong arms were wrapped around me. Holding me as we came down off our high. My head dropped down and I pressed my forehead against his collarbone, shuddering through my orgasm's aftershocks with closed eyes. Kyle stroked a hand over the back of my head, smoothing away my hair, and he let out a long, relaxed sigh.

I was supposed to climb off him, but didn't.

Even as his erection flagged and his climax dripped out of me, I stayed. There was no desire to leave as he delivered his languid kiss and stroked his tongue against mine. I couldn't even leave if I wanted to. His arms were steel bars, caging me against his body.

Time was irrelevant.

Eventually he shifted us so we were on our sides. I stretched and rolled away from him, but backed my body up against his heated one, wordlessly demanding he spoon me. All this week I'd tried to keep my distance after the sex, but now everything was different. I bit back my moan of satisfaction when his arm slipped around me.

I was still hungry since my tantrum at the restaurant had forced us to skip dinner, and we had a lot to talk about, but the emotions had taken their toll and left me exhausted. I was safe, warm, and happy beside Kyle. His slow, even breathing was gradually lulling me to sleep.

"You still awake?" he whispered.

I was, but right on the cusp of drifting off. If I spoke, it'd wake me up, and a little nap wasn't going to hurt us. I'd recharge for thirty minutes and then be better prepared to discuss everything.

"Ruby?"

His voice was soft, like a final effort to see if I was awake. I could barely hear him. I slipped further toward sleep.

He let out a hesitant breath. "I love you."

I'd never jolted so hard in my life.

The words reverberated through me as I rolled over to stare at him. Everything went still. My eyes were so wide, I could only imagine what I looked like.

His face was shock, which quickly turned to horror. He scrambled up off the bed, moving away like both it and I were on fire. He grabbed his boxers off the floor and yanked them on.

"You love me?" I gasped.

"No, I don't!" He blurted it out, his face contorting into an expression of embarrassment a split second before his feet pounded on the floor and he thundered from the room.

KYLE

Well, I couldn't have fucked that up more if I'd tried.

I was too distracted thinking about the disaster I'd just run from, so I let my subconscious handle everything else. My nervous hand poured a glass of bourbon, neat, and I carried it to the window in my living room.

I stared out at the view of the city at night, looking but not seeing anything.

My head was so heavy with thoughts, it was crushing. Ruby had been asleep. She hadn't even stirred when I'd uttered her name. The thought had struck me then; I could say whatever I wanted. I could practice.

Test the sweet nothing out on her before actually doing it.

I'd never said it before, not even to my parents or my sister. Weren't you supposed to practice before doing something? Fucking hell. The bourbon was warm as it slid down my throat.

I had one hand on my hip, and the other wrapped around my glass, and my shoulders tensed as her footsteps approached. When her arms went around me, I saw the white sleeves. She'd put on my dress shirt. My eyes closed as her palms pressed against my chest, and she flattened against me. Kisses were planted on the bare skin of my back.

It felt so goddamn nice.

"I would have stayed," I said on a low voice. "If you'd asked me not to go to New York, I would have stayed. For you."

She let out a soft cry, her body shuddering against mine. My intent wasn't to hurt her, or make her cry, but she needed to know. I was sick of holding back feelings for so long they turned to poison inside, but . . . shit. I had no idea how to get them out, either.

"I would have gone with you," she said, "if you'd asked me."

My heart twisted painfully.

Why had it been so hard for us? I wasn't afraid of much. Shove me in front of an intimidating jury and I'd excel. So why the hell had I been terrified to put myself out there to Ruby?

I took another sip of my bourbon, set it down, and grasped her hands that were pressed to my skin. She stood still as I turned, urging her to keep her arms around my waist. She gazed up at me, her eyes shining.

"We're going to do better this time around," I swore to her. No more unspoken wishes or feelings.

She nodded enthusiastically as I brushed an errant tear from beneath her eye.

"What just happened back there?" she asked.

"I didn't think you were awake."

"Did you mean it?"

My lips parted to speak. It was the first big test, and I would be damned if I'd fail, even though it was scary. It meant so much.

"That I love you?" Everything hinged on this moment. "Yes."

She filled her lungs with air. Ruby didn't blink at my

admission and her beautiful face was frozen. Like she couldn't accept it. And why should she, my brain fired back. She'd only been waiting half a decade to hear it.

The lack of response from her was pure agony. It dragged, and dragged, and I wondered if this was what I'd done to her all the times I'd been silent. It was awful, and I deserved it.

Her voice was uneven, but the words powerful. "I . . . love you, too."

Breath left me in a loud burst. Her words wrapped me in warmth, and before the desire could register, she was in my arms, her legs folded around my waist. Her kiss was ferocious.

Her hands threaded through my hair as I stumbled forward, striding toward the couch without breaking our connection.

"Please," she whispered between kisses. "Say it again."

Her plea was the sweetest thing ever; how could I not? "I love you."

I lowered her down and she cried out, as if my words were the relief she'd been desperate for her whole life. A different kind of pleasure burned through my veins. I'd been so nervous to tell her, I'd never considered how much I might actually like saying it.

"I love you," I said again, stunned at how good it felt.

She moaned as I settled her back on the couch and trailed kisses down her naked body. I moved my lips over her trembling belly and worked lower.

Each time I said it, my voice was stronger. "I love you."

"Wow," she whispered. "You feel strongly about it." A soft smile broke on her lips.

I nodded. "I do, Ruby. It bears repeating."

"I don't think I'll ever get tired of hearing it."

Tariq Crawford's counter offer of alimony was so low, it was offensive.

I stared at my email in disbelief. Crawford was making millions a year, and Courtney only wanted a fraction of that. She wasn't greedy, but if she was going to go back to school and get her master's, she'd need financial support.

Her husband had dragged her around with his career. He'd been drafted to one team and traded to another a year later, before ending up with Chicago. He'd also been on injured reserve with a torn ACL once, and she'd been the one to make sure he went to all his rehab sessions. She'd helped him get back out on the field. So in my mind, Courtney was owed her fair share of the Crawford assets.

It annoyed me this hadn't already been settled. There weren't children. Both parties wanted to dissolve the marriage. Division of assets shouldn't take this long; no one was fighting over spoons. Fucking hell, a lengthy divorce wasn't fun for anyone involved.

And the sooner Courtney put Tariq in her rearview mirror, the sooner she'd hopefully be able to see Julius as more than just a friend.

I couldn't talk about the divorce with Ruby, even in generalities. She'd know instantly which case I was referring to. She wasn't helping on Tariq's case anymore, but she was still working for opposing counsel's firm. Neither of us spoke about it, not wanting to accidentally put the other in an awkward position.

It was one of the only things I didn't talk about with my girlfriend. That, and the blindfold club.

After our failed dinner at *Celeste*, Ruby and I ordered Thai food, talked about everything, and then I'd fucked her on my ridiculous blue couch. My dick couldn't get enough of her. Actually, all of me couldn't get enough.

It'd been two weeks since I'd dropped those three crucial words, and I hadn't had an issue since. She stuttered at times of stress and perhaps I had something similar, like a stutter block whenever it came to her. But I'd discovered when I put my lips on her, it disabled the block and I could open up.

Her text message came through at a quarter to five as I was finishing up at the office.

> Are you nervous?

Noemi and Joseph were coming over for drinks tonight. Potentially more, if everyone was comfortable with that.

> No. Are you?

> A little.

> I think that's normal. Remember, it's just drinks. It doesn't have to be anything else.

> I'm excited though. Can't stop thinking about what it would be like.

I was *beyond* fucking excited. Not just at the idea of

watching her with another woman, but to give her an experience she'd been interested in for a long time. Getting to peek behind the curtain and watch Joseph interact with his sub was also something I was looking forward to.

Ruby and I had been wading in the waters of a D/s relationship, going a little deeper every few days, but tonight could be the plunge we needed to make it official.

She arrived at my place at six thirty, bringing in a box of macarons and two bottles of wine. "I didn't know if red or white was better."

She handed them to me, put her coat in the mudroom, and then looked lost. Unsure of what to do.

"You look fucking amazing."

Although her sand-colored top was loose-fitted, the way it hung flattered. The neckline was low cut, showing off her excellent cleavage, and her tight, shiny black leggings ended in a pair of *fuck me* black stilettos. The thought of bending her over the counter and fucking her right now was very, very tempting.

"Thank you." She slid up to me and laced her fingers together behind my neck. "So do you, counselor."

Her lips tasted like cherries, probably from her lip gloss, and my kiss seemed to have a calming effect on her.

We ate the dinner I'd picked up on my way home from the office, and attempted to have normal conversation, pretending we weren't going to potentially be naked in front of other people this evening. As the clock closed in on the other couple's arrival, Ruby and I grew more excited and anxious.

I'd given Joseph's name to the front desk so they could come straight up, and the soft knock on my door had Ruby leaping to her feet. She tucked a lock of her wavy hair behind her ear and flashed a nervous smile.

"Hey," I said to them when I opened the door. I tossed a hand toward my living room. "Come on in."

Noemi was tucked beside Joseph, one hand clasped in his, and a bottle of red wine in the other. She smiled shyly as they stepped inside.

"Can I take your coat?" I offered to her. Joseph was wearing a suit without a tie, but no overcoat.

It was electric when the women's gazes met; it could be felt in the air. What did Noemi think of the beautiful brunette who stood in my kitchen, one hand resting on the counter and trying to appear casual? Ruby's smile was bright, and then recognition flickered in her eyes.

"Joseph, Noemi, this is Ruby."

They shook hands while I hung Noemi's coat up, and when I joined them in the kitchen, Ruby glanced sideways at me. "Not famous, huh?"

Ah. She'd figured out who Noemi was, and the NDA probably made a lot more sense now. "You only asked if *he* was, counselor."

Without a word, Joseph picked up the wine opener off the counter, took the bottle from Noemi, and worked to get it open. It was my apartment, and yet he seemed to be the one most at ease. Of course he was. He was in charge tonight. Everyone had desires for this evening, and his was to hold the reins. He'd never had power over three people at once.

Wine was poured and glasses handed out.

We stood around my counter, chatting casually about our day as Ruby got a sense of the couple, and they got to know her. She'd set her macarons out, and I wondered if everyone ate a cookie just to have something to do. White chocolate raspberry tonight, which went well with the wine.

By the time Joseph was refilling glasses, the atmosphere had relaxed. Ruby softened beside me, laughing as she listened to Noemi describe her horror at catching her father fooling around with his girlfriend in his office.

"He'd forgotten we had a lunch appointment," Noemi said, shuddering.

Joseph looked confused. "You told me you didn't see anything."

"I didn't, but when Claudia popped up from under his desk . . . uh, I don't want to think about it."

He chuckled, and then the conversation lulled at the mention of sex. It was a key turned in a lock, setting the desires for the evening free.

Joseph's attention went to the back of the room and his gaze lingered on the bright blue upholstery. "That's some couch." He set his hand on Noemi's arm. "You and Ruby will go sit beside each other there."

His voice was light and easy, but his control fell in the room like a hammer.

RUBY

Noemi Rosso was fresh-faced pretty, and looked even better in person than she did in photos. Of course, she wasn't usually the focus of those pictures. It was her father who garnered the attention. But damn, did she look young. How old was she again? Early twenties at most.

Her fiancé looked considerably older. Joseph's hair was so dark it was almost black, and his deep brown eyes matched. His build was similar to Kyle's. Lean. Broad shoulders. Toned without being overly muscle-bound. I liked the look.

Joseph was late thirties, maybe even forty, and she was in her twenties. His hair was dark, while her long blonde hair hung past her breasts and curled softly at the ends. Joseph's expression was intense and serious, whereas Noemi's seemed bright and excited.

The juxtaposition of them worked, each perfectly complimenting the other. And the chemistry between them? It was undeniable. She flashed a smile to Joseph as she followed his command and sat on the blue couch, and he studied her intently the whole way. Examining to see if she was nervous?

I was nervous as hell.

In a good way, but still anxious. I clenched my glass of wine tighter as I made my way to the couch and sat beside her, leaving a few inches of space. Without thought, my gaze went to Kyle. When he nodded, I turned to Joseph, as if I needed to check in, show him I did as instructed, and if my proximity was all right.

It seemed to be. The men joined us, sitting in the chairs that flanked either end of the couch. If someone were to walk in right now, this would all appear normal. We'd seem like two couples having drinks and conversation. Would they sense the sexual tension swirling around us like an invisible fog? It was provocative. Seductive and so fucking powerful it squeezed my lungs.

Only Joseph seemed unaffected. He looked comfortable leaning to one side of his chair with an arm slung over the back, and a glass of wine in hand. Kyle tried to mimic his friend's posture. Both men watched us expectantly, and Noemi fidgeted with the hem of her dress.

My voice was tinted with nervous energy. "What now? You guys are looking at us like you want a show." I felt weird and didn't really want to be on display. It had been one thing to fool around with Leslie years ago. It was dark, I'd been kind of drunk, and Kyle had been right there beside me. He was so far away now.

Joseph took a sip of his wine, then rolled the liquid slowly in his glass. "I'll take care of the awkwardness in a minute. Do you find Noemi attractive?"

"Yes." I glanced at her. "You're very pretty."

"Thank you," she said warmly.

"Noemi's not pretty," he said, "she's fucking *gorgeous*. You should see her when she's naked." He took another sip of his wine. So calm and composed. "Would you like to?"

Kyle's apartment suddenly felt like the inside of an oven, and I was closest to the heating coils. My face warmed, but I pushed my nerves away and spoke honestly. "Yes."

The edges of Joseph's mouth turned up into a slight, pleased smile. "Would you like to kiss her?" he said. "Touch her?" His voice went deep and dark. "*Fuck* her?"

I could barely breathe. "Yes," I whispered, unable to contain it. "I mean, if she wants to."

His pleased smile widened. "She already gave me the signal of yes when she sat on the couch."

I guzzled my wine, hoping it'd make me relax. I was wound as tight as a spring.

"I am not your Sir." His gaze was focused on me. "But to avoid confusion tonight, you'll address me that way. Understood?"

Oh, God. I risked a glance to Kyle. A light smile played on his lips, as if he was comfortable with this, and then he nodded. I turned back to Joseph and nodded as well.

"Good. Noemi, put your mouth on her."

She didn't hesitate. "Where, Sir?"

"You can kiss her wherever you want."

I set my empty wine glass down on the table with jittery hands and too much force, so it clanked loudly, and then I rubbed my sweaty palms over my pant-covered thighs. It was a simple word, Sir, but it reverberated in the room.

I looked at Noemi, wondering where this beautiful girl was going to carry out her Dom's command, and it must have been the opening she needed. She reached out and cupped a hand on the side of my neck as she slid closer. Her eyes fluttered closed as she leaned in to me.

It wasn't a conscious thought to meet her halfway, but it happened. Her lips pressed oh-so-softly to mine in a delicate, closed mouth kiss. It was chaste. A tease, and over just as quickly as it had started. Confusion crackled through my mind. These lips didn't belong to Kyle, yet I wanted more. I sensed everyone in the room wanted *more*.

There was a sharp inhale of breath from her as I grasped her shoulder and pulled her back to me. This time my mouth sealed over hers, and I gave her just a hint of tongue. A sliver of the full kiss I wanted to share with her.

Her hand on my neck began to ease downward, her palm pressed against my collarbone. Inching her way toward my breasts as she opened her mouth and her tongue sought mine. She answered my intensity and desire with her own.

"Fuck me, that's hot," Kyle said. It caused me to grin, but I didn't stop kissing her. Her lips were so soft, and her delicate tongue sliding against mine was erotic. Wrong or right didn't apply. Kyle's voice had been loaded with satisfaction, and it shot a bolt of pleasure deep in my belly.

Also, there was her hand. She'd tucked it inside my shirt and slipped her fingers beneath the strap of my bra, toying with it. Toying with not just me, but with the men watching. I wanted her to go further. My nipples strained beneath the lace of my bra, begging for attention.

"Do it, baby girl," Joseph said.

Our sighs mixed together as Noemi's fingertips traced lower and grazed beneath the cup of my bra. She found my nipple and gently pinched it between two fingers. I grew hot and damp between my legs in a flash. Before we'd started kissing, I hadn't wanted to put on a show. But now? Oh, I was enjoying it.

As we both became bolder, so did our kiss. Her teeth snagged my bottom lip and nibbled on it, while my hand slid from her shoulder down to cup a handful of her breasts. There was a wicked male chuckle which sounded like Joseph, but I was too preoccupied with her to confirm.

I squeezed the globe of flesh and reveled in the sexy moan I pulled from her.

And the next second she was gone. My eyes flew open and I gazed up in surprise. Joseph was on his feet, as was she, and he had a hand on her elbow, like he'd tugged her upright there.

His tone was authoritative. Strict, but still hot as he spoke it near Noemi's ear. "Take your panties off. You'll watch Kyle as you do it."

Whoa. I locked my knees together, holding back the rush of desire. There was something lewd yet enticing about this concept. Noemi turned to face Kyle and bent at the waist. Her hands went up her skirt, disappearing beneath the purple silk shift dress. Kyle's blue eyes were zeroed in on her movements, and he followed the gradual descent of black lingerie as it skated down her legs.

When it was over, her underwear was abandoned on the gray flooring, and Kyle turned his attention to me. Lust was a dark shadow on his face. Not so much lust for her, I believed, but for me. For me *with* her.

The couch jostled as Joseph guided her back down into her spot beside me. "Sit back," he said. "Ruby, on your knees."

This command punched the air from my lungs with an audible sound. My heart banged in my chest and threatened to catapult from my body. It seemed pretty apparent what this was leading to, but . . . could I do it? I wanted to, yet this felt like we were skipping ahead in a choreographed dance and now I didn't know the steps. He'd given an order, though, and I was supposed to follow it unless Kyle vetoed it.

I poured myself over the side of the couch until my

knees were on the hard floor.

Joseph's dark eyes were intense. "May I touch you?"

When Kyle and I had discussed limits for this evening, I'd said I would probably be okay with that. It'd be hard to play with anyone else if we were hung up on something like touching. I nodded, and even though I'd given him my approval, I still startled when Joseph bent and grasped my wrist in his hand.

It was so he could set my palm on her knee. He leaned over and repeated the action with my other wrist, so I had one hand covering each of her knees.

"Open her legs."

The room was quiet, save everyone's deep breaths, and the blood rushing loudly in my head.

Messing around with Leslie had been short and sweet. We'd all been fumbling around together, not sure of how far to go or what to do. This was *nothing* like that. Joseph's dark commands and Kyle's heavy gaze ramped up the intensity of it until I was so turned on I worried I'd come with one wrong move.

Christ, just Kyle's hand caressing over my pants and between my legs would probably set me off.

I inched forward on my knees, positioning myself before her, and watched her expression as my palms pressed her open, forcing her skirt to ride up. I parted her legs until the fabric cut across the tops of her thighs, just barely concealing her nakedness from view. Well, from the men's view. I could see beneath her skirt and how beautifully bare her pussy was.

Noemi's face was teaming with desire. Her hands were splayed beside her on the blue couch, and her pink manicured nails dug gently in, as if wanting to hold on for whatever happened next.

Joseph's hand once more wrapped on my wrist. He didn't command me verbally, choosing instead to guide my hand up along her thigh. Goosebumps dotted her smooth skin, and as I reached the apex of her thighs, she began to quiver.

I turned my unsure gaze up to Joseph, but he smiled. "She trembles when she's really turned on." He stepped away, leaving us hanging right at the edge of serious girl-girl action. Was I supposed to take the final leap? What if I did something I wasn't supposed to? He returned a moment later, holding a nearly full glass of red wine out to Noemi.

Her voice was breathless. "No, thank you."

"I'm not asking." His tone was direct. "You won't drink it. You'll hold that glass while Ruby goes down on you, and you won't spill a drop on Kyle's couch. There will be consequences if you do, besides them never inviting us over again."

She took the glass in her hand, and her eyes were impossibly wide as she watched the wine slosh with her tremble. It was cautiously lowered down until the base of the glass was supported on the armrest and she gripped the stem securely. When her focus shifted from the wine to me, I swallowed hard.

Pressure pushed me forward like invisible hands, urging me to do it. She was spread before me as I shifted, settling back on my heels to a more comfortable position. He was right; she was gorgeous. Her pale, flawless skin begged to be touched, and my hands smoothed up and down her long, quivering legs. Then, I dipped my head, bringing my mouth closer until no more space was left between us.

"*Oh.*" It was a soft gasp of pleasure from her as my tongue tentatively glided through her valley. She was wet, warm, and incredibly soft.

"That's it," Joseph said. "Good girl."

Was he speaking to her, or me?

Joseph's praise could apply to both of us, or neither. Were we good girls? I was performing oral sex on his fiancée, all while my boyfriend watched. My tongue fluttered over her lush skin, and it unleashed a moan from Noemi. Her satisfaction gave me a shiver of pleasure.

Joseph's voice rang out again. "Sit beside her on the couch."

This command was for Kyle, and his footsteps got louder as he came closer. Then, he was there beside Noemi, his blue eyes staring at me and a carnal expression smeared on his face. He looked at me like I was incredible, and warmth spread through my already overheated body.

I had too many clothes on. So did he.

But we took orders from someone else tonight, which was new and interesting, and I got the feeling our clothes wouldn't come off until we'd been given permission. How did Kyle like being under Joseph's control? And . . . how did Kyle feel about another man telling me what to do? It was sort of dangerous and exciting.

Since my hands were already there, I used one to push back Noemi's skirt, and the other to spread her further open to my mouth.

"Oh, fuck, Ruby." Kyle's voice was audio sin. "Jesus, you look amazing doing that."

I shuddered under his praise, and closed my eyes, enjoying the feeling he gave me. Noemi's breathing went labored as my tongue lapped at her, building into a flurry.

She took over holding onto her own skirt, her hand gripping the silk, so I walked my fingers across her leg and onto Kyle's thigh. I pushed further up, wanting to massage his dick through his tented pants while I was also pleasing her—

There was a sharp sting on the side of my neck, gone before it finished registering, but enough to give me pause. I turned toward the sensation. "Did you just . . . *flick* me?"

The weight of Joseph's gaze was crushing. "You need to ask permission to touch him."

"I'm sorry," I blurted out, embarrassed. I didn't want to make mistakes or disappoint. "Can I touch him . . . *Sir*?" The word was erotic coming out of my mouth.

Any displeasure disappeared from him. "Keep it over the clothes."

I resumed what I'd been doing, both to her and to Kyle. I closed my lips around her clit and sucked gently, while stroking my palm over his firm dick. Need had focused into a sharp point between my legs and the throb was persistent, clouding my mind.

Noemi's body was slack as I licked her, my face buried between her thighs. Her head was tipped backward and rested on the edge of the couch, her gaze up to the ceiling, and she looked a bit like I was torturing her. Her quiet whimpers and moans said otherwise. The wine in the glass stayed calm, even as I sucked harder on her swollen flesh.

Could I make her come with my mouth, and would it be enough to get her to spill at least a drop? Did I want to get her in trouble with her Dom? She seemed to be getting close. Her moans were coming faster now, and louder, too. My hand on Kyle slowed as I focused on getting Noemi over the edge.

"Joseph!" She gasped it like a warning.

"Stop." The command from him was reinforced with a hand on my shoulder, urging me back. "I'm the only person who makes her come."

He took the glass from her and pressed the rim to his lips, drinking a long sip, and then set it on an end table. A hand was smoothed down the line of buttons on his dress shirt, and his attention went to Kyle.

"Ruby has too many clothes on. Take off her top and pants."

It seemed like Kyle was happy to follow this command. He stood from the couch and helped me up in a rush, moving so fast I was barely on my feet before he was tugging my shirt up. I wasn't concerned about being naked in front of the couple now, not with what I'd just done, and I'd never been overly shy in the first place.

The shirt was off my body and in his hands, and then it sailed onto the chair he'd been sitting in earlier. I kicked off my shoes as his fingers worked to undo the slide clasp at the top of my pants. My zipper rang out, and then the leather was peeled down.

We weren't paying much attention to them as Kyle undressed me, and it wasn't until I was standing between the coffee table and the couch in nothing but my black lace bra and panties, that we realized Joseph had taken off Noemi's dress and undone her bra.

She stared at me as the bra slipped down her arms and fell to the floor.

Naked, other than her heels.

Her breasts weren't as large as mine, but they were perfectly proportional to her petite frame, and looked sexy as hell. Part of the allure was the way she held herself.

There wasn't an ounce of embarrassment or shame in her expression. She was confident, and why shouldn't she be?

I was older than she was, but less experienced, so I chose to mimic her confidence. I knew Kyle desired me, and Noemi was looking at me with a fair amount of lust, and it made me feel powerful. It was addicting.

Joseph brushed her hair back behind her shoulder and dropped his mouth close to her ear. "Get a good look, baby girl. I'm about to take it away."

I didn't understand until he retrieved something from the interior pocket of his suitcoat. She held perfectly still as he lowered the black blindfold over her eyes and adjusted the straps in the back, which pinned her hair in place.

Joseph's gaze floated from his fiancée to land on us. It was strange the way he looked at me. As if he was pleased, but not leering. Like he had little more than mild interest.

No, his interest was definitely focused on her, and it sparked an unexpected romantic emotion. She was wearing a blindfold, so she couldn't see his reaction to my nearly nude body. But there was no sexual reaction toward me. He only had eyes for her, the woman he loved.

Joseph motioned to the couch. "Kyle, sit down in the center. Ruby, sit in his lap, facing away from him."

Kyle sat, clasped his hands on my hips, and lowered me down to sit on him. His hard-on was pressed to my ass, so I wriggled against it, and grinned to myself when he let out a tight groan of pleasure.

Together, we watched Joseph clear everything off the solid and sturdy-looking coffee table, and then he led Noemi to it and guided her down. "On your hands and knees. Ass up." As she got into position on top of the table, his attention briefly turned to us. "You can touch and kiss each other during this, but don't get distracted or I'll take that privilege back."

I gazed at the girl before us. She rested her forearms against the tabletop, her palms flat and straight out in front of her. Since she was on her knees, her hips were higher than her shoulders. Her head was in line with her spine, sloping downward, her back flat. Ready and waiting for her Dom.

"She looks amazing," I whispered to Kyle. Her lithe body and her offered submission were a seductive combination. He murmured a sound of agreement as his lips coasted along the spot where my shoulder met my neck.

"You look amazing," he added.

I closed my hands on top of his as he caressed my bra-covered breasts, and tilted my head to the side, encouraging him to keep kissing me. It gave me shivers in the best way possible, even as I was on fire.

Joseph retrieved Noemi's large purse from the counter, brought it over, and as he set it on the floor beside the coffee table, he pulled out a black paddle. The fingers inside my bra slowed to a stop, and Kyle's lips froze on my skin. We'd both checked off spanking with props on our willing lists; floggers, crops, and paddles, so I knew Kyle was interested, but we'd yet to try any of it.

Joseph's stance was confident, while his expression remained businesslike. It was playtime, only playtime was serious. His dark eyes focused on Kyle. "You'll want to understand the different sensations you can create with each tool you use." The paddle was lightly placed against the round curve of Noemi's ass, and he rubbed it in slow circles as he continued speaking. "Try them out on yourself first and build up intensity. If you can't handle it, it's unlikely your sub can."

The black leather was hypnotic as it skimmed over her backside, like he was priming her. Or teasing her. Either concept worked for me.

"Determine thresholds. Just because she can take it, doesn't necessarily means she should." He lifted the paddle away. "For example, Noemi's not a pain slut."

Joseph moved efficiently, almost surgically. He brought the flat side of the paddle crashing against the roundest part of her ass, generating a loud, sharp slap and making her ass cheek jiggle. She didn't break her position, but a gasp fell from her lips. He instantly pressed the fingers of his free hand against her pussy, stirring in lazy strokes.

His voice was dark as sin. "No, she's a slut for *pleasure*."

She was the one who moaned, but I felt it deep inside my own body, and beneath me, Kyle's cock twitched. He was enjoying the display as much as I was. His arms wrapped around me and pulled me tight against him, and I sighed in contentment.

Joseph knew what he was doing positioning us this way. I kept my head tilted to the side, which allowed us both to watch, while also allowing Kyle to run the tip of his tongue along the edge of my ear. His breath was warm and felt great on my sensitive skin. His hard body molded perfectly to mine.

It was quite the show in front of us, and my face warmed with a flush as Joseph volleyed a series of strikes against her ass. His hand on her pussy never ceased moving throughout the spankings, but he drove a finger deep inside her when her hips began to swivel.

"You want to come, Noemi?"

She spoke, but he slapped the paddle against her reddening skin and the crack was the only sound we could hear.

"What was that?" he demanded.

She was clearly saying yes, but he continued the game and swatted her again, covering her words.

His face and tone were ruthless. "I can't hear you. Speak up."

Her fingers tensed into fists and her head hung until her forehead rested against the wood. "Oh my God, please make me come."

The paddle thumped to the floor. "Aren't you forgetting something?"

Her head snapped up, like alarm pulled it up on a wire. "Sir," she said quickly. "Please make me come, *Sir*."

Joseph splayed his hands on her enflamed skin, massaging it. It had to burn, but I knew if it were me, I'd enjoy that burn. Kyle had become an expert at turning my ass a delicious shade of red.

"Half," Joseph said, and lowered to kneel behind her, his hands still on her cheeks.

You'd think he'd just told her she was getting sued. Her mouth dropped open as she strained her head to turn toward him. Not that she could see with the blindfold, but her frustration was clear.

"Half?" The repeated word from her was like she couldn't believe it.

"Yeah, half." He looked annoyed. "If I have to tell you twice, one of us is doing something wrong." His large hands slid down so his thumbs could manipulate her clit. "You use Sir as a sign of respect, or have you forgotten?"

Her body slumped just a degree, like his thumbs were distracting her from whatever she was upset about.

"No, Sir."

"You know I could have said none. Be grateful I didn't."

She let out a tiny whimper and bit down on her bottom lip. Was she fighting against the pleasure he was giving her? I knew what it felt like. One of Kyle's hands had wandered down south and was stroking on top of my panties. He gave a wicked chuckle when he realized how soaked they'd become.

Joseph glanced over at us. Was he checking to make sure we weren't getting distracted?

"Noemi's orgasms average twenty-two seconds. I've trained her to control their duration."

I'd swear I felt Kyle's jaw hit the floor, because it was right alongside mine.

"You trained her to . . . stop her orgasm?" Kyle asked.

"Yes."

Holy shit. It sounded like the cruelest thing ever, and yet, it turned me on. That kind of dominance was abso-*fucking*-lute.

I squirmed against Kyle, trying to increase the pressure of his touch, but he must have known, because his strokes went feather-light. I shoved a hand inside my bra and pinched my nipple, only for him to seize my wrist and push it away.

"Please?" The ache inside me was racing toward critical meltdown.

"Not yet."

It was a simple expression of control from Kyle, but fuck me, it felt incredible.

Joseph leaned forward and put his mouth on Noemi. *Rimming her.* The image of him fully clothed in an expensive suit, kneeling behind the beautifully naked girl perched on all fours on a coffee table was decadent. It was an obscene art display and I didn't want to blink. Didn't want to miss a fraction of a second.

He used both hands on her, one to rub furiously back and forth on her clit, and the other to pump two fingers in and out. They were wet and glistening. His eyes were closed as his mouth was between her cheeks, and when she began to rock with pleasure, he moved with her, never losing contact.

"Oh my God," I whispered, overwhelmed with desire and craving for relief.

The side of Noemi's balled fist slammed against the table with a thud. Her biceps flexed and her back arched. "Oh, oh, Joseph. I'm gonna come!" She gasped again. "I'm *coming!*"

He kept his fingers inside her, but straightened and laid his other forearm over the small of her back, turning his wrist so he could stare at his watch. "Eleven. Ten. Nine. Eight."

She moaned repeatedly as the ecstasy rolled through her. Her left leg was quaking so violently, it was amazing she hadn't collapsed. He continued to count down until she'd have to stop, and it had the inverse effect on me. Every number brought me closer to satisfaction.

"Three. Two. One. Stop."

Joseph studied her critically, watching her every cue. Noemi half-sobbed as she shook and pressed her lips together. There seemed to be tension rippling in every muscle of her as she clamped down and tried to shut her pleasure off. A deep breath was drawn in through her nose, and as she exhaled, she relaxed.

She'd done it.

His fingers withdrew from her body.

He launched to his feet, grabbed her shoulder, and yanked her upright, only so he could slam his mouth over hers, one hand cupping the back of her head. "Oh, you good girl. Such a good girl, Noemi." His tone was so pleased, it was like she'd amazed him. "You're so, fucking, *perfect.*"

I wanted to hear that tone from Kyle. I was desperate to please him like that.

She was panting as if stopping her orgasm had taken its toll and had been exhausting, but Joseph's kiss was giving her much needed energy back. I'd thought the sex act we'd just witnessed was hot, but it paled in comparison to this passionate kiss. She clutched at him and he held her right back, strong and secure as he drew her up off the table and wrapped his arms around her.

Kyle used the opportunity to turn my head toward him.

His stare was . . . hungry. It made me believe I was the only thing that could satisfy him. Electricity clung in the air as he moved in, bringing our mouths together in a long, drawn-out kiss. Like he was slow fucking my mouth.

I had fallen so deep into him, I hadn't realized the other couple had moved until our kiss ended. Noemi stood on her heels before us, her hands hanging at her sides. There was a soft squeal as Joseph dragged the heavy coffee table away, clearing space, and she flinched subtly at the noise.

My gaze traveled the curves of her nude body. Her nipples were taut and pink. Her waist narrowed and her flat belly encouraged me to keep looking, all the way down to the delicate, feminine slit between her legs.

"You're stunning, Noemi," I said.

Her chest lifted with a deep breath. "Thank you."

A smile warmed on Joseph's expression as he

came back to her. "I think it's time to show Ruby some appreciation."

He grabbed a throw pillow off the chair, dropped it to the floor, and urged her down onto her knees so she knelt between Kyle's legs. Mine as well, since my legs were hung over his, spread even wider. The electricity in the room ramped up until all the hairs on my arms were charged and standing on end. As if in slow motion, Joseph placed her hands on Kyle's knees.

"Find the lace," Joseph whispered to her, brushing a kiss over her cheekbone. "When you do, you'll put your mouth on it."

Chapter

THIRTY-FIVE

KYLE

Ruby's hands were resting on her thighs, but when Joseph issued the command, she lifted them and seemed unsure what to do. She didn't want them in Noemi's way.

Joseph read my mind and beat me to it. "Ruby, put your elbows together behind your back."

It made it easy to clamp one hand around them and hold her, while keeping my other free to touch. To explore. To direct. At least, when Joseph permitted it. So far, he hadn't ordered me around much, and it hadn't been a problem. I'd agreed to his requirement of him topping the scene, and he'd said as long as I didn't get in his way, there shouldn't be any issues.

The only issue so far was I was sure I was going to die. Watching Ruby go down on Noemi had been so hot, it'd been stamped permanently in my brain with a branding iron. When I'd been instructed to move by the girls on the couch, I'd gotten a much closer look, and every flick of my girlfriend's tongue on another woman's pussy was better than a stroke on my cock.

I ached to slide inside Ruby's tight, soaking pussy and feel her grip me. I needed her. How the fuck had I existed before her? Before *us*? I'd been a shell. A man going through the motions of life, checking boxes of what I thought was required of me. She unleased all these . . . feelings.

There were hands on my thighs, and as they slid up over my pants, I had to close my eyes against the sensation. Noemi's sensual touch didn't last long. She was on orders from her Dom, and for the second time in my life, my fingers tangled with another woman's as we both touched Ruby's breasts. Since I held her elbows, it forced her to arch, and the back of her head rested on my collarbone.

The sound Ruby made . . . *fuck*. It was a soft whine, loaded with need. All of my thoughts, she produced in audio format. I moved out of Noemi's way before Joseph had to say anything. I wrapped each hand around Ruby's arms, just above her elbows, and as I listened to her struggle for breath, I gently sank my teeth into the side of her neck.

Noemi's lips traced over the lace holding back Ruby's full breasts. Joseph had moved to his knees behind her, and leaned over, dropping kisses along the length of her spine. It was seductive. Sensual. His hands moved, sliding all over her skin. Caressing her breasts, stroking her back, disappearing between her legs.

I was sweating.

My pulse rushed along, blood roaring in my veins. Noemi's sweet kisses on Ruby's bra were taking too long. I wasn't sure which I would find hotter, Ruby going down on Noemi, or Noemi returning the favor, and I was desperate to find out.

He didn't tell me, and I didn't ask for permission, but fuck it. I undid the clasp on Ruby's bra and urged the straps down. Joseph had a watchful expression, but as Ruby struggled out of the bra, there was a hint of a smile from him. He approved of my action, thank fuck.

It sparked a primal emotion in me as Ruby's bare breasts came into view. Her tits were magnificent, and she was my woman. I was proud to show her off. *Look at how gorgeous she is, this woman who's chosen to be with me.*

Noemi's hands touched bare skin where the bra had just been. Her fingers glided over Ruby's hard nipples, exploring and learning.

"Uh oh," Joseph teased. "Find some new lace."

She sighed, only it was sexy. Anticipatory. The only lace left on Ruby was the small band covering her hips and between her legs. I secured my hold on her elbows once again, inching my legs apart a little wider. It forced her to open up to the blonde, blindfolded girl who used her hands to see.

Noemi's tone was pure surprise when her fingers moved down. "Oh my God, she's wet."

Dark, nasty thoughts burned in me. I wanted to see Ruby's wetness smeared across Noemi's lips. Dripping off her tongue. Yet it was hard to get a good view from over Ruby's shoulder, so I shifted her to lean to our left, and peered around the right side of her body. Better. Now I could see Noemi's tongue gently licking the crotch of Ruby's panties, and I enjoyed the squirms it gave her.

Ruby ground her ass against my cock. "Are you trying to tease me, or ride Noemi's face?"

"Which do you want it to be?" she answered, breathless.

The younger woman was focused on her task. She had one hand on Ruby's leg, and the other on mine, supporting herself as she brushed her tongue over the strip of lace that kept her from truly tasting Ruby. Neither girl seemed to care as Joseph's hands undid his belt. His zipper. I couldn't see what was happening because Noemi's body blocked my view, but it appeared he'd dropped his pants and underwear, and was stroking himself.

Once again, I didn't ask permission. I could use the upcoming moment to my advantage, and I committed to it. Joseph's arm flexed. I assumed he was holding himself at the base to steady his dick, and then his hips pushed forward.

Noemi's mouth ceased on Ruby, rounding into an "*Oh.*" She needed to take a moment as he entered her, and I moved, hooking my fingers around the crotch of Ruby's damp panties, pulling them aside. The blindfolded girl had no idea the lace was gone, too preoccupied by her fiancé's cock sliding deep inside her.

"Don't stop," Joseph ordered, a wide, evil grin spreading across his face. He'd seen what I had done, and . . . Yeah, he really fucking approved of this.

The contact of Noemi's tongue on Ruby's bare skin made both girls jolt, only Ruby's was more acute. She cried out with pleasure. "Oh, fuck me. Again."

Noemi hadn't recovered from her shock, and Joseph's hand was on her head, gently easing her forward. "You heard her."

His first real thrust into his fiancé drew a moan from her, and his expression hooded as she set her mouth on Ruby.

Inhibitions had been abandoned the moment Joseph had ordered Noemi's panties off, and I let my mouth run. "Do you like eating my girlfriend's pussy as much as I do?"

She moaned. Not like she could really answer. Joseph's hands were braced on her hips and he was giving it to her. Rough, and fast, and she struggled to keep pleasing Ruby as her body recoiled from his devastating thrusts.

Ruby groaned. Her fingers were digging under her ass, trying to find my dick. She wanted to touch me. Was it the sensation of another woman going down on her? The restraint of her hands behind her back? Or the people fucking right in front of us that turned her on so much?

I wanted her to touch me. I wanted to put my mouth on her tits, but this position made everything impossible. Had Joseph put us like this to torture me, or save me? I probably wouldn't last a minute if Ruby had full access to my dick.

"How does it feel, Ruby?" I asked. "Do you like it?"

"Yes," she gasped.

The moans of the women echoed in the space, occasionally overpowered by the sound of hard bodies smacking together, or a deep groan from Joseph. I started to get envious. I wasn't sure how much more teasing I could take, but as soon as I had the thought to slip out from under Ruby, it died.

A tremble swept up her legs, and she swallowed down a big gulp of air. Her signal that her orgasm was arriving. I squeezed harder on my grip on her elbows, reminding her of my presence and my dominance. Noemi might be the one to bring her to orgasm, but I was the one allowing it.

"Oh," Ruby cried. "Yes. Fuck yes, right there."

There was a shift in the room. Everyone now sensed her approaching orgasm, and I'd swear Noemi redoubled her efforts. Joseph rained down words of encouragement to his fiancée. I sat up straight, bringing my lips to the base of Ruby's neck, and whispered how fucking dirty she was.

How much I loved it, and her.

Ruby came first with a loud cry, which was more like a scream.

Noemi let loose a panicked moan, and Joseph's expression hardened with what seemed to be concentration. "All of it, Noemi. You give my cock every goddamn second of your orgasm."

She seemed to set him off. It was an orchestra of groans and gasps, moans and sighs as they jerked and spasmed through their release. Noemi's head rested on my knee, still gripping my leg as she tried to recover.

Joseph's curious eyes watched Ruby, not that I could blame him. Her epic orgasms always made me want to stop and enjoy the spectacular show. She shook violently from head to toe, flinching with aftershocks, and sometimes I was envious of her. How much pleasure was coursing through her body right now? I wanted to experience that, but watching her go through it was the next best thing.

I dropped my grip, released my hold on her panties, and curled my arms around her. I loved holding her like this. Her hair smelled faintly like fruit, and goosebumps pebbled on her soft skin as I pressed my lips to the side of her neck.

Slowly, the electricity in the room subsided, one ragged breath at a time.

There was rustling as Joseph did up his pants and helped Noemi to her feet. The blindfold fell to the floor beside her feet.

"Bring me a towel, please," Joseph said quietly to her, breaking the spell of silence. Noemi's heels clicked away toward the bathroom. The door shut with a soft thump, and the sound of water running in the sink was heard.

Ruby slid sideways off my lap, and I had to gnash my teeth as she did it. My cock was hard and angry, begging for satisfaction. When she was seated beside me, her hand resting over my zipper, I noticed the strange way Joseph was looking at her. Like he was considering something.

"What is it?" I asked.

"Are her orgasms always like that? So . . . violent?"

The carefully selected word wasn't wrong. "Yeah."

His dark eyebrows pulled together. "How comfortable would you be if I touched Ruby?"

I didn't understand. We'd gone over limits, and . . . "I thought she already gave you permission."

He stood and loomed over us, but his expression was serious. "She did."

He reached for her, tracing his fingertips along her cheekbone until he cupped her face in his palm. There was a hint of tension in her, and I wasn't exactly sure what to make of his touch. It almost would have been better if he'd touched her in a sexual way. His fingers on her face were . . . *intimate.*

When Noemi returned from the bathroom, a white bath towel clutched in her hands, Joseph's thumb brushed over Ruby's lips.

"Open."

The single word from him was a fresh wave of lust in both women's eyes, and Ruby's hand rubbed against my aching dick. Fuck, that felt good. Noemi stood beside Joseph, watching with curiosity as Ruby parted her lips and took Joseph's thumb slowly inside her mouth.

It was seductive. His nostrils flared as her lips closed and it was clear she was sucking on him, simulating oral sex, all while she stroked me.

"I want to know," his voice was so steady and low, it verged on hypnotic, "how you'd feel if I put my fingers somewhere else in her body."

The groan from me was unstoppable, but mostly because Ruby clenched me tightly. Was all the blood in my body located in my dick right now?

Joseph pumped his thumb slowly in and out, his gaze fixed on hers. It was crazy how fast this had gone from her simulating going down on him, to him fucking her with his fingers.

"I want to teach something to Kyle, but I understand this might be past your limits."

I considered his question carefully. Ruby and I had discussed what we were comfortable with in detail, and while we'd both thought we'd be okay with it, neither of us were sure what would happen in the moment. Could I handle this? Would Ruby be all right with it?

Joseph withdrew his thumb and I leaned into her, trailing my fingertips up and down her arm. "It's up to you. I'm pretty sure I'm okay, but it's entirely your call."

She blinked her eyes slowly, as if trying to clear away a fog of lust. "I think . . . I'm okay with it, too."

Joseph's pleased smile held a strange power. I wasn't submissive. I enjoyed giving commands, not taking them, yet it felt nice having his approval. His expression was disarming.

We sat motionless on the couch as he took the towel from Noemi's hands and covered her mouth with his. The kiss was short and sweet, and they whispered something to each other afterward I couldn't hear. Was he confirming she was okay with this, too? She didn't look unhappy. If anything, she seemed interested. Intrigued.

The towel was folded and laid on one end of the coffee table, and then Joseph's gaze went to Ruby. It was spoken softly, more of a request than an order. "Come here, both of you."

My mind was pulled in a thousand directions as I stood and helped Ruby up. I selfishly wanted satisfaction, but I was eager to see what he was going to do. Anxious to learn from a man who seemed to possess a wealth of knowledge when it came to dominance.

He removed his suit coat and handed it to Noemi, who hung it on the back of one of the chairs at the breakfast bar, and then he was undoing the buttons at the cuffs of his dress shirt. "Take off her panties. I want her naked and sitting on the towel."

Ruby's breathing was hurried, but otherwise she seemed calm. I took a knee behind her, curled my fingers under the lace, and inched it down. There was the slightest tremble in her knees, but it could have been from any number of things. Was she nervous? Excited? Or was this leftover from her orgasm?

Joseph barely glanced at her once she was completely naked. He'd seen his share of naked women, hadn't he? He'd unbuttoned his shirt and pulled it off his shoulders, causing both Ruby and me to pause.

Noemi's smile was bright. "I know, right? Silas does amazing work."

Blue ink covered his shoulder, extending down to his elbow. The half-sleeve tattoo was scrolls in an intricate pattern, and the shading was masterful. It looked three-dimensional.

"It's beautiful," Ruby agreed.

"Thanks." He discarded the shirt on the chair, and his gaze fell to the table.

It wasn't lost on her what he wanted, and she complied, lowering to sit on the towel. She nibbled on her bottom lip, visibly nervous as she stared up at us. I trusted her to speak up if she became uncomfortable, but I'd also keep a close watch. If her stutter came out, I'd put a stop to all of this immediately.

"Lie back," he said. "You're going to suck Kyle off while I'm demonstrating." One corner of his mouth lifted in a smile. I was relieved. Was he aware how painful my situation had become?

He positioned himself to kneel in front of her legs as Ruby lay back, and as he gazed at me, his eyebrow curved upward. His expression was expectant.

Ruby voiced what he was probably thinking. "You want to come closer and get your dick out?"

I was on my knees beside her on the low table in a heartbeat. Ruby stared up at me, her eyes full of both nervous energy and amusement as I undid my belt. It didn't bother me that another couple was about to watch. It turned me on. I'd enjoyed watching them, and was hopeful they'd feel the same.

Ruby barely waited for me to free myself from my pants and boxers before she had me gripped firmly in her hand. I jerked at the contact and watched her stroke the length of my throbbing cock.

"Fuck," I muttered.

She smiled then parted her lips and wrapped them around the tip of my dick. Perhaps it was a side effect of not being the one in control, but I scooped a hand under her neck and guided her to take me deeper. I set the pace as she swirled her tongue and sucked.

Everything focused in on the sensation. Her mouth was burning satisfaction, promising sin with her tongue, her lips, her teeth. And abruptly it was gone. Her fist clenched at the base of my dick and her stunned gaze flicked up to mine.

Because Joseph had inched her knees apart and coursed a hand up the inside of her thigh. Noemi was kneeling beside him, her arms draped over him, watching with her lips pressed to one of his shoulders.

"Okay?" I whispered to Ruby.

She nodded, hurried, and held my gaze. Out of the corner of my eye, I could see the movement, but didn't dare look away from her. Her lips fell open just enough so she could sip air and her eyes widened subtly as Joseph eased a finger inside.

I could sense he was watching me as much as her, and for a split second I was grateful he'd requested to be the one in charge tonight. It was demanding having the control. Being responsible for Ruby's pleasure took effort, so to be responsible for three people? If tonight didn't go well, Joseph would be the one easiest to fault.

Her eyes fluttered closed, and her mouth found me again. I sawed my cock between her pursed lips, one slick glide at a time, until she opened and took as much as she could. Her tongue flattened against the sensitive underside, and desire heated my blood to a boil.

She moaned when I was deep, the tip of my dick pressed against the tight spot at the back of her throat, and the vibration was fucking amazing.

"Her G-spot," Joseph said. I lifted my head, trying to

think over my lust and the sensations that tingled at the base of my balls. He used two fingers of his other hand to tap low on Ruby's belly. "I start slow, and build up to it. I use two fingers, but you can try three if she likes that."

It was hard to comprehend Joseph's words when I teetered at the edge of losing control. His tone was professional, but it was in conflict with the two fingers disappearing inside my girlfriend. Was there something wrong with me that I didn't want to punch him in the face?

Ruby's soft moans probably helped. He had his palm up to the ceiling, and eased his first two fingers in and out at a slow, steady pace. It allowed him to go deep, and she was enjoying it.

So far, he wasn't showing me anything I didn't already know, but I kept quiet. Ruby's mouth shut down most of the systems in my brain anyway.

"Touch her," he said.

I hadn't realized I'd been holding back until he gave me permission. I put my hand on her breast, squeezing her flesh. God, she was beautiful. Her fist slid back and forth on my wet dick, and her cheeks carved into hollows as she sucked.

I wasn't going to be able to hold off too much longer. It felt way too good, and it was insanely hot watching her writhe on Joseph's skilled fingers. I wasn't sure where to look. Her pink lips wrapped around me, glossed with saliva as I fucked her mouth, or down to her pussy where another man was touching her.

My legs were quaking and I pinched hard on her nipple, focusing elsewhere than the pressure building inside me. I bit back a groan as she tried to take me even deeper and gagged, backing off for a moment.

"She needs to focus. Kyle, come on her tits."

His filthy order threw me into chaos. I wanted to come, but this wasn't how I wanted to do it.

Joseph wasn't finished, though. "Do it. Remind her who she belongs to."

Aw, fuck. The vision of my cum painted on her sexy breasts was too enticing to say no to. I yanked myself from her lips, wrapped my fist around my cock, and pumped as fast as I could. Never would I have thought I'd want to do this in front of anyone else. The act seemed . . . uncivilized. Too raw, and Ruby deserved better.

Only she appeared as excited about it as I was. She cupped her breasts and pushed them together, waiting.

Joseph was fucking her with his fingers, but she was mine. The need to show ownership was powerful. So powerful, it shoved shame out of the way, and I came in a fiery explosion, streaking ropes of cum across her chest.

Fuck, fuck, *fuck* . . .

It went on and on as pleasure twisted all through me, leaving me weak as it faded away. I dropped my grip, resting the head of my dick in the mess I'd created as I struggled to catch my breath.

"You naughty boy," she whispered, grinning.

One half of a chuckle released from my lungs. All my dirty fantasies were brought to life by Ruby Carter. Was I the same for her?

"You look so good like that," I said. If it had been just us, I'd have ordered her to run her hands through it and spread it all over her tits, but I filed it away for another day.

Now that I'd come, my brain was operating again. I tucked my flagging erection into my pants and zipped up, then turned my attention to him. He'd slowed almost to a stop when I'd groaned in pleasure, letting Ruby focus on that. Now he gestured for me to move beside him as his attention went to her.

"I want you to rub your clit," he said. "No one can get a woman off better than herself."

His fingers drove deep inside her, and she let out a whimper, as I joined him. Her back arched as her hand reached down and the pads of her fingers fumbled over the bundle of nerves at the top of her slit.

"Good girl." His tone was soothing. "Relax. Whatever you feel, I want you to go with it." His two fingers pumped faster, and hers moved quickly to match his pace. I was so busy watching, I barely realized he was addressing me. "Do it exactly like I am."

His hand retreated all the way out, and he shifted out of the way. He wanted me to take over? I set my left hand on her knee, and eased my first two fingers inside her, where she was wet and hot. When Joseph had stopped, she'd slowed her own movement, but it resumed as I thrust inside her, aiming for the same angle he'd been using.

"Here," he said, once again tapping the spot low on her stomach, directing me.

Her eyes were half-lidded. "Mmm . . . shit, that feels good."

Joseph slipped an arm around Noemi's waist, but his gaze stayed on Ruby. "You're going to think the word 'go' now. Visualize it." His tone was hypnotic. "Faster, Kyle. What word are you thinking, Ruby?"

I pumped my fingers in and out. Her eyes were shut, her face twisted with concentration, and the word was breathless. "Go."

"That's it, good. Keep repeating it in your head. Over

and over." His voice dropped low as if only speaking to me. "Get stable, because you're going to pick up speed. Her knee might give out. If it were me, I'd put my other hand on the tabletop."

I leaned over her, supporting myself on my knees and the hand flat on the wood as I moved faster.

"Oh, fuck," she moaned. Her hands slapped against the table, then one reached out and latched onto my arm. Her feet were on the floor, but she rose on the balls of her feet, tilting her pelvis.

"Faster," Joseph ordered. "Go as fast as you can and you don't stop until I say so."

I gazed at the woman beneath me and focused. I slid my fingers in and out of her body so fast, my hand was a blur. The force of my rapid thrusts made me vibrate. My chest heaved with the demand to maintain the furious tempo, but I kept up.

"Go, Ruby," he ordered. His tone was like mine could be, only his was even more demanding "Go, Ruby. Go, go, go—"

She grunted out a sound that was beyond pleasure, and her body seized. It clamped down on my fingers, tighter than I'd ever felt before, and liquid heat burst from her. She erupted in a scream so loud, the neighbors had to have heard it.

I continued to fuck Ruby even as she was coming, and she grew wetter, and wetter. It poured from her in a gush, drenching the towel beneath her. It soaked my hand, and as I pumped, more slung out onto the towel.

"Okay, Kyle," Joseph said over Ruby's loud moans.

As I slowed, everyone could hear how wet she'd gotten as soaked skin met soaked skin. It wasn't like the fake shit in porn; it was more of a rush as she came, and it was infinitely hotter. Her grip on my arm was fierce, and stayed tight while she climaxed, bucking on the tabletop. The orgasm was continuous. Pulse after pulse inside squeezed on me and I stared at her with disbelief. My cum was still on her chest, and I watched the rise and fall of it as she slowly drifted back to earth.

Her hand loosened and thumped to the table as she was finally spent.

"Are you fucking kidding me?" I said. "Holy shit, Ruby. You're so fucking sexy. Goddam, sweetheart. Fuck."

I withdrew and launched forward, clasping her face in my hands and planting my lips over hers. I tried not to overwhelm her as she was still panting, but I was greedy. I wanted the connection to her.

Her voice was exhausted but trying to stay strong. "I hope you took good notes. I'm going to want to try that again sometime."

I gave a wicked laugh. "You better believe it."

We stayed like that on the table, kissing softly as she continued to recover. My tongue dipped into her mouth and slid over hers. I couldn't use it to find adequate words, so I my kiss would have to do.

We were poor hosts. We lingered, making out on the coffee table while our friends washed up and dressed. Eventually, I asked Noemi's help in grabbing a shirt from my closet, and took the towel from beneath Ruby to help wipe her off.

Noemi reappeared. Had fate forced her hand in selecting the oversized t-shirt? It read "Randhurst Law School" on the front as Ruby slipped it on.

Joseph and Noemi gathered their things. He offered

to move the coffee table back, but I declined. I sensed the evening was over between us, and was anxious to have some time with Ruby all to myself.

"We had a great evening," Joseph said as we followed them to the door. "We should do it again sometime."

The t-shirt on Ruby hung almost to her knees, but as she wrapped an arm around my waist, it crept up her thighs. She nodded and glanced at me.

"I think we'd like that," I said. "Thanks for coming."

The statement hung awkwardly for a moment, but he didn't seem to care. He extended a hand for a shake while the girls hugged each other. "Invest in towels. Now that she knows she can, it's more likely to happen."

I had no idea what to say to that.

He seemed to know, and smiled faintly. "Not a lot of women can do that." His words went heavy with meaning. "I hope you know you're a lucky man."

"I do." I exchanged a look with Ruby and squeezed her. "I'm very lucky."

When they'd gone, I scooped her up into my arms, ignoring her startled cry, and carried her toward the bedroom.

"What are you doing?" she asked.

"Taking you to bed."

"Can I wear this shirt while you fuck me?"

"God, it's like you can read my mind. My dirty, dirty mind." I set her down on the bed and began to strip. "What am I thinking about right now?"

"That I'm amazing, and you love me?"

I couldn't have smiled wider if I tried. "You're absolutely right."

Joseph's Porsche was already parked in front of the club, and I went past, choosing to park down the block. It was expensive and a pain in the ass to own a car when you lived in the city, so most cars on the road were nicer, but I still didn't like grouping my Range Rover near his. Even if the blindfold club was in the nicest part of town, which it wasn't, I didn't want to attract attention.

He met me at the door and gave me a warm smile. "How're things?"

"Good." Obviously good, because I was here. We hadn't seen each other since the night we'd played together a week ago, and I was worried things would be uncomfortable, but of course they weren't. Joseph was so confident, it overruled awkwardness.

Neither Joseph nor I had time to make it out to the suburbs again, so he'd arranged for his supplier to meet with us at the club after dropping off the monthly delivery of new 'equipment' this afternoon.

"How about you?" I asked. "How are wedding plans going?"

He smiled faintly. "I didn't think I would, but Noemi says I have an opinion about everything."

"Let me guess, the wrong one?"

He chuckled as we walked through the front door, surprising the guy sitting on the stool just inside. The man was huge, and as he lumbered to his feet, he recognized Joseph. "What are you doing here, man? Haven't seen you in a while."

"I have an appointment with the supplier," Joseph said. "It's okay, I already ran it by Julius."

"Shit, he must have forgot. He didn't mention it." The bouncer leaned over and pressed a button, buzzing us through the second door. "He's in his office, supervising a regular in room six. Supply guy's not here yet, but he's gonna start in room four."

There was a slight pause as Joseph held the door open for me. I doubted the bouncer noticed, but Joseph's body language hinted at something. We made our way through the first holding room, where the small bar on the side was dark. The club didn't operate during the week, and not during the day.

"Something wrong?" I asked.

"No." But his tone suggested it was. Abruptly he pulled to a stop. "It's not my place anymore, he can run it however he wants, but I made it a rule not to take off-hours appointments. Especially not when a delivery is being made."

I knew how the place worked. When I'd handled Julius's case, I'd had to understand the transactions from start to finish. The client's privacy was the foundation Joseph had built this place on. Sometimes the johns left the blindfolds on, not for the experience, but to keep their anonymity.

"I'm sure it's fine," he added. "Some of the regulars are hard to say no to."

We moved on. The long hallway had a bank of doors on the right, each adorned with a single brass number. Like last time I'd been here, I tried not to think about how many times my sister had been in these rooms, selling sex to strangers.

We reached the door to room four, and Joseph grabbed the handle, pushing it open. I stood still in the hallway, hesitating as I peered into the dark, ominous space.

"Something wrong?" he asked.

"No, I—"

The door to the last room opened abruptly and a tall guy stepped out, his stunned gaze finding Joseph.

"Monsato," he said. He seemed just as surprised to see Joseph as the bouncer out front had been.

Shit!

Shit, shit, *shit!*

"Mr. Crawford," Joseph said.

Tariq pulled the door to his room shut. "Thought you didn't own this place no more."

"I don't, but I help out from time to time."

I needed to get the fuck out of there before Tariq recognized me. I turned on my heel to head back down the hall, but swift, heavy footsteps rang out. Too late. A strong hand latched onto my shoulder and jerked me around by the lapel of my suitcoat.

Tariq stared at me like he was letting the recognition set in, and fury burned in his dark eyes. I was prepared for a fist to come flying my direction, and for it to hurt like a motherfucker.

Only he didn't throw a punch. He let go of me, put his forearm in Joseph's chest, and slammed my friend against the wall with an enormous bang. Joseph let out a surprised grunt of pain.

"What the fuck is this?" Tariq shouted.

Joseph's face was shock and confusion, but then his gaze went down to the forearm pinning him to the wall. "I've no idea what you're talking about, but you better get your fucking hands off me."

The amount of malice in Joseph's tone was stunning. Tariq was a weapon of muscle and power. On the field, he was fast, strong, and ruthless. Off the field, he didn't have to play by rules, and he could crush my friend easily.

"Tariq."

The deep voice came from the base of the stairs where Julius's hulking form occupied most of the space.

Tariq turned his head, but didn't release Joseph. "He set me up!"

"No, he didn't. Let him go." Julius moved closer, his posture a silent threat.

Joseph was released with a shove, and he straightened his suit, eyeing the larger man with disdain.

Tariq didn't give a fuck. His gaze bounced to me. "Yeah? What the fuck is my wife's lawyer doing here, then?"

Joseph's mouth dropped open, finally clued in on what had set the football player off and why he'd been throttled against the wall. Did Joseph grasp the severity of this? What Tariq was doing was illegal, and worse, if it got out, it'd be a scandal too big for the NFL to ignore. Crawford had been coming to the club long enough to be labeled a regular. Long enough to know Joseph used to run the club.

Years of cheating on his wife, and with prostitutes.

The attorney in me now had the bargaining chip I needed to get whatever I wanted on Courtney's behalf. If my father were her lawyer, he'd be a shark and go for every last cent he could squeeze from Tariq.

But there were two very important things in play. First, the club was under FBI protection. They'd never let the scandal break because it'd jeopardize their sophisticated sting operation.

And second, I wasn't my father's son. I wasn't going to put money ahead of everything else.

"I'm not here for you," I said to Tariq, trying to keep my voice calm and professional. "I didn't know—"

"Shut your mouth, ain't nobody talking to you!" Abruptly Tariq began to pace in the narrow hall. He pushed his dreads back out of his face and seemed lost. Was he picturing his career unraveling?

He skidded to a stop and glared at Julius. "How'd you know he didn't set me up?"

Julius's expression twisted. The damage was done; there was no going back. He lifted a hand, gesturing for his friend to remain calm. "He was my lawyer."

"Wait, what?" Tariq took off pacing again, this time just one tight, frantic circle, and then he got up into Julius's face. His tone was laced with betrayal. "You did this?"

"I told you not to come, T." Julius's expression was pained.

Tariq threw his hands into Julius's chest and attempted to shove him back, but it had barely an impact. "I thought you were my boy. What the fuck?"

"Yeah." Julius's deep voice was heavy with anger. "What the fuck? How could you do it to her, man? I'd kill to have a girl like that, and you don't care. You're here, buying pussy week after week, throwing her away. You don't deserve her."

Joseph sensed it at the same instant I did, the terrible shift in the air as their friendship headed toward a violent end. We both straightened and tensed, preparing to do whatever we could if these two freight trains decided to run at each other.

"Man, shut the fuck up," Tariq barked. "You think

you're better than me? Who've I been buying pussy from, Julius?"

"Didn't say I was better than you. I kept my mouth shut too long. Court deserves a man who ain't gonna cheat on her every chance he gets."

Tariq scoffed loudly. "Fuck you, you don't know what it's like. I'm getting it from all sides. Sometimes I just gotta get out and be me."

"Yeah? Lemme help you." Julius's tone was as dark as his expression. "Get out of my club, and don't fucking come back."

Disbelief ran over Tariq's face. "Her? You gonna pick her, over *me*?" He slapped his palm to his chest. "We played ball together. You and the whole D line were my brothers."

Julius shook his head. "You and me . . . We're not those guys no more. Go, Tariq, before I make you."

Tariq's sneer was ugly. "Like you could."

"By myself, nah, maybe not. But I'm not alone. Guess you didn't notice the enormous white boy when you came in."

The sneer slid away, and although Tariq tried to disguise it, he seemed to realize he was outnumbered. His narrow gaze swung from Julius to the exit, and then landed on me. My pulse roared, but I steeled myself.

He cleared his throat and spat on the ground, like the whole situation left a bitter taste in his mouth. "Fuck you all, and fuck this bullshit."

Julius's large hands curled into fists at the disrespect, but he stayed silent as his former teammate stalked down the hall, and Tariq disappeared into the payment room.

I watched my friend's shoulders sag as he spoke into

his earpiece and called for Nina to report to room six, most likely to assist Tariq's girl, and his sad eyes focused on me. "What are you doing here?"

"I asked him," Joseph said. "I'm sorry I didn't mention it. If I'd known you were taking clients, we would've met Mr. Dufrane somewhere else."

Julius waved the statement off. "Nah, you didn't do anything wrong. I forgot you were coming." He turned and headed up the stairs, getting us to follow. His voice boomed on the narrow, steep staircase. "I shoulda never told him about this place. Shoulda turned him away."

We trailed behind him into his office, and as he sat in his chair, he looked defeated.

"I was the one," Joseph said, "who gave him membership, so you could say that's on me." His expression was plain. "But it isn't. Half the members here are married. A guy like Crawford? He's getting ass somewhere on top of this place, guaranteed."

Julius's gaze darted away, staring off vacantly. So, he already knew that for a fact.

"It's no one's fault Crawford's a piece of shit," Joseph added, "except his own."

"Does Courtney know?" I asked. "How he's been cheating on her?" She'd never brought it up with me.

"Maybe." Julius hung his head. "But I don't think she ever called him out about it. It'd hurt her too much." He ran a palm over the smooth dome of his head and dropped his hand on the desk with a thud. "Do you have to tell her, Kyle?" His gaze lifted and trapped mine. "Can I talk you outta it?"

I didn't want to tell a woman her husband was a frequent visitor of a brothel, and I certainly didn't want to explain who was running the establishment. "I'll do my best to avoid it, but it depends on what he does. I might not have a choice."

He nodded, but looked resigned.

The supplier arrived. After we left Julius in his office, it was hard to pay attention. I was distracted while considering what Tariq would do. A wise man would accept the alimony offer I'd suggested and hope everything would conclude quietly. Only, Tariq was a loose cannon on the field. I assumed his emotional, fiery temperament extended to his regular life, too.

That led my thoughts to Ruby. I wanted to talk to her. Get her take on what to do, only I couldn't. Thank fuck she wasn't on the case anymore. I stood beside Joseph, not paying attention while he talked about products, and I hoped any moment my phone would buzz with an incoming email from Sterns and Clifford. It would announce Crawford's acceptance of terms, and we'd finally put the divorce to bed.

In the end, I only bought one thing. A simple black flogger, and Joseph explained how to vary the technique to maximize Ruby's enjoyment of the experience.

My phone chimed with a text message from Payton when I was back at my office and had just finished going through settlement papers with a client.

Are we still on for dinner tonight?

Yes, I've got us reservations. Meet at my place at 6:30?

Sounds good.

I was looking forward to Payton and Dominic officially meeting Ruby. My days of being the third wheel were behind me. My sister seemed cautious, but happy I was in a relationship.

Yet there was no need to be cautious.

I loved Ruby, and she loved me, and nothing was going to come between us now.

Chapter

THIRTY-EIGHT

RUBY

The day was dragging, and yet going too fast.

I had anxiety about dinner tonight. Of course I was pleased Kyle wanted me to get to know his family, but my first run-in with Payton had been less than stellar. Her attitude toward me was barely warmer than the weather outside. At least she didn't seem to view me as an enemy.

I had a feeling if she gave me a chance, Payton and I would get along just fine.

Kyle didn't say it, but he didn't have to. Tonight was important. His sister would see how much we cared about each other, and it would put her fears to rest of me hurting her brother again. And I was excited to lay eyes on the man who was always pitted against my boyfriend for the silly dollar bet. Who the fuck was better looking than my boyfriend? No one.

An angry male voice carried through the office. It unfortunately happened from time to time. Emotions ran high, especially when a lot of money or divorce was involved, and I'd heard several of my colleagues getting an earful when things weren't going well. Hell, I'd been on the receiving end once before. My personal favorite was, *"What the fuck am I paying you for?"*

The shouting up front grew louder. Whoever he was, the guy wanted to see Henry, and he wanted to see him right this very moment. Wasn't going to happen, though.

Henry had worn his power suit early this morning as he'd swung through the office, which meant he'd be in court for the day.

I tried to tune out the noise, but then he yelled my name. *Shit.* It had to be Tariq Crawford. A split second later my phone lit up, and FRONT DESK blinked on the screen.

My heels tapped out a quick beat as I marched to the front, and sure enough, Tariq stood beside the receptionist's desk, his eyes blazing and his expression furious. He looked intimidating, both his size and demeanor, and the administrative assistant cowered behind her desk.

I forced myself to look pleasant and stay calm. "Mr. Crawford?"

His wild gaze swung toward me. "Now we getting somewhere. I need to talk to my guy. It's an emergency, and he won't answer the damn phone."

"I'm sorry, Mr. Reed is in court."

"Then you gotta help me." His face was pained.

No, I couldn't. It was a major conflict of interest. And what on earth had happened that was so urgent in his divorce? I glanced to one of the side conference rooms and saw it was empty.

Not that I really wanted to close myself in a small room alone with this large, wild-looking man who'd hit on me, but what was the alternative? If he told Henry I'd turned him away, one of the biggest clients to come through the door at Sterns and Clifford, I'd be in serious trouble.

I motioned to the room. "Do you mind if we talk in there?"

The only response from him was a look of relief.

I'd barely sat down before he unraveled like a hot mess. Tariq set his hands on his forehead, then swiped his palms backward, stroking back his thin, neat dreadlocks. "Okay, I—"

"Wait," I said. "Before you say anything, I need to disclose I've been removed from your case due to a conflict of interest."

"What?"

God, it was embarrassing enough having this conversation with Henry two weeks ago. Both men had witnessed me losing my temper at Kyle, and heard me in the elevator afterward. "Your wife's attorney and I have a personal relationship."

He scowled and shook his head. "Yeah, I already know that. I remember you cussing him out."

"Right." I gnashed my teeth. "Except our relationship is ongoing."

Tariq blinked slowly, and suspicion crept into his eyes. "What's that mean? You sleeping with him?"

I narrowed my gaze and struggled to pull in a deep, calming breath. *Keep your cool, Ruby.* "Yes, we're dating."

He stared at me with a dubious expression, and then the suspicion grew exponentially until his whole face was sour. "No, you ain't."

I wasn't going to waste time arguing. "It's in your best interest to wait for Mr. Reed."

"I don't have time for that. I need a . . . I dunno, a gag order or something."

I gave him a skeptical look. "A gag order?"

"I need protection. The press can't find out about me going to the club, or I'm fucked."

What the hell was he talking about? "I'm sorry, what?"

The strange, sickening gleam in Tariq's eyes made unease flood my stomach. It announced whatever this 'club' was, it couldn't be good. He leaned forward. "I'm about to use some adult language, girl. You seem like you can handle it. The blindfold club is where I go to get good pussy."

My face grew hot with a flush. I wasn't an idiot. The lives of professional male athletes in Chicago ran the gamut. Some were wholesome family men who went to church every Sunday, and some partied harder at night than they did in the arena. A sports town as big as Chicago always had the rumblings of scandals with players.

I kept my voice even. "A strip club."

"Nah, it's not like that. It's a classy, expensive whorehouse."

Sweet Christ, I didn't need to know this. If Kyle had that kind of info, he'd eviscerate Tariq, because I would if Mrs. Crawford were my client. "Mr. Crawford, let me remind you—"

"If the league finds out, forget it. I'm fucking done. I gotta know he's not going to talk about it."

"Who?"

His eyes were deep pools I couldn't look away from, and his tone was pointed. "Your boyfriend."

I swallowed hard and my voice went grave. "Mr. Mc-Creary knows you've visited this club?" If so, Tariq was right. He was fucked.

"Yeah," he said, and the sick gleam was back. "He was there today."

My brain buzzed as the information sunk in, but I battled to stay logical. I repeated it, but my words were full of skepticism. "He was there."

"Yeah. I thought it was a setup, but . . . he wasn't there for me." His expression was lewd, and dripped with meaning.

I laughed at this total nonsense. There was no way Kyle would go to a *whorehouse*, as Tariq so nicely put it. No way he'd cheat on me.

"You think that's funny?" Anger darkened his face. "The girls at the club are up for anything. All kinds of kinky shit a vanilla girl like you won't do. They're naked, strapped down to the table, blindfolds on. I come in and do whatever the fuck I want, as long as I got the cash."

I made a face, not needing the image of Tariq fucking some girl bound to a table, and definitely not needing to know this information. "I'm sorry, I don't believe you."

"Oh, yeah? Call him. Ask him where he was at one o'clock."

Why was I even humoring him? I set my cell phone on the table with a quiet thud and stared at the scene. "Let's just pretend for a moment I do that. You think he'd tell me?"

Tariq paused, considering. "He's wearing a light gray suit, white shirt, blue striped tie. Call him."

The conviction in his words was unnerving, and my breath caught. The level of detail was hard to ignore. Was it possible he was telling the truth? I crossed my arms and leaned forward, hardening my expression. "Okay, so say you're right. What the hell was he doing there?"

He stared back at me like I was an idiot. "He was going into one of the rooms, and believe me. Only one thing happens in them."

It made no sense, and although I refused to believe it, my pulse was racing. Before I knew what I was doing, I had my phone in my nervous hands.

This was stupid. I watched the three dots dance across the screen, my heart in my throat. When the message came through, I stared at it in disbelief. I clutched the phone so hard, it was a miracle it didn't break.

Chapter

THIRTY-NINE

KYLE

Ruby didn't respond to my text, or the follow-up one I sent which was simply a question mark.

It bothered me, not just that she went silent, either. A bad feeling seeped in, took over, and it was suffocating. The feeling only intensified when I called her and it went straight to voicemail.

Keith Gillespie's face was a deep shade of red as he told me about his wife's latest antics. She'd graduated from the spoons and lamps to claiming primary ownership of the furniture. She wanted the water bed in the guest room.

A water bed.

I choked back the urge to ask if I should list the bean bag and lava lamp, too. Surely, they had those. Wasn't that included in the set when you bought a water bed?

Jesus, why couldn't I get hold of Ruby?

"She's getting that bed over my dead body," Keith said.

It was at least the third time he'd flung out the words *"over my dead body,"* and each time he uttered the phrase, it became more likely. I sort of wanted to murder him.

A sharp knock on my office door made both of us flinch in our seats, and without waiting for me to respond, the door pushed open. My father lurked in the doorway, his expression solemn.

"Please excuse the interruption, Mr. Gillespie," he said. His gaze slid to mine. "Kyle, we need your help with something. It's urgent."

He wouldn't interrupt me with a client unless it was serious. I excused myself and joined my father in the hall, only he didn't stay there and explain. He moved swiftly down the corridor, heading for the lobby. What the hell was going on? Unease chewed at me as I went after him.

He turned the corner and led me to the front desk where I pulled up short.

Ruby stood beside the half-wall the assistant's desk was behind, and she leaned on it as if using it for support to keep her upright. Her cheeks were blotchy and her eyes rimmed with red.

I didn't care that my father was standing there, glaring at me, or how Suzanne, the administrative assistant, was leering at us like she didn't want to miss a second of drama. All that mattered was Ruby was crying.

I spoke on a low voice and stepped close. "Sweetheart, what's wrong?"

"Don't!" Her voice was pure fire and she backed away, her gaze fixed on my tie as if it were offensive. "Where were you today at one o'clock?"

The lobby became a vacuum. I couldn't breathe. I never anticipated Tariq would go to her, but I should have. Fuck, I should have just told her about Joseph and the club.

I couldn't take her back to my office because Gillespie was there. "Come on," I said, hushed. "Let's find somewhere to talk about it."

"No! Just answer the goddamn question."

I clenched my jaw, feeling my father's gaze digging into the back of my head. I just needed her to calm down enough for him to leave, and then I could explain. "I went out to lunch with Joseph."

She banded an arm over her stomach, practically doubling over, as if my words had struck her painfully in her center. As her anger seemed to rise, so did the volume of her voice. "I know that's not true, and you promised no lies."

It was both firm yet desperate. "Keep your voice down."

"Don't tell me to be quiet, just tell me where you were."

Control was slipping away. She already knew my answer. If I gave her anything but the truth, it'd push her temper to redline. I glanced over my shoulder. Robert McCreary studied me the way he studied a witness on cross-examination, and I sighed. "I've got this under control. Can you tell the client in my office I'll be another minute?"

"No," Ruby said. "You don't have this under control."

I felt the imaginary knife she stabbed me with, every inch of it as it sliced into me. She wasn't operating with all the information, but she was at least supposed to *know* me. She should trust I'd never, ever cheat on her.

Fucking hell, we were right back at Randhurst. Had nothing changed? How could she think I'd fuck anyone else, and prostitutes, at that? My body tensed with a surge of anger, but I maintained a grip on my emotions.

One of us had to right now.

I summoned the strictest tone I possessed, the one I only used with her behind closed doors. "You're going to let me explain."

The statement implied guilt, when the only thing I was guilty of was trying to protect my sister. Ruby's face went ash-white, and I could see the exact moment I lost her to her temper. Her eyes burned with the fire of a million suns.

Time decelerated.

I sensed it, yet was surprised when she lashed out, her hand slapping me hard across my face. The assistant gasped loudly. My cheek stung, but it burned hotter with embarrassment and how unjustified her action was. For a sliver of a moment, I saw nothing but red.

She was shaking violently, and tears spilled from her eyes, but she didn't seem to be aware.

"In private, now." I was so pissed at her, it was difficult to think. Her scene had just thrown me into deep shit. I slipped a hand under her elbow to guide her toward a conference room, or the kitchen, or the bathroom . . . anywhere out of my father's view.

I pulled her stumbling along, even as she tried to break free with a defiant jerk of her arm, and I pushed the door open into the first empty space I could find. Lights blinked to life in the tiny filing room, and she whirled to face me when I released her.

The door had barely shut before she spat it out. "I just left a meeting with Tariq Crawford."

Fuuuuck.

"Are you trying to get us fired?" I growled under my breath. "Do you want to be disbarred?" Because whatever Crawford had told her was subject to attorney-client privileges. "You know better than this."

Chaos teemed in Ruby's beautiful eyes. She was so lost in her hurt, she wasn't thinking at all. When we got through this, we'd have to work on her anger issues, but right now I had to find a way to defuse the situation.

"I have a good reason for going to the club, trust me," I said.

"S-S-So you admit you were there."

Her stutter tore a hole in my heart. "Yes. I need you to

calm down so I can explain."

"Forget it, I don't want to hear—"

Asking her to calm down always had the opposite effect, so I had no choice but to match her intensity. "Shut up, Ruby." Anger had pulled my muscles taut. "Goddamn it, you're going to listen to me."

She froze, so I pushed on.

"The guy I bought those restraints and other stuff, he agreed to meet Joseph and me at the blindfold club today."

Her eyes narrowed down to slits.

"I didn't go there to fuck someone else. I went there to buy things to use while I was fucking you."

My explanation had no impact on the shield of her temper. "Tariq said you knew both owners of the place. You'd been there before."

"Yes. You and I know one of the owners . . . intimately."

Her face went blank with shock, and perhaps a little horror. "Joseph? He owns a whorehouse?"

I grimaced at the word. "No, he doesn't own the *broth-el* anymore. He sold it to someone else when he fell in love with Noemi."

"Oh, good lord, Noemi." Ruby was probably thinking if the story broke that her fiancé was selling sex at some high-end club, it'd ruin the heiress. But her concern for our new friends slipped away and was replaced with her earlier suspicion. "And the other owner?"

"I met Joseph, and the other owner, through Payton. She used to . . ." Fucking hell. "She used to work there a few years ago."

This statement got through to her, judging by her jolt of surprise. She could see clearly it wasn't a lie, and her anger flagged. "Oh."

As her anger faded, mine grew. "This is not the time or place to discuss it. We'll have to do it later." My cheek still stung from where she'd slapped me. "You embarrassed both of us by coming here."

Her posture sagged. It was like my disappointment was physically crushing her. "I . . ."

"I've got a client in my office. You need to go."

Fresh tears welled in her eyes, but she blinked them back. Even if they fell, I was too angry to let them get to me. Did she realize how badly she'd fucked this up? I went to the door and tugged it open, not looking at her as she exited.

"I'm sorry," she whispered as she lingered in the doorway.

It came out colder than I intended. "Yeah, me, too."

I escorted Ruby to the elevators, not saying a word. Disappointment churned inside my stomach like bile and blotted everything out. She stepped into the empty car, turned to face me in the lobby, and her expression was haunting. She wore guilt and remorse in equal parts, but I wasn't going to waver. I crossed my arms over my chest to steel myself.

When the doors began their slow slide shut, panic overtook her, like she worried this would be the last time we'd see each other. Her voice was broken. "Goodbye."

I said nothing.

The doors closed and the elevator carried her away.

Ruby had rendered a guilty verdict before I'd had a fucking chance to defend myself, and I'd never been so angry in all my life.

Oh, wait. No, I thought bitterly. She'd done this to me before, hadn't she? What had I expected? I was a fool. I deserved to get brutalized by her a second time. I'd been dumb enough to let it happen.

My feet were blocks of concrete as I walked back to the front desk. The audience of two who'd witnessed Ruby's outburst was still there. Suzanne's gaze dropped down to her desktop, but my father's didn't waver. It put me under a microscope which he turned up to the highest magnification, until he could see every flaw.

"My office," he ordered. "Now." The edge to his words was a crack of whip. Then he turned and instructed Suzanne to ask Mr. Gillespie to reschedule.

As a partner, my father's office was easily twice the size of mine. It was decorated to be elegant and precise. There weren't any pictures of family. Not one. I'd overheard him joke once to another attorney at the firm how he did that on purpose. It was easier for his clients to see him as less than human that way. He didn't have emotions or family obligations to get in the way of his job. They were supposed to believe he was fully dedicated to their case.

It was pure bullshit.

He didn't have family photos because he didn't care. He had a newspaper article framed from the first big case he'd argued and won. Money, power, and winning. These were the things that mattered to him.

"What the hell was that?" My father's voice grated on me. I was too upset about what had happened to give much of a shit about his impending lecture. "We can't have one of your girlfriends coming here. Jesus, Kyle. I've never seen something more unprofessional. Thank the lord no one else saw it."

Whatever. I turned and gazed out his window. He had a better view of the lake, and I stared at the icy edge of the water where it had frozen to the shore.

"And thank God no one heard it."

"Yeah, I feel real lucky right now."

He didn't notice how flat my voice was, or how dead my expression had to be. All he was worried about was how this could negatively reflect on him. "That cannot happen again. Do you understand? I won't tolerate it."

He scolded me just like this when I'd come home with a B on a report card once.

"Okay," I said.

He halted his movement, looking visibly thrown. He'd expected me to defend myself, or at least plead my case, but I didn't have the energy.

"Okay?" he repeated, stunned. My single word agreement seemed to take all the wind out of his sails, and now he was adrift, unsure where to go.

"Yeah."

He lived for the fight, and had no idea how to handle a surrender. "Don't you care about how that scene made us look?"

"Not really. You don't care about me, so why should I care about you?"

He scowled. "Don't be ridiculous, of course I care about you."

"All right." The urge to prove my point was too powerful to resist. "Who was that woman out front, and what's her name?"

The question screwed him perfectly. I'd only loved one woman my whole life, and he didn't even know her fucking name, even though I'd mentioned her at least twice this week.

I let him flounder for a moment, and then set my jaw.

"Don't worry, I doubt you'll see *Ruby* again."

I threw open his door so hard on my exit, it banged against the wall, and his precious framed newspaper article rattled on its hook, threatening to fall.

319

RUBY

I was a mess. The fire of my rage earlier had consumed so much energy, I didn't have any left to cry, and certainly not enough to make therapy macarons. I sat alone in my dark kitchen, my palms flat on the table, hoping if I sat still enough, I'd turn to stone and all my feelings would go away.

I couldn't call Grant. I didn't want to talk about what had happened. I wasn't sure what the fuck I'd tell him, since I could barely admit to myself what I'd done.

When the anger took over, the smart, logical woman I was disappeared. It made everything hazy. I'd confronted Kyle in front of his father and boss. I'd slapped him. And I'd done what I always did when I felt overpowered by emotion . . . I lashed out, hoping to strike where it'd do the most damage. It was a great tool in the courtroom, less so anywhere else.

My phone chimed with a text message from Kyle.

> Call me when you're ready.

I couldn't dial fast enough. I'd been a little terrified I'd never hear from him again. "Kyle, I'm so sorry."

There was a cold tone in his voice that made my blood turn to slush. "Crawford probably made it sound like I had, but I would *never* cheat on you. You should know that."

Alone in my dark kitchen, my face crumbled. He was

absolutely right. I'd fucked this all up so horribly. I whispered it into the phone. "I know. I'm sorry. I lost my fucking mind. He said there was no other reason for you to be there. He was convincing."

"You did it again, Ruby. You automatically assumed the worst of me." His accusation was loaded with pain.

What do you know? Tears are possible.

When I closed my eyes, they streamed hotly down my cheeks. "I didn't believe him at first, but he kept talking, and the idea of losing you . . ." I sniffled, trying to stuff my emotions back inside me. "It's not an excuse. I fucked up, and I'm sorry."

"Yeah, you mentioned it." His voice fell like a rock.

I wasn't going to say it needed repeating. Things were too serious to crack a joke, and it felt like he was pulling away from me. I put my palm on my chest, trying to stop it from hurting.

"Please," I gasped. It was the only word I could choke out. *Please forgive me. Please don't let this be the end. Please, please, please . . .* "I love you." I'd do whatever he wanted. I'd beg until my voice was hoarse and there were no more tears left in my body. Anything. "I'm so sorry. Kyle, please. I love you so much."

"You've a funny way of showing it."

I deserved whatever he wanted to throw at me. "I know." I swiped my fingers quickly under my eyes, wiping at the tears. "I won't overreact again. Ever."

He issued a noise that sounded like exasperation. "Gotta be honest, that's not a promise I think you're capable of keeping."

"Not without your help," I whispered.

It was deathly silent on the other side of the

conversation, and my insides turned to broken glass.

"Please," I begged. "Let's not do this over the phone. Come over." I'd stall him any way possible. I was desperate. "I love you."

"Look at the evidence you've given me to support your claim." It was icy, probably to mask his pain.

"I love you, and I can prove it."

"Yeah?" He was pure sarcasm. "How?"

"I'll keep loving you," I broke on the inside as I said it, "even if you stop loving me."

The lengthy pause stretched between us, and I held my breath.

"I need to go," he said. "I need time to think about things."

I nodded slowly, and to myself. "I get it. Whatever you need."

"Goodbye, Ruby."

The words tasted like dust in my mouth. "Goodbye, Kyle."

When he disconnected the call, I crossed my arms on the table, dropped my head onto them, and cried myself to sleep.

Chapter

FORTY-ONE

KYLE

I hung up, and Ruby's haunting goodbye echoed in my mind. Her voice had been full of worry, like she thought this might be the last time we spoke.

Did I want it to be? No. But I also wanted her to trust me, and I was learning the hard way I couldn't always get what I wanted. Goddamnit. I set my palms on the counter, spread wide, and hung my head, feeling weary down to my bones.

Why couldn't she love me the same way I loved her?

I reached for the bottle of bourbon on the counter, and stopped when I saw the box of mint chocolate macarons Ruby had brought over the other night. A new recipe she'd tried out, just for me, because it was my favorite flavor combination. They hadn't come out perfectly, according to her, but they were still delicious.

The box went in the garbage. I wanted it gone from sight.

I poured my drink but didn't take a sip. I stared at the caramel-colored liquid with a scowl. Was I going to have to pour it down the drain? It reminded me too much of her.

As did the blue couch.

And the whole fucking city.

I closed my eyes, but even there I couldn't escape. If anything, it was worse. There was nothing to distract me from the memories of her. How she laughed. How she gasped my name when I made her come.

How she looked when she was standing in my firm's lobby with tears streaking down her face.

"Fuck!" I threw the glass in the sink, slinging the bourbon everywhere, and it shattered on impact. I stared at the gleaming shards at the bottom of my sink, stunned. I wasn't one to have emotional outbursts, but then again, I wasn't one to have much emotion at all.

Not before her, and not after her, either.

It ate at me, the box of macarons in my empty garbage can. I'd seen firsthand how difficult those damn cookies were to get right; she'd worked too hard for me to just throw them away. I lifted the lid on the can, dug the box out, and set it on the counter.

They weren't perfect, but things rarely were on the first try. She'd told me how sometimes she could have all the right ingredients, but still not have them come together as she wanted. It might even take her a few more attempts before she finally got it right.

Jesus. What if that was us? We had all the right stuff, but needed to refine our process until we got it how it was supposed to be.

I was still picking glass out of my garbage disposal when Payton and Dominic arrived; I'd forgotten completely about our plans to go to dinner. I tried to get out of it, but Payton could be just as stubborn as our father, and I found myself seated at the restaurant, recounting the ordeal.

Once again, I was a third wheel.

I glanced occasionally at my phone, wondering if Ruby would reach out to me, and if so, what she would say. I'd told her I needed time, and I did, but as I stared at the empty spot beside me in the booth, I missed her. All these emotions twisted inside me.

"I know he looks perfect," Payton said, her smile directed at Dominic, "but no one is. Even he fucks up."

"Rarely," Dominic corrected. "You meant to include the word 'rarely.'"

Payton ignored him, turning her focus on me. "Sounds like she's got trust issues. You know, you kind of reinforced that by abandoning her after graduating."

I frowned and pressed my lips together. Even though it was true, it rankled to hear it.

Payton pushed on. "You need to figure out if you can deal. If you love her, you will. It's cheesy as fuck, and I know you're going to tell me not to talk to you about love, but that's what it is." She leaned into Dominic. "You don't just stop loving them when they make a mistake."

Wasn't that exactly what Ruby had said to me? How she would keep loving me even if I no longer loved her?

My sister snuggled closer to her husband. "And, come on, Kyle. You're like me."

"A pain in the ass?" I shot back.

She gave me a dirty look. "I was going to say smart. I bet you can find a way to fix the problem you helped create."

"I don't want to talk about it," I grumbled.

"Okay." She flashed a smile at Dominic. "Kyle's all pathetic looking. Let's find someone and win your dollar back."

Courtney Crawford stared at the divorce papers I'd handed to her, and her gaze floated down to the bottom of the page, presumably lingering on Tariq's signature.

I hadn't handled a lot of divorce cases. It had never been my area of focus. Too much emotion, and I didn't know what to do when a client broke down in front of me. I'd never had a shoulder to cry on, although that was partly my fault.

My sister had been there, but we'd both been too afraid to reach out to the other one while we were growing up. Dominic had changed her, and although the concept of her working at the blindfold club would never sit easy with me, if the place hadn't existed, they wouldn't have found each other.

I was restless last night, thinking about Ruby so much I couldn't sleep, and the goddamn sheets smelled like her. The alarm clock went off too early. I dragged my sorry ass into the office, hating how I felt like a mopey teenager, but the upside was both of my parents steered clear of me.

The email from Tariq's attorney had arrived swiftly this morning, accepting all the terms I'd laid out for Courtney.

"Do you have any questions?" I asked. She had a pen clutched in her hand, but didn't sign.

"No, I just . . . need a minute." Her sad gaze drifted up to mine. "Is that okay?"

Her marriage was ending, and I mentally kicked myself for trying to rush her. "Of course. Take all the time you need."

"I don't know why this is so hard. Tariq and I have been done for months. We both want this." She seemed frustrated with herself. "But signing, it's so . . ."

"Final," I said.

"Yeah. Exactly."

My lack of sleep must have gotten to me. "Can I ask a

personal question?" She nodded. "When did you know it was over?"

She took in a sharp breath and her gaze flew away from mine.

Shit. "I'm sorry. Please forget I asked. It's absolutely none of my business, and—"

"He cheated on me." She didn't seem upset, it was more like disappointment, which made me think she'd known about it for a while. Courtney looked at her hands clasped in her lap, but her posture was strong. Like she wasn't defeated. "It was the second time I'd caught him. He'd been so drunk after the Minnesota game, he thought he was texting his driver. Instead, he was texting me."

I bit my tongue. I wanted to tell her what an asshole I thought her about-to-be ex-husband was, but refrained.

"So, it's four a.m., and I'm staring at this message about how great the random hookup my husband just had was, and you know the first thought I had?"

"He's a son of a bitch?" It was more profane than I usually got with clients, but a tame version of what I wanted to say.

A half-smile darted across her lips, then disappeared. "No, it was, what could I have done differently? What was I not giving him that he needed?"

My mouth dropped open. She was worried about what she'd done, and not the cheating bastard?

"Want to know what my second thought was?"

"Please tell me it was that he's a son of a bitch."

Her smile was bigger this time. "That was my *third* thought. My second one was nothing was wrong with me. Tariq is who he is. He isn't going to change, and I realized I couldn't love the man he is. I tried."

She laid the document down on my desk and signed beside the sticky tab pointing to the signature line. When it was done, she handed it to me, letting out a breath. A sigh of relief?

"Just my opinion," I said, "but it doesn't sound like he ever deserved you."

A soft laugh bubbled out of her. "That's what Julius keeps telling me."

"He's a smart guy." I saw the opportunity and seized on it. "How's the divorce going to affect your friendship with him?"

She contemplated for a moment. "He was Tariq's boy before we met, but . . . I dunno. We talk a lot now. Ever since Tariq got traded and we came to Chicago, Julius has been there for me." Was it the afternoon sunlight coming through my window that lit her eyes, or the thought of him? "He's like *my* friend now."

It was good to hear, but I didn't want him to be friend-zoned forever. Could I plant the idea in her head? Maybe she just needed a nudge to see Julius in a new light. The question pushed past my lips before I could reel it in. "You ever wonder if he'll be interested in more?"

Her breath caught and warm color splashed on her pretty face. Her eyes shifted away, shy. Holy shit.

She *knew*.

Courtney's voice was soft. "I married his best friend. He'll never make a move."

"Then, I guess if you're interested, you'll have to do it. When you're ready."

Her eyes widened. "I doubt I can compete with the girls at his club."

I tried to be nonchalant, but my pulse quickened. "His

wine club?"

"Yes." She seemed to scrutinize me just as much as I did her. Gauging each other's response. Did she know what Julius really did? Was she trying to figure out if I knew?

"It's funny," she said, "how he owns the club. Julius doesn't even like wine."

Oh, she definitely knew. But how? Tariq acted like she didn't.

"That is funny," I said. "It's also strange how he got his start there. I wouldn't think a wine club would need such heavy security." The meaning was clear on my face. "How'd you hear about the kind of wine they sell there?"

"Another player's wife. She, uh, goes to the club with her husband." A blush washed over her face. "Anyway, when she told me it pretends to be an exclusive wine club, and what part of town it's in . . . It wasn't hard to put together."

"You haven't talked about it with Julius, though?"

Courtney shook her head slowly. "Yeah . . . I don't know how to start that conversation. I guess I'll wait for him to tell me."

Would he, though? It didn't sound like she knew Tariq was visiting the club, and although she seemed to accept what Julius did, it might be a different story if she found out *everything*.

Both our gazes sank down to the divorce papers on my desk.

"Is that it?" she asked quietly.

"I'll file these with the judge and let you know when it's official." When she stood, I rose from my desk. "I'll be in touch."

I escorted her to the front, passing by the main

conference room where both my parents were seated with a team of attorneys. My father's gaze tracked me the entire way. If I had followed exactly in his footsteps, right now I'd be thinking about the nice paycheck heading my direction. There'd been a lot of billable hours, thanks to Tariq's stalling. Instead I was thinking about Julius and Courtney, and if they'd be able to develop their relationship into more.

I was becoming less and less like my parents every day. I'd fled Chicago, hoping the distance would prevent me from turning into them, but it was back here where I felt like I'd truly broken free.

Courtney gave me a soft smile as she slipped on her coat. "Thank you, Mr. McCreary."

She was friends with Julius, as was I, and I genuinely hoped to see her again. "It's Kyle, and you're welcome."

My phone chimed with a text message and I glanced at it as she stepped into the elevator. A single line of text from Ruby.

Don't give up on me.

She had stirred up all these feelings, and when they spilled out, it brought other ones into play. She'd changed me for the better, more or less.

Was it possible? Could I do the same to her?

RUBY

I sent the text message to Kyle yesterday in a moment of weakness. His radio silence was torture, but not receiving a response from him after? That was pure agony.

I'd called Grant in a panic this afternoon, and after work was over, he'd gotten us a spot at the back of the gastro-pub one block over from my apartment. It was tiny, like they'd tried to cram too many booths along the wall, and he looked uncomfortable. He barely fit in the space.

The tabletop was decorated with our empty drinks, more of them his than mine. The place was dark and our booth was tucked in at the end, so the server rarely came around to check on us or clear away our empties. I was glad. It gave me privacy to explain my fuck-up.

"There's a place here in town," I said. "It's an illegal, high-end brothel."

Grant's stunned gaze flicked up to me. "Sorry?"

"I can't talk about the situation, other than to tell you I made the very wrong assumption Kyle was a client, even when my gut was telling me otherwise." I should have trusted myself. No, fuck that. I should have trusted him. "Now, a normal, sane person would call their boyfriend and talk to him about it. They wouldn't go to his office and accuse him in front of his boss, who also happens to be his father."

"Rube, you didn't." He appeared horrified on my behalf.

The words were full of self-loathing as they came out. "I don't even know what happened. Sometimes I get carried away, but with him . . . it's a whole new level. He disables my brain." My gaze drifted down so I could stare vacantly at the paper coaster pinned beneath my drink. "He explained what he was doing at the blindfold club, and I believe him. I apologized a bunch of times, but . . . I don't know. He asked for time, and I haven't heard from him since." Could Grant hear the tremble in my voice? Could he see how close I was to breaking down? "I'm pretty sure I'm going to lose him over this."

A long moment passed with no words between us. There was only the sound of the noisy bar in the background.

"You recognize you made a mistake," he said finally. "Can you take back what happened? No, but you apologized. If he loves you, he needs to not be a McAsshole about it, yeah?"

Grant's expression skewed, as if he wasn't sure what else to say, and I couldn't blame him. He took a sip of his beer, shifted in his seat, and opened his mouth, only to snap it shut a second later.

"Out with it," I prompted.

"The place he went to . . ."

"The club?" I scanned his face, finding curiosity there. My mouth went dry. "If you're thinking you want to do a story on it, you can't." I'd made sure to leave both Tariq and Payton out of it, but I couldn't have my friend digging. "This conversation is off the record."

"It's off the record," he said, nodding. "How much do you know about it, the club?"

"Nothing," I lied.

He looked disappointed, but not ready to give up. The

high-class brothel had attracted Tariq Crawford. It stood to reason there were other celebrities frequenting it, maybe even politicians. The story could be a goldmine.

"You called it the blindfold club. Why?"

"I'm told the girls wear blindfolds."

"Why?" he repeated.

"Sorry, no idea." We needed to get off this line of questioning. "I didn't mean to hijack this evening and make it all about me. We came to help you get back up on the horse, so to speak. I see two options for rebounding, the redhead by the—"

"Nah."

"Oh, yeah. You like blondes." My sister had been blonde when they'd dated, as was Morgan.

"I meant, not sure I want to pick someone up tonight." He glanced around, surveying the bar crowd. "People who go out to the bars on a Wednesday night are strange."

I shot him a plain look. "We are out on a Wednesday night."

"Proves my point."

My phone vibrated, and as I glanced at the screen, my heart stopped. A text message from Kyle.

> We need to talk.
> I'm at your place
> but you're not here.

The pull between relief he'd reached out, and dread over his 'we need to talk' statement threatened to tear me in two. I swallowed thickly and tapped out a response.

I glanced up at Grant. "It's Kyle. He wants to talk, and he says he's already at my place."

"You need to take off just now?" he said, his tone casual. "It's okay."

I frowned. "I'm sorry. I'm not trying to ditch you, and this is the second time I've done it. He's not more important than our friendship. I don't want you thinking I'm blowing you off, but—"

"It quite all right. I know that's not what you're doing." He smiled softly. "Talking for you two is good. I understand you need to."

Of course he did. "You're kind of awesome, you know that?"

Grant's deep laugh was warm. "See if you still think so when I say you're picking up my tab."

I smiled and thumbed out a response to Kyle.

Hopefully sooner if we could get the server's attention. Assuming things could be smoothed over between Kyle and me, I'd make introducing him to my friend a priority.

As the front door of the bar swung open, it no longer became necessary.

Kyle stepped inside and his gaze swept over the crowd before settling on me all the way at the back. Had he come straight from the office? It seemed like he wore a suit beneath his long dress coat. There was a scarf knotted around his neck and the ends tucked inside the coat. He shifted the manila envelope he was carrying from one hand to the other as he tugged off his black leather gloves, shoved them in a pocket, and approached the table.

His gaze never wavered from mine, and my breath hitched. His expression was stoic. A total fucking enigma. I couldn't tell if he was happy to see me, or ready to get this over with.

I knew how I felt, though.

The air crackled with sparks. I leaned subtly forward in my seat, my body aching to be just a little closer to him. It was snowing outside, and the dusting of snowflakes melted on his hair, glinting in the low light.

When he was close enough to reach out and touch, his attention jumped from me to Grant, and his shoulders snapped back. His eyes narrowed sharply. The ends of his mouth turned down into a scowl, like he was pissed off just at the sight of my friend.

"Who the fuck are you?"

I gasped. Kyle's tone was adversarial, announcing he viewed this other man as a threat. Did he think Grant and I were here on a date?

The booth was elevated, so Grant swiveled in his seat, put his feet on the ground and rose to his full, impressive height. "That's funny, coming from you. I'm the one who's been around for the last five years after you left without saying a single word to her."

Kyle's chest lifted as he took in a deep breath, but otherwise there was no reaction from him; he wasn't intimidated. His face was blank. A duck floating calmly on water, where no one but me could see the feet beneath the surface churning furiously.

"The question is, who are you?" Grant said. "Besides the guy who broke her heart?"

There were other sounds in the bar, but I couldn't hear them now. All that filled my ears was the sound of Kyle's sharp inhale. His focus shifted away from the enormous man and found me.

I stood from my seat. "Kyle, this is my friend Grant."

Kyle looked at me with total disbelief, like I was nuts. "You said he plays cello."

"I do." Grant was visibly annoyed.

Kyle had probably pictured a slight, dorky looking guy, but Grant was the opposite. There'd been plenty of times he'd been practicing at home, drawing the bow across the strings while nursing a black eye from rugby.

Kyle's gaze bounced from mine, to Grant, and back again, as if needing confirmation. I nodded.

"Well, shit." Kyle looked sheepish. "You're on her wall, and I thought you two were . . . Doesn't matter. I'm sorry." He thrust his hand forward. "Let's start again. I'm Kyle."

"Grant." They shook hands stiffly, and then both turned their attention to me. Grant gave an easy smile. "I'm heading off. Thanks for the drinks." He nodded back to Kyle. "Nice to meet you, McAsshole. Have a good talk."

Kyle blinked. Was he deciding if he wanted to let the comment slide?

"Hey," I said softly, pulling his focus to me. "Let me just get the check and we can talk at my place." Every cell in my body was tight and on edge. Was this the end?

He stared at the empty booth, set down the envelope on the seat, and began to peel off his coat. "Here is fine."

Oh, God. I pressed my lips into a line to hold back the

tremble. I slid down into my seat slowly, wondering how long the waitstaff would let me stay here after Kyle left. I'd sat on his doorstep at Randhurst for hours, and things would be so much harder this this time around.

He'd barely settled in across from me before the server sashayed up and began to load her tray with the empty glasses. "Another Amstel?" It was then that she looked up and paused. "Didn't you used to be a big, gorgeous guy?"

"He had to leave," Kyle said dryly. "I'll have a bourbon and Coke."

When she turned to me, I shook my head, and she flitted away with her tray. It opened up room on the table, and he pulled a napkin from the dispenser, wiped away the condensation from the drinks, and dropped the envelope on the lacquered surface.

"W-W-What's that?" My voice was small. *God-damn stutter.*

He laid his hand on top of the envelope, and the action struck me as odd. His fingertips rested on it delicately. Whatever was inside was important, and potentially difficult. Every second of silence from him made my heart climb higher in my body until it was pounding in my ears.

"Last time we spoke, you made me a promise, which I told you I didn't think you could keep." His blue eyes seemed deeper in the dark lighting, and they sucked me in. "Do you remember what you said after that?"

I nodded so slowly, it might not have registered to him. I'd promised not to lose my head again with him. "I said I couldn't keep my promise without your help."

He looked pleased and the envelope slid toward me. "Exactly. This is my offer."

Frantic energy buzzed through me as I bent the metal

prongs inward and lifted the flap. Inside was a single sheet. A contract, judging by the format and the signature lines at the bottom.

I made it one line before I burst into tears.

Kyle was out of his seat in a flash. "Ruby."

His palms were warm on the sides of my face, his lips warmer still against my mouth. His kiss was overpowering. Emotion swept through me in a deluge, flowing outward to the tips of my fingers and toes.

He pushed me back into the seat cushion, not letting up on his devastating kiss. The angle was adjusted, deepening the connection between us, and his tongue pressed against the seam of my lips. Was he asking permission or tempting me with more? Didn't matter. I parted my lips and stroked my tongue against his. It was slow, and wicked, and I felt it all the way in my center.

I was sure in this moment I'd been put on this earth just to kiss him.

My hands found their way inside his suit jacket. I wanted it fucking gone. All his clothes, any barrier between us needed to be removed. The two days without him felt longer than the five years, and it seemed to be the same for him. He was passionate. Desperate.

His thumbs brushed over my cheeks, wiping away my tears, and then one hand traveled backward to gently grip a fistful of hair at the nape of my neck, tugging me back so his searing mouth could further claim me. A small action, but it lit a fire in me like a powder keg. Now that I'd had a taste of his domination, I always craved it.

"Your bourbon and Coke, sir."

The server's pointed tone wasn't lost on either of us.

Even though we were in the back of the place, Kyle was standing over me and we'd had our lips locked in a kiss that bordered on indecent.

As she departed, he straightened and peered down at me, his hold still in my hair and his power poured over every inch of my body.

"Why'd you order a drink?" I whispered. "All I want to do is take you home and let you fuck me into tomorrow."

His smile was kind of evil and insanely hot. "We have business to discuss first."

I sighed as he let go and sat back down, all the way on the other side of the booth that had once felt tiny but now was much too big. I'd dropped the partnership agreement on the table when the waterworks started, brought on by the last sentence of the contract.

He'd put the biggest term in the final paragraph of our last partnership agreement, so I had chosen to start reading there this time. Before, he'd attempted to leash our emotions and prevent our relationship from going too far. This new one had very different language.

It stated that in the event of marriage, the partnership agreement would continue to apply.

Marriage.

He saw a future for us, the same one I hoped for someday, which neither of us had said out loud. I picked up the contract and began to read from the beginning while Kyle watched and sipped on his drink. I read it twice, set it down, and lifted my gaze to meet his.

"Thoughts?" He asked it casually, but I could tell he was far more interested than he let on.

This new partnership agreement was shorter. It stated in any situations of confusion, or if one partner acted rashly, they were required to take five minutes to organize themselves and then communicate with the other. If this didn't happen, there would be consequences. Even punishment, if necessary, to negatively reinforce that the behavior didn't continue. It would be up to their partner to decide what form of punishment, and how much.

So if I lost my head as I seemed to do around him, I'd have to calm down and speak to him like a fucking adult, or . . .? The image of me bent over his lap, his hand preparing to strike my bare ass, sent a shiver of pleasure through me. Only, he wouldn't give me what I wanted as negative reinforcement, would he? Maybe he'd withhold his kink instead.

"I like this," I said finally. Who was I kidding? I fucking loved it, but tried to keep my cool. This agreement was a fail-safe. If I lost my damn mind, it at least required him to stick around long enough to punish me. It all but bound us together and forced me to be rational.

"Is it retroactive?" I asked, nervous.

Surprise darted through his eyes, like he hadn't thought about it. "We've both made mistakes. I think we should start fresh."

"Oh." A new wave of relief surged in me. "Good." I stared at the neat type, my gaze tracing the last line and blurring a little with tears I blinked back. Enough crying, even if they were happy tears. My voice was thick with emotion. "Thank you for this."

I'd never seen him look so surprised. It might have been silly to thank him for drafting a contract, but it meant so much more than the words on the paper. Our first agreement had been about sex, but this one was about love.

His voice was uneven. "I'm sorry it took me so long to

present it to you."

It wasn't a marriage proposal, but he'd taken a leap and put himself out there with the last line. It made sense why he'd hesitated. "What changed your mind?"

"Changed my mind?"

"I mean, what made you decide to forgive me?"

He smiled like I was talking nonsense. "I love you, Ruby. There's nothing that's going to change that." There was more emotion on his face than ever before. His eyes filled with longing. "It's *always* been you."

My heart threatened to explode and I put a hand over it, shielding him in case it happened.

Kyle wasn't finished, either. "I wish I could go back in time, kiss you outside your apartment at Randhurst, and get this thing we have right the first time. But as long as you sign my offer, it doesn't matter. We're together now."

It was a miracle I was still functioning. His words had rendered me a useless mess of emotion. I sat perfectly still, worried if I moved in the slightest I'd break down and they'd spill out.

His gaze landed on the contract before me, and concern overtook his expression. Was he worried I hadn't moved? How I hadn't signed? "Do you . . . have questions?"

"Just one." My voice was a ghost. "And it's important."

He drew in a preparing breath. "Go for it."

"Do you," I said, drawing it out, "have a pen?"

He moved like a flash of lightning, producing one from his interior pocket, and a smile broke so large on my face, my cheeks hurt. I scribbled my name on the signature line, just below where he'd already signed, and stared at it as the ink dried.

Two signatures on one sheet of paper. I'd seen

hundreds of contracts during law school and my career, but there'd never been a more beautiful agreement than the one in my hands, and certainly not one that ever made me this happy.

thank you

As always, thank you to my husband. With your support, I was able to follow my dreams, and perhaps one day these dirty books will be so successful I can return the favor. I love you vastly more than any hero I've created. You know all their best parts I stole from you, anyway.

To my beta readers, Joscelyn Freeman Fussell, Andrea Lefkowitz, Rebecca Nebel, Nikki Terrill, and V. I got lost writing this book, and not in a good way. You guys pulled me back on track, not just with your notes, but with your unwavering support. Plus, you put up with my weekly lies of, "I'm going to send it to you tonight!" for over a month. When I turned in the first draft, I hated it and wasn't sure it could be saved. But you did it. I feel like this book is just as much yours as it is mine, and I hope you're as proud as I am of the result. Cock and balls, 4ever!

An extra special thank you to Andrea for answering my random legal question at strange hours, and for all the extra work you put in to help save Kyle and Ruby. I can't express how much it meant to me, because saying it was *a lot* isn't close to accurate.

To my editor Lori Whitwam. You are amazing. Thank you for continuing to work with me, even when I can't get my shit together. This is our sixth book as a team, so I suspect you're used to it by now. (I just realized six books, that's bananas!) Hopefully there are many more to come!

To my publicist Heather Roberts. Thank you for championing my work, for going above and beyond, and for being my friend.

To the readers and bloggers who enjoyed my work enough to share it with others. I am so honored, and incredibly grateful.

...and to you, reader, right now. Yeah, you! Thank you for reading. You're awesome.

What had originally started as a novella and bloomed into a full-length novel, then a series, has been an absolute joy to write—one I could not stop, much like a drug. Thank you so much for taking the time to read Kyle and Ruby's story. If you enjoyed it, would you be so kind as to let other readers know via an Amazon review or on Goodreads? Just a few words can help an author tremendously, and are *always* appreciated!

about nikki

Nikki Sloane landed in graphic design after her careers as a waitress, a screenwriter, and a ballroom dance instructor fell through. For eight years she worked for a design firm in that extremely tall, black, and tiered building in Chicago which went through an unfortunate name change during her time there.

Now she lives in Kentucky, is married and has two sons. She is a member of the Romance Writers of America, also writes romantic suspense under the name Karyn Lawrence, and couldn't be any happier that people enjoy reading her dirty words.

Find her on the web: www.NikkiSloane.com

Contact her on Twitter: @AuthorNSloane

Send her an email: authornikkisloane@gmail.com